Praise for the novels of Heather Graham

"Heather Graham delivers a harrowing journey as she always does: perfectly.... Intelligent, fast-paced and frightening at all times, and the team of characters still keep the reader's attention to the very end."
—*Suspense Magazine* on *The Final Deception*

"Taut, complex, and leavened with humor, this riveting thriller has...a shade more suspense than romance, it will appeal to fans of both genres."
—*Library Journal* on *A Dangerous Game*

"Masterfully told and deliciously engaging, *Seeing Darkness* will keep you turning pages late into the night."
—*J.R. Wallace of JathanandHeather.com*

"An enthralling read with a totally unexpected twist at the end."
—*Fresh Fiction* on *Deadly Touch*

"Graham strikes a fine balance between romantic suspense and a gothic ghost story in her latest Krewe of Hunters tale."
—*Booklist* on *The Summoning*

"Will keep you glued to the pages...[with] the danger, drama and energy."
—*Fresh Fiction* on *The Seekers*

"An intense murder-mystery that kept me turning the pages. Graham never fails to pull me in.... Each [of her books] offers rich history, an interesting murder-mystery and a new... romance."
—*Caffeinated Book Reviewer* on *The Seekers*

Also by *New York Times* bestselling author
HEATHER GRAHAM

For more titles, visit TheOriginalHeatherGraham.com.

* * * * *

Look for Heather Graham's next novel
THE FORBIDDEN
available soon from MIRA.

HEATHER GRAHAM

THE
UNFORGIVEN

mira

ISBN-13: 978-0-7783-3182-7

The Unforgiven

This edition published by arrangement with Harlequin Books S.A.

For questions and comments about the quality of this book, please contact us at CustomerService@Harlequin.com.

Mira
22 Adelaide St. West, 40th Floor
Toronto, Ontario M5H 4E3, Canada
www.Harlequin.com

Printed in Lithuania

To Patrick DeVuono, musician, teacher, writer...
Kind, giving, bright and thoughtful. All-around great guy!

And my cousin, who also grew up with stories of
banshees and leprechauns, and a feisty great-gran
and a few other delightfully crazy Irish
who gave us gifts of stories, art and songs.

THE
UNFORGIVEN

Prologue

There was nothing like being in the water, and nothing at all like diving. The sea, all around her. The calm, rhythmic sound of her breathing through her regulator, the sun streaking through the water, catching on the brilliant colors of a yellow tang, a blue angelfish or the orange of a clown fish.

Larger creatures swam by as well: snappers, grunts and even a giant grouper that must have been hundreds of pounds.

Katie Delaney was in ecstasy.

She had gotten her junior PADI diving certification at the age of ten. At five, she'd wanted to be a mermaid. Her parents had laughed and assured her that as soon as she was old enough, she could get her diving certificate and become the next best thing. Now that she had turned fifteen, she'd upgraded to the certification that had no *junior* attached to it, and she was proud and delighted.

She loved the water, the sun, the sand and the sea.

It ran in the family. Both of her parents had been in the navy; her dad had been a SEAL.

Today, they were diving out of Key Largo. There were

so many places she wanted to go. But their home was Key West, and while she wanted a trip to the Great Barrier Reef and other renowned dive sites, her dad had assured her many times the reefs off the Florida Keys offered fine diving.

They were lucky—she needed to realize that. They lived right by the only living continental barrier reef in the United States. And while she might go down time after time, she would never see all the wonders there—right in her own patch of the ocean—that might be seen.

Naturally, she had her favorite things to do in all the islands of the Florida Keys. And that morning, she and her parents had done one of them: Captain Slate's Creature Feature. They had fed nurse sharks and rays and other incredible sea beings, and the fish would come and play with the divers. A giant nurse shark had been swimming right above her head!

Today was a birthday and *congratulations* present from her parents. They had done the Creature Feature with Captain Slate's crew, done a second dive with them and then gone back in to shore just to go back out again to maybe dive on their own.

And now, they had been joined by her folks' best friends and a younger couple the two had recently met when they'd been out at a local restaurant or somewhere. Her mom and dad were happy to bring out-of-towners out on their boat with them for the day.

Katie didn't care—today was her *birthday for her folks* day.

Her actual birthday had been last week, and she'd spent it with her friends, including her boyfriend, Brad. Her parents had been great about it.

But being fifteen didn't change her love for her family or

the water. In fact, it brought her closer to her dream. She'd go to college. She'd learn how to run a business. Because eventually, she'd have her own company, be a certified dive master. And *then* maybe she'd get serious about boys. And if Brad was still around, and still hot, well…

Yep. She knew she was envied by other girls her age because Brad was hot. She grinned around her regulator mouthpiece. He just wasn't as good a diver as she was yet.

One day she would change that!

You never, ever dive without a dive buddy. The best divers in the world might perish when a problem could be easily solved or alleviated if a partner was just at hand.

Her father had hammered that lesson into her.

She suspected that during her father's time in the navy, he had been in the water a few times on dangerous missions when a partner had not been with him.

But she wasn't alone today; she was following the rules.

She'd thought maybe the young woman they'd just met, Jennie, who was with a guy named Neil, might have wanted to get in the water again. But Jennie seemed to be a bit of a prima donna: she wanted to be on the boat but not in the water. She said she *could* dive, she was certified, she just didn't feel like being all salty with wet hair.

That was all right. Katie wasn't alone. She might have wandered a bit from the anchor line, but her mom's friend, Anita, was in the water near her somewhere. Mrs. Calabria was always cool: she might have wanted to stay onboard with the other adults, but if so, she hadn't let Katie see that. She had just enthusiastically excused herself to her new friends, Dr. Neil Browne, doctor of what Katie didn't know, and his girlfriend Jennie *someone*, from *somewhere* up north. Katie didn't know much about Dr. Browne or Jennie, but they were a younger duo, full of energy, eager for new experiences—except for getting wet, so it seemed. They seemed nice enough, though she had to wonder if her parents and George and Anita might be trying a little too hard to keep up with them. Like her folks, George and Anita were older now.

She'd known Anita and George all her life. They, along with her mom and dad, had been career military, and then her dad had done a stint as a cop while her mom had worked in a library when they'd first been married. Her dad had been over fifty when Katie had been born, and because her mom had been forty-one, Katie was considered something of a miracle child. They'd moved from New Orleans—her dad's family's home—to the Florida Keys before Katie was born because of their love for the water, boats and diving. Katie had grown up with that love and shared it with a passion.

She hadn't wanted to push it. Her parents, she thought, were too tired for a third dive today, no matter that the charts said they could do more time at this easy depth. But Anita—bless her—knew Katie was in seventh heaven because of her birthday and adult certification and so had risen to the occasion and come in with her. And they had been together until...

Katie had noticed a curious barracuda lurking by a reef and had followed his glittering silver body at a distance. Barracuda were okay, as were most creatures, if you left them alone. And while they weren't diving in John Pennekamp State Park—where the waters were protected, there was no fishing, and fewer underwater plants and animals offered any danger as their natural food supply was healthy—they were close enough to the park so the fish had a ready food supply and most probably would not be after people.

And she had just been watching, keeping her distance. Of course, there were sharks in the water; she knew not to thrash around, and she never wore jewelry while diving or did anything to attract any kind of predator.

Still...

She realized now she didn't see Anita anywhere. And she'd been so wrapped up in her own thoughts she didn't even remember when she had seen her last. They'd only planned a thirty-minute dive, but...

She winced. Thirty minutes were up. Anita was going to be very angry with her for swimming off. Just as her parents were going to be angry.

She had to face the music.

She had promised to stay near the boat. Her father had wanted to head back as soon as this last dive was over; it was a bit of a ride to get home, even once they cut through a channel to take the Gulf side of the island chain rather than circle around on the Atlantic. Their scuba gear had to be washed down, the boat secured and so on.

When she'd gone in, he'd reminded her, "Hey, I'm not a spring chicken anymore!"

And she had called back, "Just another old rooster running around Key West." She adored her dad.

He'd grinned, but he had been serious, too. He was ready to head home.

Where was Anita? Had she gone up without her?

Yes. Katie was going to be in serious trouble. She hadn't been paying attention to her dive buddy.

Quickly, get up there and face it.

She was generally a good kid. She was an excellent student. Most of her friends were boy crazy. She had nothing against boys, especially cute ones, but her interest in Brad was levelheaded. She never let liking him interfere with her family or school.

Surely her parents would bear all this in mind.

The boat had been anchored by one of the reefs in about thirty feet of water. There was no reason to worry about coming right up: she hadn't been deep enough to need to decompress. And so she followed the anchor line to the rear of the boat, removing her mask as she arrived and tossing it onto the little dive platform, detaching her regulator and doing the same with it.

She figured her father might be there, or her mother, or even Anita. They would be staring at her angrily, perhaps with their hands on their hips. They wouldn't scream or yell; they would just announce the consequences for her behavior.

But there was no one anywhere near the dive platform.

"Hey!" she called, banging against the edge of the platform as a wave took her unexpectedly.

Still, no one arrived.

She had, of course, learned to remove all her equipment— and put it all back on—while in the water as part of her training. She removed her tank and buoyancy-control device and flippers, setting them atop the platform, too. Then she crawled up the little two-step ladder.

That was when she first saw the blood.

A spatter of small, diluted drops on the dive platform. It couldn't be blood. Or maybe it was fish blood. That had to be it. A fish. Except her parents didn't go fishing. Maybe those other people had wanted to fish. The doctor—Neil Browne. Or his girlfriend, Jennie whatever. And her folks might have complied. They weren't against responsible fishing, they just didn't care to fish themselves.

"Hey!" she called again.

Nothing.

Then it came over her—a sensation of pure dread and terror. She had to force herself to move on from the platform to the deck. She looked up the four steps to the helm of the boat. There was no one at the wheel.

But the deck, leading to the cabin below, was covered with blood. Not thick but diluted blood, as if someone had thrown down buckets of water, or as if there had been a storm that had ravaged all aboard…

"Mom! Dad! Anita! George!"

Compelled though terrified, she walked down the steps to the cabin. Blood. Everywhere. As if a slew of razor-sharp propellers had ravaged the cabin, tearing into flesh and bone and…

Bodies.

Lying at unnatural angles. So still.

She started to scream and scream.

She backed away from the blood and bodies, not able to look away or see where she was going. Her legs caught on the edge, and she fell over the hull, back into the warm embrace of the Atlantic. The water wrapped around her; she was in such shock that it felt good, it felt right. Just let the water take her along with the darkness that was engulfing her…

She heard a dim whisper in that darkness. A man's voice, soft with a bit of a burr.

"Nay, lass, nay. Life is never easy, but death be not the answer for ye!"

She had lost her mind or she had died—despite his words about death not being the answer. Because she seemed to be looking at a powerful old man in the depths, a fellow with a full beard and mustache and flowing white hair. He was shirtless but wearing some strange kind of pants, beige, tied on with rope and cut off at the ankles.

She would have screamed if she wasn't ten feet down.

Then she wasn't down any longer. She was never sure if he pushed her or if her own instinct for survival kicked in.

She thrust up with a scissor motion of her legs, still hearing the strange man's whisper—in her mind. It had to be in her mind.

"Radio! Use the radio. The Coast Guard is near."

She stumbled back up the dive platform. Now, despite the warmth of the water and the day, she felt cold. Bone-cold—and numb. She stepped over the blood—or through it—she didn't even know. She never looked down.

She moved straight to the radio and called for the Coast Guard.

Even as she spoke, desperately, somehow managing to share her position, darkness seemed to descend around her.

Once someone had assured her that help was on the way, she stumbled back down to the cabin, reaching out to touch her dead mother's hair.

One

Twelve Years Later

"**Y**ou must think I'm terrible, hiring you to spy on my husband," Wendy Lawrence said, her back stiff as she leaned forward entreatingly. "I just… Well, you see, the family money is his, and that makes him think he can do anything he wants. His family owns five of the finest restaurants between here and Biloxi, and…"

Wendy was an attractive woman, a tiny brunette with striking dark eyes and hair, but though Dan Oliver was willing to take her money—investigating was what he did—he wasn't looking forward to continuing with the assignment.

Wendy did not come from money, and there was nothing wrong with that. But her husband, Nathan Lawrence, seemed to be an okay guy. He was a high school teacher specializing in history, civics and government. Dan had already started watching him for Wendy, and the wildest thing the man had done so far was sponsor a high school trip to the zoo.

"Wendy, I need to tell you," Dan said, "I've followed him after school every day for a week now. He's gone home. I don't know what has made you think he...that he might be using you, cheating on you, and staying married to keep his money."

"I saw the text on his phone. *You are truly the best. Thank you! Loved my time with you!*"

Dan shook his head. "I hung around at the café by the school, too. I'm pretty sure that was from one of his students."

Wendy sat back in horror. "A student! Oh, my God!"

"No, no, Wendy. Students might well have a distant crush on a teacher like that. I didn't say your husband was acting wrongly in any way. I think that text might have been from Lily Levan, one of his honor students, and it was innocent—a thank-you for the help he gave her filling out forms. She's in line for a few scholarships, but the paperwork on them can be overwhelming."

"Are you refusing to...to work for me?" Wendy asked.

"No, of course not. I'll continue on your case. But I don't think I'm going to find anything. I think your husband is honest and upright, and I'd hate for him to find out you don't trust him."

"In one set of pictures you gave me, he was with a woman," Wendy said.

"Wendy, he was with a man and a woman. They had folders out on the table; I believe it was a business meeting."

"He's a teacher."

"Yes, and he helps students decide where to go for college, he helps their parents when they're trying to figure out how to pay for college. Wendy, he didn't leave with the couple. The couple left together, and the man's arm was around the woman's shoulder."

"And you don't know who the couple were? What kind of an investigator are you?"

Dan sighed. "I can use some contacts and see if I can find out who they were. You're afraid your husband is cheating on you. Well, he wasn't cheating on you with that woman. I didn't know you wanted dossiers on all his students and their parents and every bartender or server he ever spoke nicely to in a restaurant."

"There is something up," Wendy whispered.

"Wendy, he isn't cheating. He's at school. I've followed him every other place he's been. He simply heads home at night. Sometimes he does go to a restaurant. He eats. You should end this before it goes badly. Do you really want him to possibly discover you hired me because you don't trust him?"

Wendy stood, somewhat indignant. "You're paid *not* to let him know."

Dan shook his head. "He won't know from me. That's not the point."

"He told me he had some kind of a business meeting, something that might bring a lot of good into our lives. But he wouldn't tell me what it was. He was so silly about it. Then he was just… I don't know…weird. And then he said he wanted to forget all of it."

"Maybe it was just a bad opportunity, and he felt weird about it," Dan said wearily.

"A week, just another week," Wendy said.

Dan knew he was good at what he did. Nathan Lawrence would never know he had been watched and followed. Dan didn't need this client. He was solvent; he had money in the bank. But he did do this for a living—as much as he was coming to loathe it—and Wendy did pay her bills.

He was nodding as his phone rang. He had his cell on silent, but it was vibrating on his desk.

Ryder was calling him. Detective Ryder Stapleton, NOPD.

"Excuse me. I have to take this," he told Wendy. It was probably a social call, as Ryder was a friend, but it could also be something more interesting.

She nodded and rose to leave. "One more week. I'll pay Marleah on the way out."

She headed to the door to exit his office. He watched her go, wondering for a moment just how he had managed to do this to himself. He'd been a good detective with the Florida Department of Law Enforcement once upon a time.

And he'd let bitterness over a case cause him to resign. Well, here he was—a licensed private investigator. Following errant husbands and wives, looking for rebellious teens and dealing with the emotional baggage of humanity.

Ryder was his one salvation: his longtime friend asked him in on a case now and then as a consultant for the New Orleans PD.

"Hey. Tell me you need me. Please, I'm begging you," he said into the phone.

Ryder was silent for a moment. "I need you." He seemed to be taking a deep breath before plunging in. "Dan, it's happened here. I need you to meet me in the Marigny."

"What's happened here?"

"A bloodbath. Like the case you had in Florida. I don't know much yet. We've just arrived. A family, Dan. An old man and an old woman and their health-care worker. All slashed up, hard to tell where one body leaves off and… We're still waiting on the medical examiner, can't touch them until he's here, but when I saw this… Well, I thought of you."

A stab of lightninglike pain streaked through Dan.

He'd left Florida six years ago over just such a case. They'd had the killer, he'd been certain. But in court, everything had gone to hell. They just hadn't had enough tangible evidence.

The man had walked free despite Dan believing he'd killed more than once. The guy maintained he'd been a survivor of a brutal attack on a boat—one that killed his wife and best friends, six years earlier.

But then he just happened to be around when very similar murders were committed a mere two hundred miles north of where the first murders had taken place.

He'd claimed he'd moved to Orlando to get away from the horrible memories and therefore couldn't help but be in the city where the next group of people had been heinously hacked up with an axe and a blade. But it was too much of a coincidence for Dan to ignore.

Calabria. George Calabria. The man said they'd been attacked, and he'd fallen overboard while his wife and others were murdered. He hadn't known who had attacked him— "a large, dark, shadowy figure from behind." He'd barely escaped with his own life, falling into the water when he'd been slammed in the head, and then somehow surfacing, maybe semiconscious, and he eventually made it to shore.

There had supposedly been another couple on the boat.

Where was this couple, and who were they?

Some new friends. Out-of-towners they'd recently met. Killed and thrown into the water, according to his story. Or maybe one of them was the killer.

But it was all so far-fetched and suspicious.

Dan was already standing, ready to rush out the door. "I'm coming."

"Slow down, Dan. I know this has happened similarly twice before, in Florida. But you need to understand, this is New Orleans. I'm not sure what you know about history here, but we had the infamous Axeman of New Orleans in

1919. And you know media today. They are going to start saying the Axeman is back. The guy that killed everyone back in—"

"1918 to 1919."

"Uh, right, I think. The point is the city will be in a panic. If you know anything on this, which I'm guessing you do—"

"I know what we can look for… Who we can look for."

"Okay, maybe. So I need you here. Now."

"I'm on my way. Text me the exact address. Ryder, you have to make me real on this case."

"I'm on it with my bosses. But it can be tricky. They like it better when you're hired by a victim's family, you know."

"We'll find something… I… Damn, Ryder. I mean, I know it could be something else, but this…"

"I saw your crime-scene photos from Orlando, and I'm seeing this. Get over here. We'll figure out the rest soon enough. Want you to see this before…before the bodies are moved," Ryder said.

Dan left his office, striding out through the reception area that opened out onto the street.

Marleah Darwin, his erstwhile receptionist/secretary/ assistant, called out to him. "Dan, Mrs. Lawrence left you a check. She's overpaying you. I tried to tell her—"

"Later, Marleah," he said, leaving her shaking her neatly coiffed, graying head and sighing with her usual patience.

His office was in the Central Business District or CBD. The Faubourg Marigny or Marigny neighborhood was the other side of the French Quarter. His car was parked in a garage two blocks away. An Uber or Lyft driver would probably be near, but then he saw a cab approaching. He stepped out in the street and flagged it down.

It would take a few minutes to get across town.

Time to remember the scene he'd been called to in his second year as a detective with the FDLE.

Ryder had referred to the crime-scene photos. Dan didn't need them. The precursor to what would certainly prove to be a similar scene was indelibly imprinted in his mind. The apartment had been painted in blood. Mrs. Austin, her head caved in, her face unrecognizable, her lower arm severed from her body. Mr. Austin, his lower left calf severed—his head looking like a blood stew filled with raw meat. The niece, Miss Henrietta, so mangled it had taken days for her identity to be firmly established.

The cabbie had an accent. Dan wasn't sure where he was from. People in New Orleans might be from just about anywhere. It was one of the many cool things about the city of New Orleans. And wherever he had come from, this man now knew this place. He moved out of the CBD and on to Decatur, telling Dan what streets had been closed off that day.

Dan was relieved he'd got a good cabbie.

In minutes, Dan was looking ahead at the street just beyond Rampart and a few blocks down from Esplanade.

Police vehicles and those labeled *Crime Scene Investigation* sat alongside another vehicle, the wagon from the morgue.

And they weren't alone.

He saw vans from the major news stations already out, reporters pointing to the house and speculating.

They weren't going to get any closer in the cab. Dan handed the driver a generous tip—well deserved—and stepped out to walk hurriedly down the street. At the police line, a patrol officer would have stopped him, but Ryder Stapleton came down the few steps from the small white

Victorian house beyond the vehicles, assuring the officers that Dan was with him.

Dan liked Ryder; he was glad and grateful that Ryder had asked him to come. He was about Dan's own age, sandy-haired, lean and fit. Dan could see that Ryder could be imposing, but yet possessed a warmth that could draw out thoughts and observations from a witness who didn't even know they had seen or known something.

As he approached, Ryder was shaking his head.

"The Axeman. They're already calling him the Axeman in the media—and we don't even know who the hell got through to the reporters! The bodies are inside, for God's sake. I mean, thank God, but…someone talked. They know an axe was involved in the murders—and it was left behind. Dammit, Dan! This might be your killer, but if so, he sure as hell knows his NOLA serial killers, too."

"Thank you," Katie Delaney said cheerfully as her group of seven departed her mule-drawn carriage on Decatur Street. They had been a family, one that seemed to get along remarkably well: two sets of grandparents, parents and an adorable five-year-old. The couple and their little girl lived in New Orleans, the father's parents lived in New York, and the mother's parents lived in Los Angeles.

Maybe that's why they got along so well!

She winced inwardly, telling herself not to be so jaded. She'd been young when she'd lost all four grandparents, but she remembered that both families had gotten along fine.

Looking back, she was glad they'd been so old, that the four of them had died before they'd had to see what happened to Katie's parents, their children.

"Oh, wait, please, wait just a minute!" the mom called to Katie.

Of course, the five-year-old wanted a picture with her mule, Sarah, and Sarah had a beautiful disposition, so pictures with her were always great.

"Please, do you mind being in the picture?" the dad asked.

"Uh, sure," Katie said, wrapping the reins and hopping down. "But," she said, coming around to the sidewalk, "wouldn't you rather I took the picture?"

"I can do it," a voice called.

It was Lorna Garcia, one of Katie's best friends and a co-worker at Trudeau Carriage Company. Lorna was slender, with dark hair and dark eyes that usually radiated cheer and energy, but even as she smiled and took the man's phone to use as a camera, she glanced at Katie with something less than happiness.

"Say *cheese grits*!" Lorna told the group, and they all smiled. Katie gave the five-year-old a few apple pieces and boosted her up on a knee so she could give the mule the treats.

"Café du Monde is right across the street," the dad said, tour director, so it seemed, for the group.

"Enjoy your beignets!" Katie said cheerfully, and they all waved and headed off.

"Thank you," the mom called back, smiling. "You were the best!" she added nicely. "I mean, the very best. Those are great stories you tell. Thanks again."

"No, thank *you*," Katie told her. She smiled. Her stories were good, and she did have her history down pat. She had a little *unusual* help when it came to the stories she told that were part of NOLA lore. A little inside info she really couldn't share with anyone.

It wasn't that she *wouldn't*.

It was that she really *couldn't*.

Over the years, one thing therapy had taught her was there were things you could share—and some you needed to keep to yourself because others might think that they were unbelievable.

And that you needed more and intensive therapy.

The entire group turned around one last time after they'd crossed Decatur Street to Café du Monde. They waved in unison. She waved back.

Then her group was gone, and before anyone else could approach either of them, Lorna slipped her arm through Katie's, drawing her back from the sidewalk and against the fence that surrounded Jackson Square.

"Lorna, what's wrong?" Katie demanded of her friend.

"I'm so sorry, but you're going to hear this soon enough, and I don't want you taken off guard… I mean, nothing can ease this, but…"

"But what, Lorna? You're babbling. I mean, thank you for sparing my feelings. Oh, no! Jeremy—is Jeremy okay?"

"Your cousin is fine. He called a few seconds ago. He wanted to know if we were together. It's already on the news—"

"What is? Lorna, please!" Katie said, frustrated and worried.

Lorna sighed. "Brutal murders in the Marigny. Cops are there now. The media isn't getting much, but you can see there isn't one cop car here where there are usually a dozen and… Oh, Katie! There's been no official police announcement yet, but…they believe everyone in the house was killed sometime last night. Um…murdered with an axe…"

Her voice trailed.

Lorna had been Katie's friend since she had come to live with her dad's cousin, Jeremy Delaney, after her parents had been killed. The girls had been in the same class in high school; they'd even chosen to go to Tulane together.

Of course, Lorna knew Katie's family history. That her parents had been murdered and the killer had never been caught.

Lorna also knew Jeremy had gone down to Florida with Katie six years ago when there had been another murder and they had thought they'd finally caught the killer—her dad's best friend! A man who had also lost his wife that day twelve years ago. But the police hadn't been able to prove it.

Katie didn't want to feel sick—there was no reason to assume the same person that struck twelve years ago was the same person who had struck six years ago—and now, again, today. Or last night.

No reason… Except whatever had happened was already on the news. She could see people on the street stopping to stare at their phones.

A carriage driver with one of the other companies shouted out to a group waiting for passengers. "He's back! The Axeman is back in New Orleans!"

Lorna let out a soft sigh, shaking her head. "What the hell is the matter with him? Does he want to send us all to the poorhouse? Idiot! I mean, this is truly ghastly and horrible—but come on, a crazed killer can't attack every tourist in New Orleans." She looked at Katie and winced. "I'm sorry, I'm sorry, that was just Bucky being a jerk— and clearing the sidewalk of our would-be customers. His, too. But truly, I'm mostly worried about you. Please don't be upset. This probably really is different, Katie. I feel terrible for the police—this is going to be a nightmare for them. More, I'm worried sick about you."

"Lorna, I'm all right. You know I'm a sound, normal

human being. Well, as normal as anyone else. But yes, I will be concerned. You don't need to worry about me, though."

A couple walked by them. "David, my God!" the woman said. "We have to leave—there's a crazy man out there killing people!"

"Martha, this vacation cost a fortune. We're in a major hotel. We're not going down any dark alleys."

They moved on by.

"The Axeman!" someone else said as they walked past. "How do you catch a ghost?"

"There's DNA today. Cops are way better now than they were then," their companion said.

For a few minutes, both Katie and Lorna were quiet, listening to the conversation going on around them. Katie noticed dryly that their friend Benny Morten—a human statue/mime who worked the corner of the square—had forgotten he was playing a silver superhero and reached into his pocket for his phone, as eager as anyone else to get what news he could.

Katie, too, pulled out her phone and checked her news app. There weren't a lot of details available yet, but the early reports were grisly and grim.

"It could be," Katie whispered. She looked at Lorna. "My parents were...hacked to pieces. And six years later in Orlando, an old couple and their niece were killed. And now, here. In Orlando, they wanted to convict George just because he was living there. He was my dad's best friend. His wife was murdered. His best friends were murdered. He barely survived."

Lorna, still distraught, was just staring at her.

"I loved my parents. Naturally, I was crushed by what happened. But I'm all right now. I was a lucky kid. I had Jeremy and then you and other great friends. I will be following this like a bloodhound, but I'm not going to take this personally. No matter how similar it seems."

"Katie, I just don't want this to upset you," Lorna told her. "You've got a reputation for being not only the most knowledgeable driver out here, but the most beautiful, too." Her friend smiled. "You're smart and savvy and busy with growing your business… You can't let this get in your way."

"Lorna, thank you. I'm not going to fall into a terrible depression or need any more therapy," Katie said. "I've had enough therapy for a lifetime. Jeremy insisted. You learn to live with something like this. You cling to the good memories. You manage to be rational. But you don't forget. I'm going to the police station. I'm going to tell them what happened before, what I saw. Maybe I can help." She forced a smile and hugged her friend quickly. "I love you, too. You're the best friend anyone could have. I love what I do. I love the mules and the dogs at the stables. I even love our crotchety old boss. But there is no way I can keep myself from finding out everything I can about what happened."

Lorna sighed. "The cops are all at the crime scene," she said. "Katie, no one is going to talk to you right now."

"Yes, but we're not busy this week. Mardi Gras is over, and we don't have a festival for a few weeks. The city is quiet. I'm taking Sarah and this carriage back, and when I can find out a bit more, I'm going to get myself to the right police station and talk to someone," Katie said.

"Katie, maybe you should take out more tourists today. It'll keep your mind off what is going on—"

"Seriously?"

Lorna sighed. "Okay. I'm sure Matt and I can keep business moving along. But I wish you'd wait. I wish you'd let me go with you. I mean, tomorrow we could plan—"

"Thank you for covering whatever," Katie said. She

headed back to her carriage. "You get a break today, Sarah," she announced to the mule, crawling up to the driver's seat. "We're heading home."

Sarah must have understood. Her ears pricked up, and she clopped along at a decent pace as Katie led her around the square and through the French Quarter, headed for the Trudeau stables across Rampart Street and deep into Treme.

Easy enough. Katie had purchased her own little home, a small house built around 1890, right next to the large property where Monty Trudeau lived and kept his stables. She loved it: no commute to work.

And while her cousin Jeremy Delaney had often suggested she could do more with her education and abilities, Katie thrived in her job.

Once upon a time, she'd thought she'd grow up to be a dive master, leading folks to historic shipwrecks, showing them the incredible beauty and wonder of the reefs.

That had changed. She had discovered she could throw her passion into the city of New Orleans, unique, beautiful and filled with more riches than anyone could ever truly embrace. She'd made a new life.

But there was something that had always nagged at her.

The killer or killers.

They had never been caught.

And she knew she would be haunted by that fact until the day she died.

Unless somehow, somewhere, whoever had committed such a heinous act—taking such wonderful people from the earth far too early—was finally brought to justice.

The scene had been far too familiar.

Three dead, heads bashed in, limbs torn asunder.

Blood everywhere, splashed on the walls and even the ceilings of the little Victorian house.

Their home help, a young woman named Elle Détente, had been killed in the kitchen, and every cabinet and appliance bore spots of her blood. The medical examiner estimated she'd received at least ten blows from an axe.

The elderly woman, Lettie Rodenberry, had been caught in her bedroom on the second floor—killed last, as Dr. Vincent currently believed. Her right leg and head had been almost severed. Two weapons had been used, it appeared.

A knife and an axe.

The elderly husband, Randolph Rodenberry, had been caught in the parlor.

"Shades of Lizzie Borden," Ryder had said grimly as they surveyed the man who had apparently fallen asleep on the couch there.

Dan could just imagine the man, sweetly sleeping, and then opening his eyes to see a vicious killer standing over him.

He'd been struck at least twelve times, hit again and again after death.

Dan had said quietly to Ryder, "Wow. Looks personal. Crime of passion. What stranger kills with this kind of fury?"

"Yeah, it feels personal," Ryder said lowly.

"And yet the same as the last two—six years ago and twelve years ago. The woman…her throat is slit almost ear to ear. This killer used a knife and an axe. And while it bears serious investigation, how could someone be so passionate about such diverse groups of people? This… this is extreme."

"The couple have a son, but he's deployed to the Middle East."

"Either of them known for… I don't know…pissing off the neighbors? Cheating, stealing, complaining about others?"

"From everything we've gathered so far, they were model citizens, nice and kind to everyone, living on their pensions. They were both teachers. No known enemies. And their maid had been with them twenty years. Similarly well-liked in the area, beloved by her employers who depended on her." Ryder paused and drew a deep breath. "The Axeman—the Axeman all those years ago—his murders and assaults were random. Just random."

To kill like this randomly… They were truly dealing with something terrifying.

But they were way too early in the investigation to know anything, even to come up with any kind of a real theory.

"Let's hear the doc," Ryder suggested. Dan observed Dr. Vincent's initial examination and listened to what he had to say. He watched as the photographer worked diligently to take any picture they might need in the future. As the crime-scene investigators moved through the house, they were looking for anything, any clue.

The killer had used a knife and an axe. Mrs. Rodenberry had nearly been decapitated, the slicing on her throat had been so powerful.

"What was his mode of entry?" Dan asked.

Despite being Dan's own age, Ryder winced in a way that added years to his countenance.

"He used a chisel to take out a panel on the back door, the kitchen side door. He left the panel and the chisel on the back steps," one of the CSIs said. "And the axe."

"Just like the damned Axeman," Ryder said. "That bastard always said he was a specter or a demon of some kind—a spirit, uncatchable and unkillable."

"Ryder, come on! Of course, anyone coming here to commit a murder or murders might have looked up stories about the past. What was known about the Axeman was well-documented. Except, if I remember right, there wasn't that much known. The police were grabbing suspects without evidence, they were so desperate," Dan noted. "They didn't have the same tools available that we have today."

"True. So this twisted history buff could be from out of town or homegrown," Ryder said. "Either way... Dan, is there anything different here from...from what you saw in Florida?"

"Just the mode of entry. In the Keys, no one ever knew how the killer or killers got on the boat unless, of course, they were already on the boat."

"Right. The one suspect claimed there had been a mysterious couple with them. Then again, if the boat was on the water, how would anyone get on or get away without another boat?"

"Right. One couple disappeared. Supposedly. One man, George Calabria, showed up on a beach delirious, dehydrated, and a mess. His wife, Anita, was found dead, hacked up and stabbed, along with Louis and Virginia Delaney, the couple who owned the boat. Their daughter had been out diving. She was the one who reached the Coast Guard. She and George Calabria both claimed there was another couple who were on the boat and had simply disappeared—a Dr. Neil Browne and his girlfriend, Jennie someone—neither the kid nor George Calabria remembered her surname. He believed the other couple who had been on the boat had to be dead, floating in the ocean somewhere, food for the fish. I never believed his story. Neither did anyone else. The couple seemed to be nonexistent. Well, you know. I was just a rookie back then, on the periphery. But we all heard about it. Then it was my case, the similar murders that happened six years later. At that time, the killer or killers came in through a sliding glass door at the Orlando home." He paused. "It wasn't even jimmied. The family had forgotten to lock it. Or they had let the killer in."

"Let's head to the station. One of our community outreach officers has been contacting the family. I have officers out canvasing the neighborhood, but this happened late last night, probably right before bedtime."

Dan nodded. The tinny smell of blood was almost overwhelming. He'd seen what he needed to see.

Dr. Vincent was trying to instruct his assistants on how to move the bodies onto gurneys without the bodies falling apart or without leaving bits of them behind.

Crime-scene investigators were still working. They would be doing so for hours.

As Dan and Ryder left the house, reporters were moving in.

"Detective Stapleton, Detective Stapleton!" a woman with a microphone shouted. "Is it the Axeman? Has the Axeman returned to New Orleans?"

Ryder lifted a hand. "The man who committed heinous crimes in this city over a hundred years ago is certainly long dead. So no. He hasn't returned to the city. Murders were committed. We are just beginning our investigation. I beg that you allow us to investigate and not create a sensationalist panic in the city. That's all for now. You'll have information when we have it, if it doesn't hamper our work. Excuse me now, please."

Dan was proud of Ryder. That was well-handled.

They made their way to his unmarked car.

"You're coming with me?" Ryder asked him.

"Took a cab to get here. But I'll hang outside the station for a few minutes. I have a few calls to make myself."

Ryder looked at him with a frown.

"I just need to know where a few people might be at this moment," Dan told him.

"Just remember I'm still trying to make you something official," Ryder said. "And remember we have a constitution and a bill of rights and—"

"Yeah, yeah. I still want to know where a few people might be right now. And I have friends who know how to do things carefully and correctly," Dan said.

Ryder nodded.

They were both quiet as they drove to the station. When they arrived, Dan lingered outside, pulling out his phone and started dialing.

Corey Crest was one of the finest investigators Dan had ever met. He was still with the FDLE, and while he never went out in the field, he was probably one of the most useful men who had ever worked for any kind of law enforcement.

He was a genius at finding people—and finding out about them.

He had apparently seen the news already. And he had been expecting a call from Dan.

"I'm on it," he assured him. "I'll find George Calabria for you."

"Not just him, Corey, if you don't mind. See if you can find out anything at all about the couple that was supposedly on the boat when the murders took place down in the Keys. Dr. Neil Browne and his girlfriend, Jennie. All we knew was they were friends of the Calabria couple from somewhere up north." He hesitated. "Their bodies were never found, and no one could ever find out if Dr. Neil Browne was even real. We put out a search for them back then, but we didn't have a last name for Jennie, and you'd be amazed at just how many men have the name Neil Browne."

"Right. I remember. Hey, half the guys who investigated back then think they might have been imaginary friends. There was no record of them anywhere."

"Browne was probably using an assumed name."

"And Calabria claimed that—whoever they were—they have to be remnants in the ocean by now. Bits of bone, if that. Sea creatures can do a number, along with storms, the passage of time…"

"Corey," Dan said.

"I'm on it. I'm on it." He was silent a minute. "And I'm glad you are, too. Dan, you're too good, too smart, too valuable to be running around after skirt-chasers or the like."

"Yeah, well…"

"Anyway, I'll get you whatever I can."

"Thanks."

They ended the call, and Dan headed into the station, waving to the desk sergeant and then weaving his way toward Ryder's office.

He paused outside a general-interview room. Through the open door, Dan could see an officer, who he knew as Stanley, and a woman seated in the chair before his desk. The young woman was leaning toward the officer and speaking passionately.

Dan didn't know her personally, but he recognized her instantly.

Because he had seen her before. Not here, not in New Orleans.

Back in Orlando.

She had been at the trial. She had been a witness in the case against George Calabria. For the defense.

She had been young then, just twenty-one. But she had

spoken with dignity, even though half of the time she spoke, tears had blurred her green eyes. She was tall, slim, and had hair so red it was like a fire. Not orangish-red, not auburn-red. Fire-red.

She could never be missed or mistaken for anyone else.

She was Kaitlin Delaney, daughter of the couple killed on the boat in the Keys twelve years ago.

The fifteen-year-old who had risen from a dive to find her parents in a different sea—a sea of blood.

And she was here. In New Orleans.

He'd known that she'd moved, that an uncle or someone was raising her here and she had only returned to Florida for the trial. With everything else, he had forgotten that Katie Delaney lived here now.

He inhaled deeply.

Yes, of course she'd have heard about the murders. The media was broadcasting little else.

So she was here. In New Orleans.

Where some supposed Axeman was striking once again.

And Dan had to wonder just what her involvement might be, and if she might be helpful—or if her defense of her parents' old friend just might waylay justice once again.

Two

Katie thought she'd gotten good—very good—at appearing calm, confident and assured whenever she talked about the past.

But the officer she wound up speaking with was nothing short of annoying. He was trying all her hard-earned patience.

"Listen, miss, I'm very sorry about your story, but this is New Orleans. And you're trying to tell me about something that happened twelve years ago over five hundred miles away."

"Not only twelve years ago," Katie said. "Six years ago, too. The killers were never caught. My parents were killed on their boat out in the Gulf. Later, an elderly couple and their niece were killed in their apartment in Orlando. The murders were carried out with two weapons according to the medical examiners. An axe or hatchet and a knife. The bodies weren't completely dismembered, but they were torn apart, a limb here or there, cut so thoroughly as to be detached or almost off. The medical examiners did consult, they believe the murders were committed by the same killer or killers. You need to know this. You need to consult with law enforcement in Florida because this is quite possibly the same killer, and anything they can share might help you find them."

"Miss, again, I'm sorry," the officer said. "We have important business to get through here. We just don't have time for amateur hour, though if your story is true, again I'm sorry."

"Stanley, that's enough!" a deep voice rumbled from the doorway.

Startled, Katie turned around. And she frowned, confused and oddly filled with a strange little sizzle of déjà vu and anger.

She knew the man who had spoken. Well, she didn't *know* him, but she'd seen him before.

He'd been with the cops trying to prove George Calabria was a psychotic killer. Six years ago, when she'd gone down to George's trial in Orlando, she had been an excellent character witness for him. She'd been infuriated the police had wanted to skewer the poor man just because he'd been living in Orlando.

The man's wife had been brutally butchered along with her parents; he'd had to be in a different place if he'd planned on starting over after all that happened.

The officer who had been speaking with her—Stanley, apparently—looked up indignantly. "Hey, come on, Dan! You don't work here. I'm not even sure what you're doing here. You can't just—"

"Stanley, I'll take over," another man said as he stepped into the office. The way he seemed to own the space suggested to Katie this might be the detective she was waiting for. "Dan, what's going on?"

Dan spoke without taking his eyes off her. "Ryder, this is Katie Delaney. Her parents were killed twelve years ago in waters down by the Florida Keys. She has every right to be here. You're going to want to listen to what she has to say."

He was helping her? He was still the enemy. He might be trying to find a way to prove that poor George Calabria was here, in New Orleans, and chopping people up again!

"Miss Delaney? I'm sorry for your loss. I'm Detective Ryder Stapleton. Please come to my office if you don't mind."

She had to crane her neck to take in the detective. She was seated; maybe that was why the two men seemed so tall. But, of course, she'd seen the one before, the Florida cop or agent or whatever. His name was Daniel Oliver. He stood a good six-three, had a broad-shouldered and lean-muscled body, a clean-shaven face with high cheekbones and a sharp jaw, dark hair and piercing amber eyes. He was probably considered good-looking by most, but she had noted that for only a few minutes back in Orlando. Because after she'd seen him testify—seen the way he'd looked at George with fire in those eyes—she'd written him off as a complete ass, rude and ridiculous.

And here he was again.

But at least he was getting her to a cop who might listen to her.

She'd see him long enough to get where she needed to be, and then he'd be out of her life again.

She briefly wondered what the hell he was doing in New Orleans.

It didn't matter.

"Miss?"

"Thank you," she said to the detective, rising with all the dignity in her, nodding briefly to the officer who had been so quick to dismiss her, and heading in the direction Ryder Stapleton indicated.

The detective was about the same age, she thought, as Dan Oliver. He was nearly as tall, and a little kinder-looking, with a broader face, fine cheekbones, warm gray eyes and sandy hair. He looked tired; she figured such work had to make you a little worn-out.

He had his own office—not huge, but comfortable—and there were two chairs in front of his desk. He indicated she should take one of them while he walked around the desk. Dan Oliver waited until she was seated.

Then he sat next to her.

She gritted her teeth. And then she almost smiled.

They'd beaten him once. Because George wasn't guilty. The man had obsessed over George because of circumstantial evidence.

But they'd beaten him.

If he started up on George now, they'd beat him again. And maybe this time, he'd realize that George wasn't involved.

"Thank you," she said, looking at Ryder. "Trust me, I understand murders take place all over the country, and many may be similar in method and madness. But as, uh, Mr. Oliver explained to you, I saw firsthand the work of a madman." She sighed deeply. "I'm a tour guide here in the city. I'm also aware there were a number of axe murders here in New Orleans and environs, taking place back in 1918 and 1919. I understand more fully than most people how myths can grow, how stories can be exaggerated and, yes, how killers can carry out copycat actions."

Ryder watched her, nodding gravely.

At her side, Dan Oliver was silent.

"I, of course, was not at the crime scene in Orlando, but I believe Mr. Oliver was." She glanced his way at last. "Or Special Agent Oliver or Detective Oliver or whoever he is now. I experienced the one scene. He saw the other. And the crime scene today?"

Dan Oliver was staring at her with those piercing eyes of his. She realized suddenly he most probably hadn't just gone after George Calabria out of meanness. He had been deeply horrified by the crimes committed, and to him George had appeared guilty.

She turned back to Ryder quickly.

"I know killings often have motives. I also know they can be random. I've read a lot. I'm not an investigator, of course, but I've read that serial killers seldom stop, that they stay active until they're incarcerated or killed themselves. There have been exceptions or times when they take a break. There might have been killings in other places—other countries, even—that we don't know about. And this killer might have discovered the unsolved case of the Axeman and decided New Orleans might be the right place to strike. My parents were killed twelve years ago, and the killer—or killers—struck again six years later. And now. There might be a pattern here. Something in the motive that means killings must happen six years apart."

"Six years... Maybe there is something to the number six," Dan said quietly.

"All right, Miss Delaney," Ryder said. "I can understand why you're so concerned, and why you think these killings are related. Sure, you've read, so you know about copycat killers. These cases could be totally unrelated. Even your case in the Keys and the one in Orlando might be separate."

"Yes, I know."

"Your parents were killed on a boat," he pointed out.

"But the older couple and their niece in Orlando were killed in their home. Just as these people were killed now."

Katie glanced at Dan Oliver again. She couldn't begin

to fathom what he was thinking. His face was totally impassive.

"Listen," Ryder said, "I understand how you both feel. And yes, murders like this aren't common, thank God. I will bear in mind during the investigation all that has happened in the past."

"Ryder—" Dan began.

"Look, I called you, right? I want to solve this. I want every piece of information available on this killer. If it is the same guy, I want to get him this time. If it isn't, I'm still interested in seeing how this killer—or these killers—are copying the Florida murders or the old Axeman of New Orleans. We're all on the same side here," Ryder said. "Our forensic teams are still going over the scene. You know that, Dan. We'll do everything in our power."

"That means calling Florida for every record available," Dan reminded him.

"I will get everything transferred," Ryder promised. He looked at them both. "I'm sorry. I'm truly sorry," he said to Katie.

She nodded. "Thank you. If you need me to describe what happened, what I found on the boat that day, I can do so."

"I don't see a need to make you go through that now, Miss Delaney. When I've read all the reports…well, I may ask you to come back in."

Katie nodded. There was nothing else she could do. She stood. "Thank you," she said to Ryder. It somewhat pained her, but she turned to Dan Oliver, who had risen as well, and said "Thank you" again.

Ryder also rose. They all just stood there for a few seconds, and Katie turned to leave at last but then turned back.

"Are you a cop here now?" she asked Dan.

He seemed to take a long time to answer. "Private investigator."

"Ah. Well, please, don't forget, if I can give you anything at all, do call me."

She didn't ask them to keep her abreast of any information.

She was just a civilian. They wouldn't tell her anything.

She headed out of the office and the police station at last.

Outside, she walked to her car, a little SUV that allowed her to tool around the city, including the French Quarter, with comparative ease.

Sitting in the vehicle, she couldn't help but relive the awful day when her parents had been killed. And the trial when George had been accused of the Orlando murders.

Something inside told her the killer was the same.

And while a half dozen law-enforcement agencies had searched for information on Dr. Neil Browne and Jennie, nothing, *nothing* had been discovered on them. They might have been ghosts—except they hadn't been. They'd been flesh and blood.

They had either become shark food in the Atlantic, or...

They had been the killers. George said he didn't know much about them. Yes, he had said they were friends. He and Anita had met them at a dockside bar in Coconut Grove. They'd been so nice. They'd claimed they were from New York. Thinking back, he'd never even asked if they were from New York State or New York City. They had simply been so friendly, so engaging, that George had asked her dad if it was all right to ask them out on the diving adventure they'd planned.

She was startled, jumping in the driver's seat, by a tap on her window.

She turned. It was Dan Oliver.

Katie rolled down the window.

"It's the same guy," he said flatly. "Or duo. I don't think more than two people could be involved."

"George didn't do it," she said.

He shrugged. "Let's hope he didn't. I mean, your testimony was so passionate, I'm pretty sure it's the reason he got off."

She forced a smile over clenched teeth.

"Or he might have gotten off because you had nothing but circumstantial evidence."

"Well, if it proves he's not in New Orleans, I'll believe you."

"George isn't in New Orleans. After the trial, he said he was moving far away. He wanted to forget everything, change careers even, anything that could fill his mind with something else. He...he hasn't stayed in touch. He needed a new life." She hesitated. "I know he lived just about a block away from the house where the people were murdered in Orlando. And he was on the boat when my parents were killed. But George isn't a killer. I knew him well."

He nodded. "Well, you might prove to be right. One way or another, I sincerely believe we need to rehash everything. Something has to give this guy away."

She nodded.

But Dan didn't leave. After a moment, he said, "I have a question. I still don't understand how George knew nothing at all about what happened when, as you said, he was on the boat."

Katie sighed. "Yes, he was on the boat. He knew another boat was approaching, but Anita was coming up on the dive platform, and the other boat was sidling along on the forward port side. I'm sure you read his testimony." She paused. "According to George, Anita came up worried because the two of us had become separated. My father was a stickler for diving dos and don'ts, such as you always dive with a partner. So George was talking to Anita, trying to calm her down, assure her I did know what I was doing. Next thing he knows, he gets a blow to the head. He was still looking at his wife, in midsentence. Then nothing. He woke up on the beach with vague memories of realizing he was in the water and had to survive somehow. How he got there, I don't know. Luckily, somehow, maybe he grabbed onto a piece of flotsam, and it brought him in to Annie's Beach. He's a great swimmer and diver—or he was. He's like me now. He hasn't been in the water since. Anyway, he made it to Annie's Beach. That's where he was found. He was airlifted to the hospital on the mainland. His doctors can tell you that he sustained a serious blow to the head." She paused again, staring at him hard. "You know all this. You have every report on what happened. You have his statement. I don't understand what it is you don't understand."

"I don't understand *a blow to the head*," he said. "There were six people on the boat. Your parents, George and Anita, and the mysterious Dr. Browne and Jennie Whoever. Browne and Jennie, disappeared. Your parents and Anita, dead. And George, alive, survived an axe murderer and the open ocean all the way to the beach while only semiconscious?"

"Think what you want. This is going to make you think again," she said.

"Maybe your good buddy will prove to be innocent," he said. "I promise you, though, whether he had anything to do with any of the murders or not, I won't stop this time. I won't stop until we have the truth and solid, irrefutable evidence."

"But you're not even a cop anymore. Or an agent of any kind."

"No, I'm not. I'm a licensed private investigator."

"And living in New Orleans?" she asked dryly.

"Yeah. I have family here, too."

"Right," she muttered. "You knew I was here. Is that why you came?"

"What?"

"Were you following me after the trial, trying to see if I'd crack or something?"

"What? No, God no! I told you, I have family here. Don't be so...full of yourself!"

She controlled her temper and gave him an icy smile. "Right. Well, anyway, excuse me. I need to get back to work. I'm sure you do, too. Private eye, huh? Guess you're on the big cases!" she said in a mocking tone.

He didn't reply. He stepped back from the car.

Katie revved her engine. She'd been sitting too long.

And ridiculously, the day was still young. Well, it was about three in the afternoon, but for many in New Orleans, that was early. The French Quarter did have a nice supply of locals, but it was also a tourist-driven city.

Plenty of rides awaited her in the afternoon and early evening. And working might—hopefully—keep her mind off things she couldn't control.

Even as she drove, heading back to Treme and the stables, she groaned aloud.

Tonight, everyone would be talking about the murders. And they'd have heard there had been an axe murderer busy in New Orleans just over a hundred years ago.

And that's what they would all want to hear about tonight: the grisly deeds of the long-gone Axeman of New Orleans.

* * *

"Listen," Dan said, striding back into Ryder's office, "I—"

"I knew you'd come back," Ryder said, sighing. "Dan, come on! I called you. Obviously, I want you involved. You're one of the best investigators I know. But you know as well as I do that investigations demand patience, too. I have cops out in the neighborhood going door-to-door. We have the medical examiner prepping the bodies today, autopsies tomorrow, as you also know. Our forensic people are gathering everything."

"I know. I want to make sure I am a consultant on this case. Officially."

"I've asked the powers that be. Don't go making them think you're obsessed or personally invested, or I won't have any luck."

Dan frowned, taking his seat in front of Ryder's desk again. He thought Ryder had hesitated, that he was thinking or worrying about something.

"What?" Dan demanded.

"You know… Well, the great powers that be tend to be more generous toward outside consultation when there's a reason, when a victim, survivor or family member has hired an investigator. For two reasons. Gives us extra manpower and makes sure the victims know we're doing everything humanly possible."

"Well," Dan said, "since the Rodenberry's son is on maneuvers in the Middle East, it might be days before he even knows his parents have been murdered. Their closest other contact—their live-in help—was killed with them. What other family is there?"

Ryder hesitated. "Well, better than nothing, there's Miss Delaney."

Dan's frown deepened. "Her folks were killed twelve years ago in Florida."

"She's still an interested party, since we might be dealing with a serial killer."

Dan sat still and silent. The likelihood of Katie Delaney wanting anything to do with him was slim. "That doesn't seem probable," he said finally.

"But not impossible. Talk to her. She may want your help."

"Aw, come on, Ryder. Your department hired me on the drug murders last year that took place in the Seventh Ward. And the year before that—"

"This is different. Sad but true. In a city the size of NOLA and with the tourism and everything else that haunts this town, there are bad things that happen. This is different. This is going to put the police on edge and the citizenry in a frenzy. The media will play it for all that it's worth. I'm afraid of being stonewalled. See what you can do."

"Okay. You'll keep at it in the meantime, right?" Dan asked him.

"You know it."

Dan stood to leave. Ryder was a good guy and would do all that he could for him. He knew the routine, too.

He headed out.

On the sidewalk, he took a few moments to breathe. Then to his own surprise, when a taxi came by, he hailed it and asked the driver to take him to the Garden District. He was going to go to the Garden District Book Shop and find anything he could on the Axeman of New Orleans.

But when he reached the bookstore, he looked across the street at Lafayette Cemetery.

He hadn't lied to Katie Delaney: he had plenty of family

in New Orleans. However, most of those family members were in a vault in Lafayette Cemetery.

It was beautiful, the oldest of the city-operated municipal cemeteries. Like in all the burial grounds in New Orleans conceived utilizing aboveground vaults, those spaces bore the mark of time, adding to a haunting and somewhat mystical appearance of the place. Begun in 1832, it held more than seven thousand dead, and while that was nothing compared to a few of the big cemeteries in New York, like many of those NY cemeteries, it held the dead from dozens of countries and American states. There were at least a thousand family vaults, laid out in a crosslike pattern with beautiful avenues and foliage where possible.

His family's tomb was in a row behind the horizontal beam of the cross. The name *Oliver* had been carved into a stone archway at the top of the tomb. The first Oliver who had come to New Orleans had immigrated from Ireland around 1810, along with large numbers of other Irish as well as German immigrants who had settled the Irish Channel area around the same time. While Louisiana had a city named Lafayette west of New Orleans, Lafayette was once the area now encompassing the Irish Channel, the Garden District and the cemetery, hence the name of the cemetery.

He wasn't sure why he'd come to stare at the family tomb.

While he'd been born in Florida himself—his mom had been a Gainesville native—he'd always loved New Orleans.

He was still fond of his home state, but he'd been haunted by the murders there—and the feeling that justice had not been served.

He'd had to leave.

As, apparently, had Katie Delaney. Then again, her

cousin had been here. He had become her legal guardian. But, as an adult, she'd chosen not to go back.

He understood.

He could be interred in this tomb himself one day if he chose. Ashes to ashes, dust to dust. In New Orleans, one became ash pretty darned quickly: the blazing heat was said to cremate a body fully within a year and a day. And when one did, their remains were swept to join other remains in a holding cell to allow more of the dead to join the family.

He wasn't sure what he wanted yet, and he hoped he had a while to decide.

Even if the life he had wanted was one that invited danger. Not that spying on errant husbands seemed to offer much danger at the moment.

"Buck up, cowboy," he heard.

The soft voice was feminine and teasing. He turned to see a woman leaning against his family's tomb.

New Orleans was known for the strange. For those who liked dress-up and masks.

This woman was dressed for a 1920s dance hall, in a form-skimming sheath with sequins and fringe, stockings and heels, and a cute little cap that was slightly askew on her head. She was posed with a long cigarette holder complete with a cigarette.

It didn't appear the cigarette was actually lit, but she took a drag on the mouthpiece of the holder anyway.

"May I help you?" he asked her.

"I'm here to help you."

"Really? And what is it that you think you can help me with?"

"You're losing your mind over the recent murders, aren't you?" She looked distressed, wincing in a way that drew her face into a truly pained expression. "I know. Trust me. I know."

Dan stood straighter, frowning as he looked at her. "Forgive me, lady. Yes, I have a lot on my mind, and yeah, I'm worried about the murders. I don't know how you think you know that—or me—but I'm not in the mood for playtime or dress-up."

"Dress-up?" she demanded indignantly. "I rather think I chose amazing apparel. And luckily. Lord, I loved my sister, but Evie would have dressed me in a tunic or something if I hadn't left a will. Not that I expected to die at thirty, but…one should always be prepared."

He shook his head. "I don't mean to be rude, but I came to the cemetery to be alone."

He decided to walk away. He felt her following behind him.

"Okay! Again, I don't mean to be rude, but leave me the hell alone!"

He was startled when he realized he was near the gate and some other people coming in were staring at him in surprise.

"I'm sorry, excuse me. She's just driving me nuts," he said.

A woman with a teenage girl skirted far around him. Two college-age kids who looked like they were intrigued tourists shook their heads, looking at one another, laughing.

"Buddy, what, are you off your meds?" one demanded, nudging the other.

"Hey, hush," the other murmured. "He's way bigger than us and talks to himself! Let's get out of here."

They rushed by him, too.

Dan swung around. She was still there, the woman in the flapper dress.

"Dan, give it a rest. They can't see me. I'm dead."

He stood absolutely still, feeling as if the light breeze suddenly turned chilly.

He reached out to touch her. She inched back, but not in time. His hand went straight through her arm.

"I've taken this too personally," he muttered. "They warn against that in law enforcement."

"Don't you see?" she asked him, her tone heartsick. "I'm here to help you! I lost my best friend to an axe murderer once, and I'm not going to see someone get away with this again."

He stared back at her. His mind scrambled to explain what he was seeing. If she was an actress with her image being projected into the cemetery, she was damned good.

Was such a thing even possible?

And if so, why had no one else seen her?

Second guess: he was truly losing his mind.

Because she couldn't be real. Ghosts didn't exist.

Three

Katie felt as if she was going to either explode or implode. What information there was about the murders was being blared on every radio and television station known to man. And in the city, there was no way around every tourist on her rides asking about the Axeman murders of 1918–1919.

She went to work because, otherwise, she'd have been crawling up the walls.

"I can tell you what was known, but to this day, no one can really say who the killer was, if it was just one killer... There are theories, and one woman claimed to have killed him," she bantered as she directed her mule through the streets.

Her carriage held two couples, both in their late forties or early fifties. They were from a small town in Ohio, and it seemed everything about New Orleans fascinated them.

Both couples had become empty nesters, with kids recently off to college, and wanted to do everything wild that New Orleans was known to offer: Bourbon Street, packed clubs, over-the-top drinks... Fun things for adults who were suddenly free to let loose in the world.

Katie had chatted with them when they had first approached her carriage. They'd liked her mule, and she'd given them a bit of info on Jackson Square just in conversation and pointed out that, yes, they were just across the street from Café du Monde.

But now, though she'd gone into history regarding the French founding of the city, the pirate Jean Lafitte and General Jackson, they wanted more recent history.

"It was early in the 1900s, right? They were killing Polish people...or Jewish bakery owners?" one of the men asked.

Katie had known to expect this. She was ready. "Supposedly, there were axe murders that took place in 1911, but a few literary authors have done intense research and could find no record of the victims or anything to suggest that such murders did occur. Catherine and Joseph Maggio were killed on May 23 of 1918—I believe that most scholars see them as the first victims. They were immigrants to the city, and there was already a large Italian immigrant population here. Some people thought the murders were Mob-related, that it was a Mafia retaliation of some kind."

"All the victims were Italian? I thought the killer wrote the press about being Satan or a demon or something like that," one of the women said.

"No, not all the victims were Italian, and a few survived. There's a theory the killer was a man named Momfre and he was shot and killed by the widow of the last victim, a man named Pepitone, in California. The problem with all of it is that records were sketchy in the early 1900s. People were arrested but later released. Previously, there had been an uncaught killer known as the Cleaver in New Orleans, but he took money. The Axeman never took anything. He broke into residences by chiseling out portions of doors. He used a knife and an axe—"

"The news this morning said this killer is using a knife and an axe," the husband said knowingly. "They're suggesting he—like the Axeman—might be some kind of a demon."

Katie arched a brow, glancing back quickly. "A legitimate news station suggested the killer is a demon?"

"Well, no, they mentioned the old Axeman had claimed to be a demon."

"He sent a letter to the *Times-Picayune* on March 13 in 1919," Katie told them. "He claimed, yes, to be some kind of a demon."

"And he made people play jazz!" the other woman said.

"Yes, he said he wouldn't kill anyone playing jazz on a certain night," Katie said wearily. "Four days later, the night of the nineteenth."

"And?"

"People played loud jazz. No one died that night," Katie told them. "We're going to be passing Lafitte's Blacksmith Shop Bar. It's one of the oldest structures remaining. There were horrible fires that ripped through the French Quarter, destroying much of what was original to the city. The bar might have been where the Lafitte brothers sold their booty. They were popular among the people!"

No matter how she tried to change the subject, her group was obsessed with the Axeman of New Orleans.

She hadn't memorized all the facts and figures regarding the Axeman, but in her training to be a guide, she'd learned about the attacks. There were different ideas, of course. And at the time, there had been arrests—wrongly, in one case. A surviving victim had accused her neighbors—an old man and his seventeen-year-old son. They'd gone to jail, looking at the death penalty, and the woman had later recanted. Many of the journalists who had explored records believed the po-

lice had pushed her into identifying her neighbors. Others
believed she had done so out of jealousy or spite.

Katie's tour ended. As the group crawled down from
the carriage—tipping nicely and giving her their thanks—
she saw an older man was waiting. He was watching her.
He had to be waiting for her, she thought, because he was
at the curb by her carriage, and she couldn't imagine any
stranger choosing one of them over the other.

The man might have been around seventy or perhaps
even a few years older, but she'd seldom seen anyone so
straight, lean and dignified. His soft, silvery-white hair
was cut short, and the customary wrinkles of age couldn't
change the fine contours of his face.

He was wearing a gray suit, white shirt and a vest that
matched his suit. He looked like a man about to walk into
an important business meeting, not a tourist eager to hear
the history, lore or ghost stories of New Orleans.

For a moment, she wondered if he was real. *Living.*

Yes, he was real. He was speaking with Lorna.

Lorna didn't see the dead. Nor had Katie ever shared
with her friend, or anyone for that matter, the fact she was
able to see and speak with many of the ghosts that filled
the city streets.

Her uncanny talent helped a great deal in her relaying
the stories that abounded in the city.

It had started that horrible day her parents had been
murdered. The ghost of Billy Battle—privateer, not pirate,
as he assured her—had come to her in the water. He had
probably saved her life, since she'd been floundering, heedless of whether she lived or died. She had seen him only
once again, one night on the beach, since she had left the
Keys so quickly after her parents' deaths. But he had been

kind and had given her so much comfort. In her new world, the dead were not to be feared; they were to be embraced.

"Katie!" Lorna called to her. "This gentleman has been waiting for you."

"Oh?" Katie offered the man a polite but questioning smile.

He smiled back. "Yes, I've been very much looking forward to meeting you," the man said.

"Oh?" she repeated.

The day was going from tragic to strange to stranger.

"May I?" he asked, indicating the step to the carriage.

"Uh...yes, of course. Do you want more of a historic tour or a ghost tour?"

"Ah, well, a good ghost tour is all about history, isn't it?" he suggested.

"Well, yes, I've always felt that way."

"A little of both, please," he told her.

He seated himself in the wagon, in the passenger seat to the right side, making it easier for her to glance back and look at him.

Lorna waved from the sidewalk, curious. Then her attention was diverted as a couple approached her for a tour.

Katie glanced back at the man. He was studying her curiously, intently, but with a smile.

"Katie," he said quietly, "I was waiting for you specifically because I suspect you're someone who can help in the current situation."

She groaned. "You mean the murders. I drive a carriage. I'm not a cop of any kind. I'm not an investigator. Do I think they're all associated? Yes. But I can't personally do a damned thing about it."

"No, but—"

"But?" she asked, wanting to like him, but exasperated.

"I knew your father, Katie."

"Okay..."

"Your dad was gifted."

"Yes, he was extremely gifted, wonderful, brave, gracious and kind. I adored my father. I'm grateful to hear you found him the same."

"I believe you might be gifted, too."

"I like to believe that I'm a decent human being, so, um, thanks."

His easy smile deepened. "Gifted. You talk to the dead, Katie. Your dad did, too."

"I've already made a pile of the books I think you might find relevant. Another agent is down at the archives, seeing if there might be anything missed in the old public records."

Dan wasn't an easily startled person, but the voice that spoke to him as he strolled down the nonfiction aisle at the Garden District Book Shop still seemed to come out of nowhere.

Except he knew the voice.

It was Axel Tiger, an old friend from Florida, who currently worked with an elite unit of the FBI. Because he was originally from South Florida, Axel had often been called down on strange cases in the state.

Axel's special unit was known for investigating the most bizarre cases. When he was with the FDLE, Dan had heard them jokingly called *the ghostbusters*, since they seemed to get any case that had any hint of the otherworldly about it.

He glanced at his watch—it was almost five in the afternoon, and he shouldn't have been surprised. Crime scene, police station, cemetery and bookstore. But had Axel just been in New Orleans? Or had they gotten a call at their Northern Virginia offices already?

"You're here on the murders discovered this morning?" Dan asked, staring at him. "Already?"

"Already," Axel said.

His friend and occasional former coworker stood looking at him with a shrug. "I know you believe the murders in Florida and here had to be related. Naturally, Feds follow events like this that have crossed state lines."

"How the hell did you get here so damned quick?" Dan demanded.

"Our fearless leader is down here, too. He can order the jet whenever he chooses."

"Jackson Crow is here?" Dan asked. He'd worked with Axel's field director in the past, too.

But Axel shook his head. "The big cheese is here. Seems a friend of his was killed years ago, in a similar brutal manner, out on a boat—"

"Louis Delaney."

"Yes, the man's name was Louis Delaney. They had met at a charity function sponsored by military vets and became friends. Anyway, Adam has been haunted by that case for years. He sent an agent down to Florida when the murders occurred in Orlando, and now… Well, we're here."

Axel lifted his hands with a shrug. He was Dan's own height, a solid six three, and the kind of man who was hard to miss in a crowd. His hair was almost jet back, and his eyes were a curious gold-green color. He had mixed Native American and European background, which seemed to add to his commanding presence.

"So, I headed to the police station," Axel continued. "You had just left. I figured this was going to be your next stop—I know you like to research—though it did take a while for you to get here. Did that have something to do with your friend?"

"My friend?" Dan said, and turning in the direction Axel had indicated, he saw *she* was still with him.

He swung back to Axel. "You see her?" he demanded.

"I do."

"Then, she's real?"

"Define *real*."

Axel was his friend, but at that moment, Dan wanted to haul off and slug him. That was not the answer he was looking for.

Axel wasn't afraid of Dan, but he might have recognized his confusion. And disbelief.

"She's real, just dead. Maybe you could introduce us," Axel said.

Dan blinked. "You see dead people?"

Axel nodded. "And I'm guessing you do, too?"

"Never." Dan shook his head. How was he having this conversation? Discussing ghosts as though it was neither impossible nor surprising.

"But she's standing right there."

"Please, tell me this is a prank. That there's a ridiculous new reality show where they take bets on how long it takes a person to figure out the trick."

A woman—very solid and real—was coming around the corner of the aisle. Axel quickly stepped back—she was a large woman. She stared at the two of them and then walked on past, sniffing. "You'd think the cops would be finding out what the hell went on instead of chewing the fat in a store!" she muttered.

Dan looked after her, annoyed. "I'm so sorry, ma'am, but I'm not a cop."

She turned, looked at him, sniffed, and kept right on going—and shivering as she passed by the woman Dan was coming to think of as his flapper.

"Maybe we should buy these books and talk somewhere else," Axel said. He picked up a stack of books and headed to the cashier. The flapper followed him. Dan stared after the two of them for a minute. He couldn't hear what was being said, but he saw the flapper was talking to Axel, and while Axel did nothing obvious in response, it was evident—to Dan, at least—that he was listening.

She was probably complaining about him.

He stood still for a moment, barely breathing. He could hear the thump, thump, thump of his heart as his mind raced.

Axel wasn't the kind of man who played tricks on others. And he'd heard Axel's unit, the Krewe of Hunters, referred to as *ghostbusters*.

It couldn't be real.

And yet…

It seemed it was. Could he simply accept it?

Axel, bag of books in hand, looked back at him.

Dan strode to him, heading ahead to open the door. The flapper went quickly to the door as he held it open. He looked at her.

"Thank you," she said.

"Of course. Though, couldn't you go right through it?"

"Yes, but…it's not always easy. Anyway, thank you."

Axel came through the door behind her. "Let's go, then."

"Hell, yes, let's go," Dan said and then paused. "You got a car here?" he asked Axel.

"Yup. I've got a Bureau car."

"Good. Then, as we drive, you can explain to me why we don't just ask the murder victims who the hell murdered them!" he said, and he gestured for Axel to lead the way.

He'd accepted it.

He was joining his old friend, Axel.

And a ghost.

Okay, never mind. He hadn't really accepted it. Not yet.

"You're coming with us?" he asked her.

"For now, yes. Then I've a little strolling about town to do, see what I can find out," she said.

"You have a name?" he asked her.

She smiled. "Mabel. Mabel Greely. Nice to make your acquaintance."

"Come on," Axel said. "The three of us need to have a good conversation, and then, well, Adam will be waiting, and we'll really get this all geared up."

Dan looked from Axel to Mabel. "Forgive me my rudeness, Miss Greely. But if you're real and you're a ghost, why don't we just ask the victims who killed them?"

"Because they didn't stay," Mabel said softly. She looked at Axel. "This poor boy. He's so lost. Much better when people realize what they can see as children. They're so much more accepting. We've so much to teach you!" she told Dan.

He felt a strange chill that was also oddly warm at the same time as she gently drew her hand down his cheek.

It couldn't be real.

Apparently, it was.

"Katie, my name is Adam Harrison. I have a fancy title with the FBI, but I'm not a special agent. Well, I'm an assistant director, but my talent isn't in finding murderers. My talent is in finding the people who have special abilities and *can* find murderers. I head a unique group called the Krewe of Hunters." He hesitated, aware she was unnerved by him and staring straight ahead as he talked. "Katie, your dad could see the dead."

"No. My father never said anything about seeing the dead. And I never saw him talking to the dead."

"You wouldn't have known."

She turned to stare at him. "I was young when my parents died. Not stupid. I was fifteen! If he knew about this—"

"You do have the gift," Adam Harrison said, sitting back.

She sighed. "I never saw my parents. If it's such a gift, I would have seen my parents."

"Some people go on, some stay. I wish I could explain why."

"Well, you'd think they might have stayed. Instead, my first experience was with an old pirate!"

He smiled. "Well, was the old pirate helpful?" he asked.

She bit lightly into her lower lip.

What the hell was this man getting at?

"Yes," she said honestly. "The old pirate probably saved my life."

"So there, you see?"

"I don't see anything at all!" Katie exclaimed. "Anita Calabria was also a friend—a dear friend. She never appeared to me."

"So who does?" he asked quietly.

She had turned up St. Ann, not really paying attention to what she was doing, and then made another turn onto Bourbon Street. They were about to pass the LaLaurie Mansion, one-time home and torture house of Madame LaLaurie and her husband, Doctor LaLaurie. The couple had found infamy by torturing their slaves and performing medical experiments on them. A cook had set fire to the house while chained to a stove, unconcerned with dying if she could only bring an end to the monstrous things going on in the house.

"Rose!" she said, pointing to the house. "Rose, she died as a beautiful young girl. She loves walking down to Royal Street and looking at all the styles at Fifi Mahony's, a wig shop and hair salon. The wigs are incredibly clever and wonderful. And Rose..."

Her voice trailed. She looked over at Adam Harrison. "My father had this?" she whispered. "He had it, and I have it, and yet..."

"Your parents loved you. They were good people. I don't have all the answers. I knew your father and mother, and they would have wanted to stay by you, I'm sure. But most of the time, the dead do go on. They were together. I don't have all the answers. In fact, I see my son, who died when he was a teenager. But... I'm lucky in that. And it wasn't right away... It took practice, from both of us. I don't know how any of this works. I just know sometimes it does."

"So you're here to solve the murders?"

He smiled and shrugged. "No. I'm a horrible investigator. But I do know how to put the right people together."

"The right people?" She looked at him warily. He couldn't mean Dan Oliver. He wasn't any kind of law enforcement anymore. He was a hack. A private eye!

"I have an agent down here."

"Ah," she said, relieved.

"He's currently trying to connect with the former FDLE agent who worked the case in Orlando, Dan Oliver."

Katie winced. "Listen—"

"Katie, you know you're going to be obsessed with this. And..."

He was staring out to the left. They were passing Lafitte's Bar. She wasn't sure she was leading her poor mule anywhere. Adam Harrison wasn't with her for a tour.

"Mr. Harrison, I believe you knew my father. And that

you care about what is happening. But I can only take your word you're who you say you are."

He reached into his jacket pocket, producing a wallet-size folder with his credentials.

"Okay, let me start over again. Dan Oliver tried his hardest to prove my father's best friend—a man who lost his best friend, his wife, and his best friend's wife on the same day—is a horrific killer. Now, I believe whoever is really doing this probably knows about George and delights in seeing him suffer, but while Dan Oliver wants to see no one else but George as the killer, I want nothing to do with the man."

"Interesting. Where are we now?" Adam inquired.

"Oh!" Katie said. She'd led her mule and the carriage through the Quarter and to Rampart Street. She was heading back to the stables.

Well, maybe it wasn't such a bad idea. It was time to give Sarah a break. Mules were smart creatures, in spite of the fact that the animals, able to handle the Louisiana heat better than horses, were often considered to be their lesser cousins.

She loved Sarah, and Sarah returned the affection.

"I guess I was randomly heading home," Katie said.

"Ah, yes, you have a house right next to the stables where the carriages and mules are kept by Mr. Monty Trudeau." She glanced back at him, and he shrugged. "I'm not a great investigator, but I'm a fine director, and I am with the FBI," he told her. "I'd love to see the stables and where you live."

"Fine."

She had to hop out on the street to open the large gates that led into the Trudeau Carriage Company. But as she entered, she saw Monty come out of the office building that sat between the large enclosure where the carriages were kept and the stables.

"Hey!" he greeted her.

Monty was a big man, tall and broad-shouldered and a bit round. He had a thick head of brown hair that matched his full beard. Both were graying and long and a bit shaggy. Monty reminded her of a bear, but a big, lovable, huggable bear.

"Hey!" she called. "I hope it's okay I brought a visitor. Adam is an old friend of my dad's. I figured I'd drive back with him and just walk next door to get my car."

"Sure. Hi, Adam," Monty called. He studied the man in the carriage. "You were friends with Lou Delaney?" he asked.

"Lou was a great guy," Adam said. "You knew him?"

"Old family friends," he said, looking at Katie and smiling. "He came out here after the storm, and he and his cousin went out in a boat to help. I didn't know him well, but as you said, great guy."

"Right. And it's a true pleasure to meet you," Adam said.

Adam easily swung down from the carriage, a nimble man for his age. Striding toward Monty, he offered his hand. "Nice to meet you, sir. I haven't had a chance to see Katie now in years, but I knew she was working with you. The reviews for your company are great. I quote, *a small and personable carriage-tour business, excellent guides, animals well-tended.* And I've just experienced the same myself."

"Well, thank you," Monty said, beaming. "I think Katie's knowledge and her warm and winning ways have a lot to do with that. We are small—three carriages, three drivers and me. I have five mules—I'm always watching that my animals are in good health and ready to go. Feel that way about my dogs, too. Mr. Harrison, it's a pleasure to meet any old friend of Katie's. Katie, I'll see to Sarah and the carriage, and you and Mr. Harrison can enjoy some time together."

"Monty, that's okay. It's my job. Adam won't mind waiting—"

"I insist! Run along. I finished up all my paperwork, and I need something to do."

Katie was about to assure Monty he was welcome to join the two of them, but she refrained. She didn't want their strange discussion shared with anyone.

"Lorna and Matt are still on the job?" Monty asked.

"Yes, they're out there."

"Then, all is well. Go off. You must have tons to talk about," Monty said.

"Oh, we do!" Adam assured him cheerfully.

"There's a gate that leads to my little place just over there, by the stables," Katie said. Then she paused. She could hear the dogs barking: Jerry, Ben and Mitch. They were huge Belgian shepherds, very loving to those they protected, but no one would ever dare break in at Monty Trudeau's place. The dogs could put up such a racket when they were disturbed that could just about wake the dead over at St. Louis No. 1.

"Monty, want to let the boys out for a minute? I'd love for them to meet Adam," she said.

She also didn't want the man shredded to bits if the dogs made their way through the gate as they sometimes did.

"Good idea," Monty said, nodding gravely. "I'll get the guys."

She thought Adam Harrison looked at his watch with a bit of impatience.

Good.

Katie was unnerved and uncomfortable, and yet she believed he'd known her father. And she was also both amazed and a bit uneasy because he knew about her strange ability.

And that her father had been able to speak with the dead, too.

He'd never told her, never mentioned it.

But then, she'd never had that ability until the day she'd been saved by a long-dead pirate. She supposed her father wouldn't have said anything to her for the same reason she never said anything to anyone else. "Is everything all right?" she asked Adam.

He nodded. "I love dogs. Great to meet fellows who might otherwise want to chew me to pieces."

She smiled. When the canine siblings came out, they seemed ready to accept Adam Harrison. Monty had trained them not to jump, but they raced out to gather around Katie and then to sniff at the newcomer.

"He's good!" Monty told the dogs.

Adam leaned down to pet all three, who then began to vie for his attention.

"Okay, guys… I'll leave the gate open, Monty. They can come and go as they like," Katie said.

"Sounds good. They'll have the run of both yards," her boss said, heading to Sarah and the carriage, ready to take care of both.

Katie led Adam Harrison through the gate at the side of the stables to her little house. Giving the dogs her yard for extra room to roam in wasn't much of a deal. While Monty's place sat on four acres, her little house had about a tenth of that room. She loved it, though. She had found it the day she had applied for a job with Monty. And with the trust fund her parents had left her and the promise of a job to pay the mortgage, she'd been set. Monty had been thrilled she'd purchased the house. She didn't mind looking out for things when he had to be away.

It wasn't in any way a grand Victorian, but it had been built during the mid-1800s and offered lots of charm. A wraparound porch with wooden railings surrounded the house. Downstairs she had what had been a small parlor and music room to one side of the narrow entry hall, and another small parlor, then connected dining room and kitchen to the other side. Upstairs, there were three small bedrooms.

It was more than she needed. She didn't have family or friends come to stay. She had cut off all ties with friends in Florida when she left. Jeremy, her closest living relation, was here.

He had his own house, a place that was a grand Victorian, in the Garden District. But Katie had gone to high school and college in New Orleans and did have plenty of friends here. While they had their own homes, Katie liked to host game nights, and she kept the one downstairs parlor as a kid-safe zone for those who now had toddlers, and it was babyproofed so they couldn't get into anything harmful.

"Nice place," Adam said, as she unlocked her front door and led him in.

She noted the way he looked at the house. He was probably thinking she had no alarm system and that the wraparound porch might allow entry through a dozen windows.

"It's very safe here," she said, as if he had spoken aloud. "And you met my alarm system. Jerry, Mitch and Ben. They would do anything for me."

"Dogs are vulnerable, just like people," he said.

"Ah, well… Can I get you something? Coffee?"

"Let's just sit for a minute, shall we?" he asked.

"Okay. Yes. Sure. Let's get to this."

She led him into the kitchen and dining area, indicating they could sit at the table.

He drummed his fingers on the table for a moment but then got right to the point.

"It really upset me when neither we nor anyone else seemed to be able to discover the truth behind the murder of your parents."

"George Calabria later went to trial for the murders of a couple in Orlando. There are those who are convinced he got away with murder twice."

"But you don't believe that."

"No."

"Why not?"

"There was another couple on the boat. They disappeared."

"According to public record, they were nonexistent," Adam reminded Katie.

"Right. Except they existed. I've said it over and over again. And I know at the time people believed I was traumatized, that I wanted to believe someone else was to blame, that I couldn't accept George was guilty."

"I don't think people thought you were making it up. It was just, on record, they didn't exist. Trying to find out anything about them was a challenge for lots of law-enforcement officials."

"They existed."

"So either they were murdered but thrown into the water to disappear or they did the murdering."

"That's my assumption, yes. I think they were the murderers because, while no one was sharing information of the investigation with a fifteen-year-old, I never let it go, and I heard they didn't find any blood belonging to anyone other than my parents and Anita Calabria on the boat.

I know forensic teams—including FBI teams—went over the boat with a fine-tooth comb."

"Yes."

"They were your teams, I take it?"

"Not at the time, but yes, I had something to do with it."

"Why don't I know you?"

"You did meet me—but you were three or four at the time."

"Ah. Why didn't you see more of my parents?"

"They were busy. I was busy. But I did see your dad about six months before he was killed. He was in DC for a reunion. We were able to go out to dinner together right before I dropped him at the airport to head home." He hesitated. "He raved about you, Katie. He said you were an amazing young diver, that you might turn that love into something wonderful one day. You'd found pieces in the channels that belonged in museums over sites where wrecks had been salvaged and investigated dozens of times."

She shrugged. "I loved it once. Now," she said, offering him a smile, "I love mules. And New Orleans."

He returned her smile. "Katie, what do you remember about that day?"

"Oh, God," she whispered.

"I'm sorry. I don't mean the horror you discovered coming up from your dive. I don't want to subject you to that again. I mean, what do you remember about going out?"

"Well, my dad had the boat at a private wharf. He rented the space. The couple who owned the property could have five boats docked there. The wife kept a little shop with bait, sodas, snacks, life vests…some diving equipment. But when we out…"

She paused, remembering the day.

"We came in separate cars. I mean, my folks and I were

in one, and the Calabrias and their friends came in George's car. We met on the dock. You said you know my dad, so you know he welcomed them. And my mom, too. She liked people... She was happy to look for the best in them. And friends of George and Anita were, naturally, welcome."

"I interviewed Mrs. Jennings, who owned the dock. Mr. Jennings wasn't home when you went out that day. She did think she saw more people than just you, your parents, and Mr. and Mrs. Calabria. But she couldn't be sure. And she couldn't identify anyone."

"I know."

"So we need to find this couple."

"You said yourself law-enforcement officials from all over tried. They're nonexistent. What makes you think we'll have any luck this time?"

"I think they're here. In Louisiana. In New Orleans."

Katie inhaled. "And you think they...that they murdered the people this morning?"

"I do. Otherwise, I'd never cause you distress again. But desperate times call for desperate measures, as they say. And I know you'd go the distance to find justice for your parents. To that end, I've come to you. And to another individual who was in on the second investigation."

"Oh, no, no, no!" Katie said. "You don't mean Dan Oliver. Look, he's not even a cop anymore. I didn't know he was living in New Orleans. Go figure on that, of all the cities in all the world... But no! He was obsessed with skewering George."

"So? Maybe George did have something to do with it. Maybe he didn't. You believe in the man. You have good instincts. In that case, let's clear him altogether by finding the truth, shall we?"

"Can we find it this many years later?"

"You'd be surprised. Where is George now, by the way?"

"I—I don't know."

"You don't know?"

"After the trial, he was a mess. First, he said something about heading to the least congested island out there and burrowing himself away in a hole. Then he decided that would make him crazy. All he would do would be to sit and remember. He wanted to plunge into something else that would keep him busy and send his mind in other directions. He loved the movies, too, and decided he would look for the least skilled, most legwork job he could find with any old movie-production company. I told him to call me when...when he wanted old friends in his life again."

"But he never called you."

"No."

The dogs started to bark. Katie frowned.

Adam Harrison sat back. "That should be Dan Oliver now with one of my team, Special Agent Axel Tiger. They knew each other from Florida, so I sent Axel after Dan. Katie, please don't just sit there. Let's go introduce them to the dogs and let them in."

Four

Dan wasn't sure it was the right time for him to be arriving on Katie Delaney's doorstep.

Yet, according to Ryder, he needed her help to keep him in the loop on everything that was happening with the case.

Axel's arrival had been beneficial. Dan knew he'd comprehend just how beneficial once his head stopped reeling.

Katie came out of the pretty little Treme house along with Adam Harrison, calling to the dogs that it was all right. She reached the wooden fence ahead of Adam, talking to the dogs, telling them he and Axel were good.

Dan knew dogs. Most of the time, he thought they were far more honest and giving than people. But he knew he'd been jaded for a while now, and it was his own fault. He needed to get over the past, get over himself.

And this might be his chance.

He ducked down to pet the three giant shepherds that greeted him with slobbery excitement once they'd been assured he and Axel were friends.

He glanced up as Axel introduced himself to Katie and greeted Adam. He noted Katie was watching him. She looked wary, but at least he seemed to have gained her approval by being a dog person.

"Shall we go in? It's getting late," Adam said.

Katie didn't say a word. She turned and led the way.

She went straight to the front door, allowing the others to follow. Inside, she moved through the narrow entry hall to the parlor at the left of the house and into the dining area, where she took a seat. She sat stoically with her hands folded before her.

The others joined her at the table.

"Well, all right, I'll begin," Adam said. "Axel and I are here at the request of the local police. Because of the nature of the crime, they know they'll be dealing with rumors, truth and myth. I became involved with this on a personal level when Katie did." He stared at Dan Oliver. "I know how hard you fought to bring a killer to justice. Whether you had the right man or not, we don't know."

"It wasn't George," Katie said flatly. She gave Dan what he construed as an extremely hostile glance.

"Maybe not," Adam agreed. "And Axel is willing to start back from scratch, but he'll consider all the accumulated knowledge of the crimes that have occurred."

"What about you?" Katie demanded, her stare on Dan.

Dan nodded. "I am willing to go back over everything I know and to investigate these murders to the best of my ability."

Axel gave him a nudge with his foot beneath the table.

Dan gritted his teeth but added, "With an open mind to the fact I might have been wrong."

"Really?" Katie said doubtfully.

He met her gaze; she was so sure. As sure as he had been the man had been guilty.

"With an open mind," he said, and suddenly he meant it.

Hell, just this morning, he'd believed there were no such things as ghosts. And while the couple on the Delaney boat that long-ago day had seemed to be specters, they might well have been real.

Real killers.

"There will be many in law enforcement who believe the killings are copycats of one another, and here in New Orleans, copycats of the killer who struck in 1918 and 1919 and perhaps before that as well."

"About that," Axel interjected. "Dan has a…contact who might be able to help us with the historical murders."

"And who might that be?" Adam looked at Dan with curiosity.

Dan hesitated. Was Axel really expecting him to talk about this in front of Adam right now? In front of Katie Delaney? He glanced at Adam, still trying to grasp everything Axel had told him about the man—and his Krewe of Hunters. Adam nodded encouragingly. Dan let out a sigh. "Her name was…is Mabel Greely, and she was best friends with one of the Axeman's victims," he said.

To his surprise, no one mocked him.

Not even Katie Delaney.

"She was a friend of a victim—not a victim herself?" Adam inquired.

Dan nodded. After the different ways Katie had looked at him—most of them hostile—she was now looking at him without doubt.

She seemed thoughtful.

"Did she know who did it?" she asked.

He shook his head. "No, but she believes—as do many people who have studied this—it might have been a man named Momfre."

Katie leaned back in her chair. "First to die, as accepted

by most people as the victims of the Axeman, were Joseph and Catherine Maggio. Then Louis Besumer and his mistress, Harriet Lowe, were attacked, but they didn't die. The police arrested a man who had worked at their store, but there was no evidence against him, and he was released. Besumer himself wound up being arrested for the attacks. Harriet Lowe began accusing him of being a German spy, claimed he'd attacked her before... It was all kind of confused, and police officers wound up being demoted over it all. Harriett Lowe later died after a surgery that was supposed to relieve the injuries she had received."

"You just know all this?" Dan asked, frowning.

She shrugged. "I'm a tour guide."

"Then, go on—though, obviously, whoever it was isn't the person doing it now," Dan said.

"But our axe murderer is playing on it," Adam said.

"I think so, too," Dan said. "And I think he's going to copy a lot of what happened. He had nothing like this back in Florida—no New Orleans legend to call up—but this might be... I don't know...his main play?" He looked at Katie who was staring back at him.

She didn't seem quite as hostile as she had before.

"George Calabria has no ties to New Orleans," she told him.

"I said I'm coming into this now with an open mind. Please go on. I just bought a handful of books on the subject, but you seem to have it down pat. What then?" Dan asked.

He noted that, for the most part, Adam and Axel were sitting back, listening.

Katie glanced around at the three of them. "Okay, next, the Axeman attacked a pregnant woman. She survived and so did the child. It was a bit different. Police believed she'd been attacked with a bedside lamp, and they didn't associate it with the Axeman right away. All she could remember was a dark figure standing over her. They arrested a man that time, too, but once again couldn't prove it. The fellow ran when police came after him. There was just no kind of evidence that suggested he did it, but he had a criminal record, and the police were desperate. Because of the nature of the attack—a brutal surprise—they began to think it was the Axeman."

"What was her name?" Dan asked.

"Anna Schneider," Katie told him.

He shook his head. "Not my ghost's friend."

Katie arched a brow in his direction. He shrugged. "I was approached at the cemetery."

"Approached?"

Axel explained, since they'd had a longer conversation with Mabel as they'd walked out of the Garden District. "There's a young woman who was friends with a victim— she wasn't a victim herself. She died of tuberculosis while still young, though. In life, the Axeman murders haunted her, and I believe she's remained because she is still seeking the truth."

"And I thought it would be hard to discover the truth after twelve years!" Katie said. "Now we're looking at more than a hundred. You said her name was Mabel Greely? I'll get to public records and see what I can find on her."

"You've done that kind of research before?" Dan asked.

She grimaced. "Hey, I'm a guide. Licensed and all. We strive to tell the truth that goes along with our legends."

"Who were the Axeman's other victims?" Axel prompted.

"Okay, so next we have Joseph Romano, an elderly man. He survived the attack. His nieces came in when they heard a commotion, and like Anna Schneider, they could report on what they saw, a big man in a dark coat and slouched hat escaping as they arrived. Joseph survived the initial attack but died two days later because of the injuries he sustained. Then…"

She paused, wincing.

"Then…" Dan said in encouragement.

She shook her head. "The worst. He attacked Rosie and Charles Cortimiglia, and their daughter, Mary. Charles and Rosie survived, but Mary was found dead in her mother's arms. Only two years old. Their lives were ruined. They had lost their baby daughter, and they divorced. Mary accused an old man, a neighbor, and his seventeen-year-old grandson. They were both arrested and did jail time, and the seventeen-year-old was sentenced to hang. Mary later recanted. And with good reason. The old man was too infirm to have committed the crimes, and the grandson was too big to have fit through the panel that had been chiseled away at the back."

"Cortimiglia? No," Dan muttered. Katie's glance at him was hostile again. "Sorry, I'm sorry. Mabel Greely claimed her friend was a victim…"

He knew why Mabel had stuck around, why her passion to find justice had been so great that she'd stayed year after year. Her friend had been murdered by the man.

And he had gone on to kill again.

A child.

The Axeman had killed a baby.

"I'm so sorry," he said. "What was the surname of the first victims again? Maggio? I think Mabel said she knew a woman named Maggio, right, Axel?" He looked at the other man, who nodded. Dan went on. "She must have still been reeling from the loss of her friend when the monster struck again."

"I know. It's so hard to think about an innocent child. At least they think the baby died quickly, one blow to the back of the head or neck," Katie said. "Anyway, a man named Steve Boca came next. He woke up to find a dark-clad man in a slouched hat standing above him and went to catch him only to discover he'd been bashed in the head. He survived. Next, Sarah Laumann. She survived the attack but could remember nothing about it. Then—in what is considered to be the last of the Axeman attacks—Mike Pepitone. He was killed, and his wife was left with six children. But there's much more in between all that. Mrs. Pepitone wound up in Los Angeles where she purportedly shot and killed a man named Momfre—with various spellings. Some researchers claim they can find no such incident. I don't know. In that theory, she claimed the man who broke in on her in Los Angeles was the same man who killed her husband. All in all, six were killed and six survived in the number of what most people accept to be the Axeman's killings. There were incidents before about dark, shadowy men attacking people, back in 1910 and 1911, but in those cases, the killer wanted money. It was over a hundred years ago. It's unlikely any more evidence will come to light, so no one can prove anything one way or the other. Researchers just go with what is out there and make their best educated guess. But the Axeman didn't take things. He hacked, sliced and killed."

"And it's believed the letter sent to the *Times-Picayune* came from the real killer?"

"Yes, the letter was received on March 13, 1919, and in it he claimed he was more than a man, that he was a demon or a devil. He refers in it to a *Satanic Majesty* and claims he is the worst spirit in any realm of the real or fantasy. He claimed he was going to pass over New Orleans on the following Tuesday at twelve fifteen at night, and he would spare those who played jazz. People played jazz like their lives depended on it, and no one was killed that night. He taunted the police. And I guess he did. They couldn't catch him. He removed panels often to get into homes, and he left bloody axes everywhere he went. He used a knife, an axe and anything he could to bash people. Maybe he was more than a man—he was a monster."

"Today, he would have been caught. Forensic science has come so far," Adam said.

"Really?" Katie said. "They never caught whoever killed my parents."

"You're right," Adam said, looking apologetic. "But if we're right, and this is the same killer, we will get him this time." He smiled and reached out across the table to squeeze her hand. "We have more than forensic science on our side this time. We have tools others don't. Katie, we're going to get this guy. Now, there is one thing."

"What's that?"

"You may be in danger."

"Me?" she asked, surprised.

"The killer missed you once. You weren't on the boat when your parents were killed. If we're right, the killer might want to finish off what they were doing."

She shook her head and smiled.

"Did you miss the fact that while the dogs aren't mine, I basically live with three giant animals that would tear you to ribbons if you tried to hurt me?"

Dan looked at Adam. If there was one thing he had learned in his years in and out of law enforcement, it was that kind of killer was not working with a full deck. Any rationality, an agenda, anything… Such a killer could be obsessive.

Determined to carry out a job.

"I'm okay," Katie insisted at their worried faces. "I'm right next to Monty. He's a great guy. If I was in danger, he'd be right there for me."

"But doesn't he work the carriages himself sometimes?" Adam asked her.

"Yes, but the dogs don't go with him."

"We'll get someone to keep an eye on things around here," Adam said, nodding at Axel. "All right, here's one thing we need right away—"

"Sketches," Dan interrupted. "We need a sketch artist, and Katie has to give us some kind of likenesses of the mystery couple who were on the boat when her parents were killed."

"I was thinking about dinner. It's gotten very late, and I'm not a young man," Adam said.

"The four of us? Go to…dinner?" Dan sputtered.

"Yes. It's a meal one eats at the end of the day," Adam said, smiling.

"But I should get back to work," Katie said.

"Katie, I'm sure you do fine. And your company will do well enough without you for a night," Adam told her.

"Uh…"

Dan could see she was worried about forging any kind of an alliance with them.

She might not have been so worried if he hadn't been there.

"Katie," he said, wincing inwardly, "I am serious. I will stop trying to prove George did these things and look elsewhere. It's best if we can both help on this…"

"All right, all right. I know a place that's local, the owner is local," Katie said. She stood. "Let me just tell Monty I won't be working for the rest of the night."

* * *

She was still wary; there was no way for her not to be wary of Dan Oliver.

But he did know the cases.

And now that she'd talked with him more, she thought Dan seemed like a haunted man. Not by ghosts—though, it appeared he was—but by the past. The murder scenes he'd witnessed had apparently done something to him. He was passionate about finding the truth.

"I think we should bring Dan into this on a double-pronged deal," Adam said. They had ordered; she'd assured him the shrimp and grits here were about the best to be found anywhere, and the table had ordered the meal along with Mama Didi's famous corn bread and salads.

"Ryder Stapleton, with the NOPD, told me I needed to have a survivor hire me," Dan said, looking straight at Katie.

She sighed. "I do all right, but I don't have the funds to hire a private investigator."

"I'll take a dollar," he told her.

The man was serious.

"Of course, we'll bring you in as a consultant," Adam Harrison said. "I believe we'll be taking lead in the case, and if so, that is all you need. But, Katie, yes—give him a dollar. Hire him officially."

"Okay," she said slowly.

Axel laughed. "Now. You need to give him a dollar now. It's a verbal contract witnessed by Adam and me."

She dug in her pocket for a dollar and gave it to Dan.

There was something in the pained look he gave her as he accepted it that suddenly made it all seem more palatable to her.

"So we're set," Adam said. "We have a great artist in

the NOLA office. We'll go to him for the sketches as soon as we've finished eating."

Their food arrived. Dan compared it to a place a friend of his owned that was in the Irish Channel.

"You really have family here?" Katie asked Dan.

He hesitated and shrugged. "I have family here—they're in Lafayette Cemetery. I do have a sister not so far away—she's living in Baton Rouge. I grew up going back and forth. My dad's family—and my mom—are in Lafayette Cemetery."

"I'm sorry," she told him.

He nodded and said quietly, "They had good lives. They were happy together. The two of them lived in Florida as their main home, but the house I'm living in has been in my family for years."

"And it's in New Orleans?" she asked.

"French Quarter," he told her.

"Ah. Well, I guess that's New Orleans, all right," she said. She was surprised to feel her cheeks redden. She felt a bit bad about assuming he'd followed her to the city when she'd first seen him.

"Katie, you remember these people, right? What they looked like?" Axel asked her.

"Of course."

"It was twelve years ago," Dan said.

"You don't forget a day like that," she said.

"No, I guess you don't," Dan agreed. "And you're right about this place. It could become one of my new favorites. Food is great."

"It is, isn't it?" Katie said.

Adam rose and was pleasant to the waitress as he asked for the check and paid at the counter.

He returned to the table and looked at Katie. "Ready?" he asked.

"Yes, but—"

"Barry Gleason is meeting us there. He's one of the finest sketch artists I've ever met. He's not just a fine artist, he also knows how to listen and adjust details of a person's features."

"It's so late," Katie said.

"Ah, well, there's the thing. Criminals don't keep office hours. Therefore, law enforcement can't do that, either. He's waiting for us."

Axel drove. Katie found herself in the back seat with Dan Oliver.

She sat politely silent and to her own side.

They headed out to the city's offices. Adam was apparently well-known; he was greeted by the security guards and then a woman who seemed to be guarding the inner sanctum.

Katie quickly found herself in a room with a desk and the artist, Barry Gleason. He was a tall, slender man with thinning white hair and a quick smile. He assured her he was happy to be working with her despite the hour.

"We're happy for any help, Miss Delaney. If you can give us a good description, I can hopefully turn it into something valuable."

She sat with the man, aware that Adam, Axel and Dan were silent against the wall as she spoke and Barry Gleason worked.

"The man I met as Dr. Neil Browne had dark hair, very dark. Almost black. He wore it short, but with a swirl over his forehead. His face… He had a young face. I thought he was young to be a doctor of anything…maybe early to mid-twenties. He had very angular features, a long face. Thick brows, light eyes. His eyes were almost a powder blue. He was pleasant, smiled a lot, his lips were thin, and as I said, his face was long, not much in the way of cheekbones, but he was still a handsome man. Part of that might have been in his manner. He was polite, courteous, liked to tease." She paused. "That doesn't help in creating a sketch, does it?"

"Yes, it does," Barry said.

He was working away as he spoke. "Computers can do these things right off the bat, but I like pencil drawings... at first, at least. So..." He added a shadowing to what he'd been doing and slid the paper in front of her for a look.

As Adam had said, Barry Gleason was good.

She nodded, feeling her throat constrict.

It was already a good likeness. Good enough to bring her back in time twelve years.

"Brow a little thicker and a bit higher at the arch. His nose was straight, dead straight. And other than that, the likeness is very good," she said.

He worked on the paper again and handed it back.

She nodded, amazed he was so good, and felt a little sick inside. "Yes, that's very much like the man. The coloring—"

"Ah, I may look like a relic, but I'll be entering this into the computer, and then I'll do all kinds of shades with you at my side. Let's get on to the woman he was with."

"On to Jennie," she said.

And Katie began Jennie's description. She had been about five foot six—unnecessary for a facial sketch, she thought, but Barry listened gravely. Katie went on. Sandy-blond hair to her shoulders, deep brown eyes, slight uptilt to her nose, clean, well-defined brows a little darker than her hair.

Hair color could change easily, Katie knew, but it was

also important in remembering and then getting down to details.

Jennie had been pretty, full of enthusiasm and, just like Dr. Neil Browne, charming. She had been pleasant with everyone. She'd had a light spattering of freckles over her nose, and her eyes were hazel, green with starbursts of brown. Also like Dr. Neil Browne, she'd had a long, lean face, but full lips and…

She paused, and Barry looked at her, waiting.

"A mole. On the left side of her face, just below and to the left of her eye," Katie said.

Barry showed her his work. Once again, he smudged, put in new lines, narrowed, widened and came up with an incredible likeness.

When he was done, he first thanked her, telling her she had an impressive memory and a remarkable way of giving him the little details that made one person different from others. Then he glanced at the trio of men who had been waiting silently through it all.

"I'm going to put these into the computer and deal with the coloring. There's coffee down the hall, and we have a fancy little machine so it's darned good coffee. I'll come get you when I'm ready for Katie."

The men all thanked him. Katie rose nervously.

"Coffee, anyone?" Adam asked. "It's late, if anyone was planning on sleep, but…"

"Hell, yes, coffee," Dan said.

He started out of the room but paused, indicating Katie was welcome to go first.

"No, no, lead the way," she said.

He did, but in the little break room, he offered to make her coffee first. There were different pods to choose from.

She knew she wasn't going to sleep that night. It didn't make any difference. She chose a dark roast.

Since she came from Miami, where Latin American powerhouse coffee was the norm, and now lived in Louisiana where they liked it just as strong, she considered anything less than very bold coffee to be nothing more than colored water.

He smiled.

She thought he approved of her choice.

Adam and Axel opted for tea but noted their tea tasted like coffee.

The offices were quiet; the only noise was from them puttering around the break room. She was afraid it was going to grow awkward, but Barry came for them, and she gratefully followed him back.

His images in the computer were amazing. She gave him only a few more changes in the way they had worn their hair and in the shape of Jennie's mouth. He accomplished all easily.

"Now," he told her, "we'll add twelve years to them."

He hit a few keys on his computer. When he was done, she could easily see she was staring at the couple she had met all those years ago as they might appear now.

"If they're guilty, they've changed everything about themselves. Hair will be different. They may even wear colored contact lenses. But unless you undergo serious surgery, there are things you can't change. These could be extremely helpful," Adam assured her.

Again, they all thanked Barry. He nodded gravely.

"I wasn't at the crime scene this morning. I understand you were," he said to Dan.

Dan nodded. "Yeah."

"If this helps catch those bastards in any way, I'm grateful," Barry said.

"We don't know, but we can't leave any stone unturned, as the saying goes," Adam told him.

They were ready to head out. It was midnight, Katie saw.

After midnight. But while many residents of the city would be in bed—ready to wake for school or jobs in the morning as in any other place—Bourbon Street would still be blaring out music.

Lorna and Matt might still be at Jackson Square getting ready to call it a night.

Or maybe Monty had headed on out to work the late shift.

Katie's mind was whirling. The day had started out so… normally.

And now she was back a thousand miles away and twelve years ago.

Axel drove to her house first, but it was Dan who got out of the car to see her inside.

"I'm okay once I'm through the gates," she told him. "The boys will be out in the yard. Really, you'd have to be one brave criminal to try to get past the boys."

He smiled. She was right, the three dogs were already at the gate, barking away. But they greeted Dan with wagging tails and sloppy licks on his hands.

"If they're here, no one has broken into my house," she said.

"Hey, I was taught to walk a lady to her door," he said lightly.

"Ah, now we're going to be…polite, nice, courteous?"

"I really am nice, polite and courteous. I was just hoping Ryder—that's Detective Stapleton—would let me work this thing."

"Because you should still be a cop?" she asked him.

He shrugged. "Yeah, I should still be a cop. Or something. Or…" He let his voice trail. He looked at her for a moment with real concern and confusion. "You… So you've seen the dead for a long time?"

She hesitated and then exhaled a long breath.

"A dead man saved my life," she said softly. Then she grimaced. "When I surfaced and saw the boat, the blood, my parents… I went numb. I fell back in the water. I would have drowned. But there was a man in the water, a long-dead pirate—or privateer, as he later assured me." She took another deep breath. "And then I came here, to New Orleans, and… Well, they like to say this is one of the most haunted cities in the country." She shrugged. "It is. Helps a hell of a lot when you're a tour guide."

He smiled ruefully. "I guess it would."

"You?"

"Today," he said quietly. "Today. My first time. And I don't…"

"Don't…"

"I've seen a lot of death. FDLE, we got a lot of bad cases. Bodies in stages of decomposition, bodies chopped to throw in the ocean…a lot of bad. Lost both my parents, though they were older, and it was natural causes." He shrugged. "As I said, my family is in Lafayette Cemetery in the Garden District."

"I'm sorry," she murmured.

He smiled. An honest smile. "The thing is… I'm wondering why I suddenly see a flapper who passed away in the 1920s."

"Maybe because you needed to see her. I saw my pirate because I needed to survive. Maybe you need her to help with this case."

He smiled and nodded again. "Well, then, let me get you to your door. I understand the NOPD and the FBI will have a task force with Adam as the titular lead, and Axel, Ryder and me—and every cop and agent in the city on it."

"What do I do?"

"Be a tour guide. I'll find you in the afternoon," he said. The dogs followed them to Katie's door, tails wagging. She unlocked her door, and Dan peeked in.

"Love this. Great little house," he told her.

"Thanks."

"You want to let these guys in for the night?" he asked her.

"Ah, well, they're following us because they want treats. But the gates between the stables and my place are open. Their job is to guard the stables, and they have nice plush beds there."

"Okay, then." Still, he hesitated. "I listened to everything you said about Neil Browne and Jennie. And I think you're really on to something with them."

"You do?" she asked. "Even with George saying they existed, it seemed the cops back then thought he had made them up, and I was a kid and didn't know better and agreed. While he was never arrested for my parents' murders, he was under suspicion. The hospital stated his condition was critical when he was first found, and there was no hard evidence he committed the crime. His story of being hit and sent flying overboard chimed with the forensic evidence they did find."

He shrugged, looking out at the night. "I've come across people like the man you described. They're charming. Pleasant, polite, devious and cold-blooded. Psychopaths. Killing someone is no different than squashing a bug to such people. Sometimes, people they kill are just in the way, preventing what the person wants. And sometimes they become fixated on an idea, and to them people need to die because of that idea. People—and statistics—show most such killers are men, but I've seen the work of misfired minds come in male and female. I think…"

"Yes?" she asked.

He was looking toward the road in front of her house beyond the gate.

"I'll tell you another time," he said. "Axel and Adam are waiting. They're not impatient types, but it is late, and tomorrow the autopsies are starting at 7:00 a.m."

"Yes, of course, go ahead."

"I will tell you," he promised, "when I see you next."

He waved, heading down the walk and out to the waiting car.

Five

Dan's morning started at the morgue with Axel and Ryder.

Adam Harrison was working at the local offices, where he could remain in contact with their main offices and gather any intel from research he could find.

Dr. Vincent was going to handle all three bodies. While the New Orleans morgue had more medical examiners—good ones—on staff, it had been agreed he would oversee the autopsies on all three victims.

And if such attacks should arise again, he would oversee the autopsies done on those victims, too. Any little detail could become important, and the medical examiner on one case might see that same detail in another.

It would be a long morning.

Despite so much that was obvious, Dr. Vincent carefully went over each body. And Dan could only imagine the scene as it had unfolded.

Dan had read Ryder's reports on the victims, and he couldn't help but think about them as their wounds were described in detail and the customary autopsy procedures were performed.

Elle Détente had been in her midforties; she had been a

beloved caretaker for the elderly couple for almost twenty years; Randolph Rodenberry had suffered from Parkinson's disease, and when their son had left home to become career military, they had hired Elle. She had been a childless, young widow; she was one of the family. Dan could imagine she hadn't suspected anything amiss, that she had been shocked to turn away from the sink where she had been rinsing a few dishes and see an axe-wielding killer before her.

Randolph might have opened his eyes to see his killer, but he hadn't seen them long. The first blow had cleaved his skull down a line that had split his face. Subsequent blows had dislodged his eyes from their sockets.

Lettie might have heard the commotion by then. She had possibly been lying in her bed to rise and head for the bedroom door to see what was happening. But she never left the room. She might have been confused, turning the doorknob to discover it was already turning, and then she was facing a man with an axe raised high in the air.

Dr. Vincent believed that she, too, had been cleaved first straight through the skull, lifted and thrown on the bed, receiving more blows there and then the slice of the knife.

Hours went by as the ME worked. Stomach contents were sent to the lab. They might give some indication as to where the Rodenberry couple and Elle Détente had last eaten, but Dan figured it may well have been at their home.

"There are two trains of thought on the Axeman killings," Ryder said as they all left the morgue at last. "One—because so many victims were Italians, perhaps it had to do with the Mob. But some of the victims weren't Italian. And there weren't any other obvious connections. So…the other theory is the victims were random. Do we think this killer just chose the Rodenberrys randomly?"

Dan shook his head. "I don't think so. I think he knew an elderly couple lived in the house and their maid wasn't the feisty kind who might carry a weapon. They didn't have an alarm system, but I think they felt safe in their neighborhood. Back in the 1900s, anyone might have had an axe lying around for firewood or household repairs. Nowadays, people have guns around because the laws allow it in Louisiana. But I don't think they were chosen for any other reason than they were vulnerable."

"So where will he strike next?" Ryder asked.

Dan shrugged and grimaced. "Somewhere he can easily get in and out. We need warnings out in the city. People need to be careful. They need to secure their windows and lock their doors."

"So who wants to give *that* press conference?" Ryder asked, looking hopefully at Axel and Dan.

"Hey, I'm barely official," Dan said.

"You are official. You're a PI hired by a victim and a consultant with the FBI," Axel assured him. He offered him a grim smile. "And there will likely be questions about the legendary Axeman *and* the Florida cases you've worked already."

"And it doesn't matter. None of us has anything to really give people," Ryder said.

"An active investigation. That's all you need," Axel said.

Dan glanced at his watch. It was already growing late in the afternoon. The conference was scheduled for five, barely an hour and a half away.

"All right, all right," Dan murmured.

Ryder nodded. "See you at headquarters," he said.

"And where are you going?" Dan called after him.

"Lunch!" Ryder replied.

Dan watched him go. Eating kept the body going.

But after the autopsies he'd just witnessed? Lunch would wait a bit.

"I'm going to the office to see if Adam has managed to get anything that might be helpful in any way. He'll have Angela on the home front following any old clue possible," Axel told him. "You're welcome to come with me."

"No, thanks. I'm going to check on...on my employer," he said.

"Good idea. You should know, we have agents out, blending in with the locals and tourists, watching out for Miss Delaney and anything suspicious. And I know Ryder has cops out on the street, too, some in uniform, some not. They'll be keeping an eye on Miss Delaney, I'm certain, but I understand your fear for her, too." Axel hesitated. "There are serial killers out there all the time, but my gut tells me that, even if we're looking back twelve years, this is somehow related. Even if there is a history of such crimes specifically in New Orleans." He shook his head ruefully. "That's why Adam wanted me to approach you."

"Yeah? Well, thank God I didn't burn any bridges. I resigned with fair notice. I didn't bash any attorneys to their faces or in the press. I just... I don't know. After that case, I had to get out of Florida. I love it there, but I was so frustrated. Such heinous crimes, and we could do nothing. I'd owned the place here for years... It belonged to my grandparents. My sister got their home in Baton Rouge, and I got the one in the French Quarter. Anyway, after the last trial, it seemed time to relocate here."

"And for six years you've been a PI," Axel said. He grinned. "How's that working out?"

"It sucks. But it was the right move at the time."

"You may be ready to move on from that, too," Axel told him. "Anyway, see you at five."

They parted ways. Dan drove home. Though he was in the French Quarter, parking for one car was easy. The old carriage house—part of the horseshoe design of the home and courtyard—was easily big enough for his SUV.

It was about an eight-block walk down to Jackson Square. He headed toward the river until he came to Royal Street. He didn't want to be on Bourbon, but he did want to see how locals and tourists were doing out among the many shops and restaurants on the popular street.

He heard constant snatches of conversation as he moved along, passing the Cornstalk House and—while he really wasn't hungry yet—he knew there was a Community Coffee shop just ahead, and coffee did seem like a good idea.

He waved to a friend as he passed by Fifi Mahony's. Mrs. Leary was one of his neighbors, who did costuming for various events and always suggested a good wig would help with any costume. He figured she was busy at work.

At CC's, he ordered their darkest coffee, black, and was starting out when Mrs. Leary came in, her most recent purchase in a box. She was shaking her head anxiously.

"You know, boy, I need to talk to you!"

Dan smiled. She was a dear from another lifetime. He let her call him *boy*.

"Okay."

"New Orleans is always wild. We're famous for wild!"

"Yes."

"Dan, those murders! So horrible."

"Yes. Mrs. Leary—"

"And people, on the streets, they're talking about buying dogs and shotguns. People are so scared! But when this is over, are they all just going to throw the dogs out?"

"I doubt that, Mrs. Leary. But guess what? I'm giving a press conference soon, and thanks to you, I will mention the fact that if people get dogs for security, they have to remember they're bringing home a family member, not to be abandoned, okay?"

"Six," she said.

"Pardon me?"

"People are getting crazy out there. There was a couple on the street. He played a violin, she was dancing. She had a card with a six on it in her hat, a steampunk getup. Then another man went up to her and ripped the card out of her hat! And he was yelling that the sign of six was not to be seen! He huffed off into the crowd, and she just looked after him, all angry. And she started shouting after him, 'Six, six, six.' What the hell? It's a number!"

"No one hurt anyone, right?" he asked her. Mrs. Leary seemed upset.

She shook her head. "Just acting crazy."

"You do have an alarm on your home, Mrs. Leary, remember? I made you get it two years ago? You remember to set it, right?"

"I will now," she said sharply.

"Mrs. Leary, you make sure that you do," he said.

"My good boy, thank you. Yes, I will." She smiled. "And, of course, I have Muffy."

Muffy was a Pomeranian, a little ball of puff. Not the kind of dog one associated with protection, though he did love his owner unconditionally.

"Muffy is great, but please set the alarm."

"Oh, yes, yes, I promise," she vowed.

Dan headed out, coffee in hand, only a few blocks from Jackson Square, the cathedral and the park with its striking statue of Andrew Jackson.

He cut down to Chartres Street and then followed the park to Decatur.

He was grateful to see that Katie's carriage was just pulling back into its spot on the curb.

"The area was claimed by an explorer, a Frenchman named René-Robert Cavelier, Sieur de La Salle, in 1682. And then the city, Nouvelle-Orléans, was founded in 1718 by a man named Jean-Baptiste Le Moyne, Sieur de Bienville," Katie said. "Lots of places' names now go back—"

"Man, they had long names back then," the boy with his dad in her carriage said, not being rude, just enthusiastic. "I see French names all over."

"The city has been under several flags," Katie said, drawing the carriage into its spot. "But the French founding runs deep."

She turned to smile at the boy. He'd been great. His father had gotten the rest of the carriage to refrain from Axeman questions because his son was in the carriage. The other passengers, a young couple and two young women, had complied. The boy—his name was Tim, and he was nine years old—had asked all kinds of questions about the city that were easy to answer. Yes, the zoo was wonderful, and they should visit. The aquarium was also beautiful and informative, and both were great for boys his age and for adults. The National World War II Museum was first-rate—and yes, they had a restaurant, and yes, she had eaten there and the food was good. It was getting near five, though, so they might want to start out in the morning. If they headed to the zoo, they could also prowl Uptown and the Garden District, and if they had time, they could perhaps start at the aquarium and spend a few hours there and then head over to the WWII Museum in the CBD. But they could look up exhibits and maps and check on times best for them. And if they hadn't done the museums in Jackson Square, those were great, too.

"I can see the document that gave us a third of America!" Tim said excitedly.

"The Louisiana Purchase, yes. You can see it. And there's the Pharmacy Museum, the Jazz Museum, all kinds of things. Tim, I think you will love both the zoo and the aquarium."

Her group crawled out of the carriage, thanking and tipping her. One of the young women paused as she and her friend took pictures with Sarah.

"You were great with that kid," she said to Katie. "And you know what? I'm grateful his dad asked us not to talk about gruesome murders. First, I was thinking he should have hired a small, individual carriage. Then I was grateful. Oh, my God, that's all anyone is talking about. And some nut this morning at our hotel was talking about six dead goats that had been found not long ago. How do you compare goats to people? Not that I have anything against goats, and I don't want any animal suffering, but...the goats, to this dude, were a forewarning. Anyway, thank you. We were happy to hear about pirates and Mardi Gras and even storms—anything other than lunatic killers." She was a pretty blond woman in her late twenties. She looked at Katie anxiously. "We're in a big chain hotel on Canal, and they have security. We're okay, right?"

"I would think you'd be okay. Just don't open your door unless you're absolutely positive about whoever is outside. I think, however, the killer—if he tries to strike again— will find a house. On a dark and quiet street. Canal... Well, there are people coming and going from clubs and Harrah's around the clock. At a big chain hotel...too many people around all the time. Just be careful," Katie warned.

The girl hugged her and gave her a nice-size bill. As she walked off, Katie saw Dan Oliver was there, casually leaned against the high fence that surrounded Jackson Square. She wondered how long he'd been watching her and if he'd been waiting for her last tour to return.

He was smiling, leaning back, one foot back up against the fence, his arms casually crossed over his chest. He was in a navy windbreaker, jeans, sneakers and sunglasses.

He did cut a striking picture.

"You're a people person," he told her.

She shrugged. "I, uh, guess?"

He pulled his sunglasses off, and his eyes met hers. "I imagine even the dead people wandering around like you."

"Who knows? Who can explain any of it?"

"Not me. I'm already beginning to doubt what I saw yesterday."

"I imagine it's a...hard thing to accept, especially when you're older."

"Thanks."

"I mean, well, I wasn't that young, but I was fifteen and was dealing with so much already. Then, of course, I realized that my privateer had saved me. I was grateful."

He glanced at his watch. "I just wanted to check on you. I need to meet Ryder and the team at the police station. We're doing a press meeting from there. Are you going to be out here tonight? What are your plans?"

She sighed. "I was awake bright and early. Sarah and I were down here by about eight this morning. I'm going to bring her back in around six. We've had a busy day, and she's a great mule, but mules need their rest and fuel just like people."

"People and animals," he said.

"Pardon?"

He laughed. "My mother would have loved you. She said people who were nice to other people were usually good, but now and then they were devious. And people who were good to people *and* animals were almost always just really good people."

"Well, I try," Katie said lightly.

"I'll come right back here," he said. "Wait for me? I'll have someone drop me, and I'll take Sarah back into the stables with you."

"That's okay. I'm capable. I've been doing it for years—"

"I never suggested you weren't capable. Maybe I need the help," he said. "I'll see you later."

A cop car was heading down Decatur, and he stepped out to hail the driver who stopped and, after a brief conversation with Dan, nodded gravely and let him into the car.

"You have all the luck," Katie heard, and she swung around.

Lorna was staring at her, smiling and shaking her head. Her mule and carriage were drawn up behind Katie's.

"I do?" she asked. Katie had never thought it good luck to have your parents brutally murdered, but Lorna wasn't thinking of the past, and she knew that.

"Damn, he's…hmm. Something."

"Something, all right."

"Where do you know him from?"

"He was a cop down in Florida when I went down for George's trial."

"Ah, and therefore, you…you what? He's here for these axe murders?" Lorna looked at her with curiosity. "It's weird. There's like this strange electricity around you both with a push and pull, a magnet, coming close…opposite ends, pushing away… Ah, then they spark again, then…"

"Then nothing, Lorna. He and a few other cops are just

asking me questions, going back into what I can remember about what happened down in the Keys."

"Right."

"Come on, it's dead serious. Bad choice of words. Someone hacked people up with an axe, Lorna. I'm going to do everything I can to help."

"Oh, of course," Lorna said, earnest then. "I didn't mean—"

"I know, I know. It's okay."

"You could have gotten stuck with an ugly detective."

"He's not a detective anymore. I don't think he was detective. I think, technically, he was called a special agent. But he's a private investigator now."

"Oh! Here, in New Orleans?"

"Yes, seems he had family here, too."

"Wow!"

"Yep. Anyway…"

There were other carriages on the street, but Matt D'Arcy, the third employee of Monty Trudeau's carriages, was out with a group.

And there were tourists on the street sizing up the guides and the mules.

"I guess we should get to work," Katie said. "And I'm calling it quits in a bit. I came out here super early today."

"Cool. I'm staying on until ten, and Matt said he'd be out here until midnight, which seems about right since he showed up an hour ago."

Their hours were loose. They just needed good reports from those who rode in their carriages. With the internet and customer reviews, it made for keeping a business nicely afloat.

"Okay, sounds good. Oh, see that little girl heading toward Sarah? I'm going to jump on it—I love taking kids these days." Katie said.

"Grab that group," Lorna said. "I see a crowd of young men coming. I'm going for them. Maybe I can meet a good one this way. I will not close my mind to the possibilities."

Katie waved at her and strode back toward the little girl and Sarah. She still had a few bits of apple in her pocket. The child's mother was near, so she asked if it was okay to let the girl give the mule the treats. A few minutes later, they were off, and Katie was glad. The little girl and her mother also had a dad and two teenage boys with them. The father told her in a whisper before climbing up that he didn't want to hear about the Axeman. She nodded.

"Hey! There's the place we had beignets," one of the kids said.

And Katie was happy to tell them Café du Monde had been there since 1862, a coffee shop for the French Market, which had also offered goods and a sales venue for many of the Italian immigrants who had come to the city as well.

New Orleans had been under the French flag, the Spanish flag, the French flag again, and then become part of the United States. People in the city were from all over the world; many still had French roots, but the English had flooded in, a revolution had caused Haitian people to come, and almost every nationality known to man might be found in the backgrounds of many current residents.

"It's a great big melting pot."

"All-American," the dad said cheerfully.

Katie was enjoying giving a tour to this lovely group. The kids loved her stories about Lafitte and Jackson and how they won the Battle of New Orleans.

She was halfway through when she heard the wife whispering to the husband. "There's a live report, Arthur. A spokesperson is talking about…events. He's warning people to be vigilant and careful, especially at night. To lock up carefully. He is also warning against becoming overly fearful and vigilantes. He believes the killer looks for those whose homes are vulnerable." The woman fell silent. Despite them wanting to keep talk of horror away from the children, she turned up the sound on her phone.

Katie could hear the press conference.

"Are you concerned that the populace is going to arm itself?" someone from the media shouted.

Then Dan's voice. "Here's the thing with turning care and vigilance into panic. The wrong person usually gets hurt. We need to keep an eye out for the unusual, for strangers haunting neighborhoods, and report anything suspicious. The police and the FBI will have a heavy presence in the city and environs. Call the emergency line. We're prepared for many instances that may be nothing. But better to check it out."

"Get a guard dog!" someone called.

"Dogs are great, but they're living beings. They're not disposable. If you decide you need a big dog, make sure you get one you intend to keep and care for. We don't need the shelters being overburdened when this is over."

"Will it be over?" someone else shouted out. "They never caught the Axeman of New Orleans back in 1919. And they never caught the axe murderer at work in Florida."

"This is the twenty-first century, and we have a lot available now in forensic science that wasn't around in 1919. We have a large population, and we're hoping vigilant people will help us every step of the way. There were two terrible events in Florida, and like this, those events shook everyone with their savagery. But we have the FBI and the NOPD and other agencies working on this as well. Every officer and agent in the city has been briefed with all information available. And New Orleans is tough. It has weathered a lot. We have you, those who call New Orleans home, those who come often and those who are visiting. With your help, we will stop this heinous killer. Thank you."

Katie couldn't see Dan, but she could imagine him stepping back. She had to admit he had done a good job, not denying any questions but working with them.

"Can we get back to the pirates?" one of the boys asked. "Whatever happened to Jean Lafitte? He was a hero, but he left?"

"He was wounded in the battle in Mexico in 1823. He was trying to take two Spanish merchant ships. Remember, in 1823, there was no internet, and records weren't as complete as they are today," Katie said. "But it's believed he died from injuries received then at dawn on February 5. He was buried at sea."

"So he was a pirate!" the other teen said.

"A hero and a pirate, I suppose," Katie said.

"Did he have kids?" the mother asked.

"Sadly, a son who died in a yellow fever epidemic," Katie said.

They passed the LaLaurie house, and she took care as to how she told the story of the woman and the doctor who had tortured slaves. The pair had escaped in their carriage after one of their victims had set the house ablaze rather than endure more. Rumors abounded about them as well.

Soon enough Katie came full circle, heading back to Decatur Street, pointing out shops, buildings and other points of interest along the way.

To her surprise, Dan was there, leaning against the fence again, waiting for her.

As he had promised.

She wondered how the hell he had gotten through the city so fast. But he'd likely been dropped off by an officer in a police car, so they might have taken a few shortcuts.

"Isn't that the man from the press conference?" the woman whispered. "Damned good-looking fellow. Think they chose him for that reason?"

"He's looking for the killer, but he's going to take a carriage tour?" the husband wondered aloud.

"He's a friend," Katie said briefly.

"Oh," the man said.

"Ohhh!" his wife echoed.

Katie sighed inwardly. "Don't worry, he'll be working," she promised. "And thank you so much for riding with me."

"Can I pet the horse?" the girl asked.

"Sarah is a mule, but yes, you may pet her," Katie said.

The family stepped down. She still had a few carrots left and let the kids all feed Sarah, and then she took a picture of the family together with the mule and carriage.

Dan had waited patiently, but now he walked up.

The family looked at him somewhat warily, then one of the boys spoke up. "We just saw you on TV!"

"That wasn't TV, that was Mom's phone," his brother said.

"Whatever. We saw you. You're really going to catch him? The hatchet man?" the boy asked anxiously.

"We will be giving it every human effort, and yes, I believe we will find him in the end," Dan told him solemnly.

"Yes, yes, leave the nice officer alone now, boys," the mom said. "Come on now, we're going to get some dinner and get back to the hotel."

"This early?" the younger boy whined. "Mom."

His brother laughed. "We're not going to Bourbon Street, huh?"

"Nelson!" his mother chastised. "Excuse us. I'm so sorry."

But Katie realized Dan was grinning, too.

"Do the best you can to be careful and enjoy New Orleans. It's a beautiful city. And, young man, it's so much more than Bourbon Street. There are amazing places to see and explore. Cool museums with neat things in them. You should see all the old planes in the World War II Museum."

"That does sound cool," the younger boy said.

"Come on," the mom said. "These people probably want some dinner, too. Thank you so much, Katie, and goodbye. Say goodbye and thank-you, kids."

Laughing, the kids waved and followed their parents, the little girl's hand clutched firmly by her mother.

"The city is full of tension," Dan said, shaking his head. "Record day at the shooting ranges in and around New Orleans."

"But is there anything new on the case?" she asked him.

"One thing."

"What's that?"

"I got a phone call from an old coworker in Florida."

"And?" she asked, a grate of impatience in her voice.

"George Calabria. He changed his name. He's going by the name George Calhoun. And he's here, just over the bridge in Gretna, in New Orleans."

Six

The sun was falling, and the colors of night were doing something spectacular. The mules and their carriages, the fence around the park, the trees, the streets, the historic buildings, all seemed to be bathed in a picture-perfect aura of soft mauves and pinks with an occasional streak of majestic gold.

But as Katie stared at Dan, disbelieving his words, just as quickly it seemed smoky shadows replaced the color all around. Darkness was coming.

"Katie, please, I'm keeping my promise to you. Just because he's here, I'm not going to make any assumptions or accuse him again," Dan told her earnestly.

She wasn't sure if his being so determinedly fair helped her at the moment or not. If he'd said *See? I told you. It's George*, she would have rushed to George's defense.

As it was, she was simply stunned.

"He's living across the river. In Gretna," she managed to say.

He nodded solemnly.

"He...he never attempted to reach me. After the trial in Orlando, he said he was starting over somewhere new.

That he had to establish a life somewhere. He'd learned to live with the fact his wife and his best friends had been murdered…and then it had happened all over again, and he couldn't bear the way people looked at him. To live, he had to…change."

"And that may be true, Katie. You ended up here in New Orleans, and I'm here, too. We didn't plan that."

She nodded and looked at him suspiciously. "But…"

"I'd like you to reach out to him. Let's go with your theory, that George is innocent. He must be freaking out now, too, and he's probably in disbelief, wondering how unlucky he could possibly be with what is happening here."

She nodded woodenly.

"Hey, guys!"

Katie swallowed hard and turned around. Matt D'Arcy hopped out of his carriage and approached them. He was smiling curiously.

Katie hadn't really spoken with him since all this had begun. Most probably, Lorna had. Therefore, he'd be curious about Dan Oliver.

Her head still seemed to be ringing. She felt as if she were in a cartoon, as if she needed a sound slap in the face to come around again.

Dan Oliver wasn't going to slap her.

Reaching out a hand, Dan greeted Matt. "Hey. I heard you are part of an amazing trio of carriage drivers and guides extraordinaire for the Trudeau Carriage Company. I'm Dan Oliver. It's nice to meet you."

Matt beamed, taking Dan's hand. "Matt D'Arcy," he said. "And to be fair, in many years I've only come across a few lousy drivers and guides. We're tested, you know, and required to know what we're talking about. Most of us do this because we love it, and because of the city."

"Well, it shows." Dan shrugged. "When I learned Katie was here, I looked up the company. You all have glowing reviews."

"Helps that Monty is a good guy. He loves his animals and takes good care of them. We all love them, too. People don't realize just how affectionate a mule can be. They get bad raps, you know. *Stubborn as a mule.* Not that a mule can't be stubborn, but…"

Matt was in his early thirties. He'd been a history and education major at LSU, and he'd told Katie once that while he'd probably never rule the world by being a carriage driver, he was truly happy. He was a night owl and slept in every morning, and he had a knack for dealing with the somewhat inebriated people he dealt with once darkness had descended. And he'd always step in to help either Katie or Lorna if they had unruly passengers. He was six feet with a full beard and mustache and looked like a man out of a Dickens novel. He was a great friend.

"You're working now, right? Until late?" Katie asked him.

"You know me. Might have been some vampire in my blood," he said lightly. Then he grew serious. "I admit, last night I was a bit creeped out. But I don't think anyone would attack a carriage driver on a busy street."

"I think you'll be okay. I pray we're all okay," Katie said. "Lots of people in the city will be frightened, but we can hope people will be smart, getting off duty at bars, restaurants and other venues in the middle of the night. Anyway, I think Lorna is out with a tour now, and I was going to head in."

He nodded. "You know me. Nothing like a graveyard shift. And I'm glad you're with this guy here, Katie," he added. "I saw your press conference. You were very cool, and I think you said things that made people aware, but not panicky. Panic is scary. But we've survived a lot. New Orleans is strong. And this time I believe you'll get the guy."

"I like to believe we will, too," Dan told him. "And thanks, pleasure to meet you. Katie, let's take care of Sarah and the carriage and maybe get that thing they call dinner."

She smiled and gave Matt a kiss on the cheek. "You be careful, anyway."

"See you," he said with a wave.

A middle-aged woman approached her as she headed back to the carriage.

"You're Katie, right? Are you available?"

Katie smiled. The lady was with a group of four women. Three of them were young and very attractive.

She thought she was about to make Matt's day.

"I'm so sorry, I'm off now. But Matt is there, right on the curb. He's majored in history, and he's great!" Katie told her.

"Oh! Okay, you were recommended to us, but—"

"Trust me about Matt! And have a great night!"

Katie hopped into the carriage, quickly followed by Dan. She watched as the woman shrugged and approached Matt.

"It's night again," she said as she headed away from the river and toward Treme.

"Yes." He shook his head. "Everyone is on edge now. But I hope people don't grow weary of being vigilant as time goes by."

Katie glanced over at him. "The Axeman worked over an extended time. May 1918 to October 1919. But Dan, if this is the same killer we've experienced before, he killed in the Keys and then in Orlando. He didn't perform like the Axeman, killing again and again in the same place."

"Right. But this is New Orleans. And there is the truth

and the legend. Let's get Sarah home then head out," Dan suggested. "I really do need some dinner."

They reached the stables, and he jumped down to open the gates. The dogs quickly came out to greet them, happy enough with Dan since Katie was bringing the rig to the stables.

He helped her—really helped her—knowing how to un-harness the rig and slip on Sarah's halter to bring her in for a brushing and her meal.

"You've done this before?" Katie asked.

"Not really. When my grandfather retired, he had one carriage. And a horse. He didn't stay out long, so his horse was fine, and he never went out during the raging days of summer. But he loved the city and loved taking people around. Especially after the storm. He was determined that the city would come back, and it did."

"Nice. Uh...where's the horse now?"

"She's happily retired on a farm outside of Baton Rouge. My sister dotes on her as if she were a puppy dog. Trust me, Arabella is doing just fine." He pointed in a westerly direction. "He had property just over that way. Small but zoned properly to keep Arabella back then."

She smiled. "Well, I guess you do have associations here and that you didn't follow me."

"No. I didn't follow you," he assured her. He smiled. "But I am going to be following you now, and vice versa, I hope. Adam and Alex and even Ryder think we're im-portant on this."

"I'm not sure why. Do they believe we can think like the killer?"

He shook his head. "I'd say it was because Mabel ap-proached me, but Axel had already come to get me. Maybe everyone is grabbing at straws and we're the straws. Okay, well, this was great, but I take it there is a washhouse out here somewhere?" He grimaced. "I did a little scooping in Sarah's stall."

She laughed. "Let's go through to my place."

He nodded, but as they headed to the connecting gate, he turned back.

"What?" Katie asked.

"Monty's place is dark."

"Well, this is his haven, but the man does go out now and then," she said.

"Sure, of course."

He followed her to her place, thanking her when she directed him to the downstairs bathroom. When he came out, his face shimmering a little from the washing he'd given himself, he was frowning.

"What?"

"Easy as pie to slip in that bathroom window," he said. "If you'll let me, I'll take care of that."

"I... Sure," she said.

"Let's just walk down to Royal," he suggested.

"Okay. You have a place in mind?"

"Let's see what appeals as we go along. But... I like the idea of walking down to the city."

"You know, there are areas around Rampart and Treme that people consider dangerous," she reminded him.

He nodded. "I think we'll be okay."

They were about to cross over to the French Quarter when they were approached by a tall figure who was completely silver.

Not a ghost, just Katie's friend Benny, the human statue/ mime.

Benny was tall and lean, an amazing acrobat, Katie knew, and a great mime. Sometimes, he wasn't on the streets because he was working a theatrical performance. But he was another person who simply loved what he did. He was about to turn thirty, something that had worried him a bit. Adults were supposed to have full-time jobs, and he was still on his own or in a show. Nothing permanent. Nothing with a pension. His background was mixed, and without makeup covering his body and hair, he was an extremely handsome man, dark bronze with flashing amber eyes and a roguish smile.

They'd been fast friends since they'd met, all but crashing into one another while in line for coffee at Café du Monde. They had both wanted enough coffee to stay awake to work long days during a long-ago Mardi Gras. She loved him and thought him incredibly talented.

"Hey!" he said, greeting her. He smiled at Dan. "Good to see you with Katie. I saw you give the press conference. I hate to think about her running around the city alone. Wait, I hate to think about me running around the city alone! But I've been the ghost of Andrew Jackson for several hours now, and I'm beat."

"Benny's place is just a block up," Katie said.

"We can watch you get there," Dan offered, shaking Benny's hand.

Benny apologized for the white that came off. Dan shook his head, laughing.

"No problem."

"I was offered a role in a play at a theater near Disney World," Benny said. "I'm going to take it—get out of here for a bit." He made a face. "I'm all on my own here."

"You're always welcome at my house," Katie assured him. "But if it's a good role—"

"It is. I'll tell you about it later. It's not just the murders, it's that people in the city are too tense. A girl this afternoon… I've seen her telling fortunes at Jackson Square—you know, in that area between the park and the cathedral—just absolutely lost it. She had cards, not tarot cards but a regular deck of cards, and she was running up and down by the shops that line the park, screaming that they were all the number six! Crazy, man. And this is New Orleans!"

"If you need help with anything, let me know," Katie told him.

Dan handed him one of his business cards. "Call if you need help, if you see anything, hear anything…or are worried about anything, even people being weird about fortune-telling. What was she saying about the number six?"

"Random stuff! 'Six, it's the time of six! Repent!' Ah, well, I'm exhausted. I need to get out of costume, chow down a giant bowl of chocolate ice cream and get some sleep."

He waved to them. Dan was silent as he headed down the street. Then he murmured, "Six."

"Bizarre, huh? But, hey. We do get people in the city all the time who think that it's a den of nothing but sin. So-called Christians carrying signs about gay people going to hell. Whether it's your faith or not, hate was not something preached by Christ. The world is filled with fanatics, and yes, I guess we're a place where most people shake their heads at whatever and keep on moving."

"No," he said. "Six. My neighbor was telling me about an incident. An entertainer on the street was wearing a steampunk hat with a playing card—the number six—stuck in the brim. A man went up and grabbed it from her, raving about the number six."

Katie frowned, remembering how the one woman that afternoon had paused to talk to her.

"One of my customers today, she said that some man at her hotel was going on about the number six, too. Something about the bodies of six dead goats having been found somewhere in the city a few years back. Oh! I wish I could remember what she said."

"Dead goats."

"Yep."

They had reached Bourbon.

Lights flooded the streets; music blared from a dozen of the clubs. People walked down the street in pairs and groups and occasionally alone.

She saw Dan was watching the street, too. He nodded to one of the two mounted policemen who were about a block away.

The policeman nodded back and raised his hand, as if assuring Dan they were on the streets and vigilant.

"This isn't where the Axeman killed," Katie said.

"No, I don't think he'll strike around Bourbon Street, either. Too much activity. He would have watched his victims. He knew they were quiet, they went to bed early. They weren't the kind to have weapons in the house. They didn't have a dog."

Katie sighed sadly. "They weren't expecting it."

He sighed, pulling out his phone. She heard him address Axel, and he told him about the goats and all the coincidental mentions of the number six and then hung up.

He smiled at Katie.

"You haven't said anything else about George," she told him.

"I told you. I'm keeping an open mind."

"But you want me to call him."

"I do."

Timing couldn't have been more bizarre. Katie's phone rang. Caller ID didn't know the number.

She looked at Dan. He shrugged.

She answered the call.

"Katie," said a man's voice, low and hushed and frightened. "Katie, it's uh… George."

She almost dropped the phone.

"George. I… How are you?"

"Scared."

"Where are you?"

"Gretna."

"I…um, I hope you're okay. You… I haven't heard from you in six years."

He let out a long sigh. "Oh, Katie, I've wanted to, but I wanted a life, and I wanted you to have a life. I've seen you work. You're great. People love you. I've seen you with your friends, laughing with the mime, having dinner with the other girl. I knew you were okay. And I had to… I had to really start over. I changed my name. It's Calhoun. George Calhoun. I've been working as a PA on one of the B movies being shot here. We're just finishing up…over in the Irish Channel. But…oh, Katie. I'm scared. No one I'm working with knows about my past. But when I heard about the murders… Oh, God. They'll be after me again. Do you think…do you think that I'm being set up?"

Dan was watching her. George was speaking loudly and excitedly then, but her phone wasn't on Speaker; she couldn't tell if Dan was hearing his words or not.

"Tell him we need to meet with him."

She stared at him, covering the mouthpiece on her phone.

"Dan! He won't see you!"

"Then, have him come to your house."

"What?"

"Tell him to come to your house. Otherwise, tell him we'll—you'll—come to his."

She winced. But she wanted to prove George innocent. She believed him.

"George, could I come to your place?"

"I'm still working, just finishing up."

"That's fine. Where do you live?"

George gave Katie his address.

"What time would you be home?" Katie asked.

"An hour? Two hours. Ten o'clock, maybe."

She repeated his address and agreed to the time. She hung up.

Dan nodded. She realized that he was just standing there listening.

"What is it?" she asked him.

"Do you hear that?"

"Music. There's always music. We're barely to Royal Street. We're hearing all the music from Bourbon Street."

He shook his head. "It's not just any music," he said. "It's jazz. It really has begun."

"New Orleans is jazz," she muttered weakly.

"Right. But with some Aerosmith thrown in. Anyway... let's get dinner."

"Okay, wherever—"

"Antoine's!" he said. "We're not far. 713 St. Louis."

"Antoine's is a bit fancy..."

"Adam is buying us dinner."

"Taxpayer money?"

"No, his money. He's a wealthy man. And he's told me I'm not to force PI pizza on you. I'm starving. Let's go for it tonight, huh?"

She nodded, wishing she could shake her feelings of unease. But he caught her hand and led the way, and soon they were seated, and she realized just how often lately she had forgotten about eating. The delicious aromas that permeated the restaurant reminded her that she was very hungry, too.

And that everyone, no matter how involved, needed to breathe in the middle of chaos.

She loved Antoine's. It had a great reputation for a reason. The food was delicious, and the atmosphere was charming. The service was customarily great.

"Oysters?" Dan asked, looking at the menu as they sat at their table with its snowy-white cloth.

"I know they're a specialty here, but I don't care for oysters."

"I don't, either."

"Oh? But you suggested—"

He grinned. "I wouldn't have stopped you," he told her. "Would you like the *escargots à la Bordelaise*?"

She laughed. "Don't care for snails, either."

"That's a relief."

"I do love their *pommes de terres soufflées*," she told him.

"Yes, potatoes! I'm in!"

They ordered iced tea and the appetizer, smiling as the waiter assured them a little sadly just what they were missing out on. They redeemed themselves somewhat by deciding that one would get the special shrimp dish and the other the *filet de Gulf poisson amandine*, as suggested by the waiter.

Katie was thoughtful. "The number six on cards around the city. Six dead goats. So far, six years between the killings."

"Well, at least you didn't suggest voodoo."

"I wouldn't. I live in this city. I know a lot of people who own shops and practice voodoo. They're good people.

They wouldn't hack you to death because in their minds, they'd be hacked to death in a manner three times worse."

He nodded. "Yeah, I got friends who practice, too. I mean, in Florida, I had tons of friends who practiced Santeria. They kept chickens, ate chickens, used chicken-feet talismans. But they wouldn't have hurt a human being in any way, shape or form. And dead goats years ago might have nothing at all to do with this."

"But the number six…"

"Six-six-six is a sign of the devil, but we're talking just six. I'm sure that there are other meanings, but you can find meanings in anything if you want. According to the Bible, God made man on the sixth day. That could be taken in a good or bad way!"

"Excuse me!" a voice interrupted.

Katie looked up startled, certain the waiter wouldn't have addressed them so.

She was so startled that she stood, rattling the glassware and dishes on their table.

It was Jeremy. He looked fierce, but then he looked at Dan, who was standing as well.

"Ah, you're here!" Jeremy Delaney said.

Her father's cousin had been only thirty when Katie's parents had been killed, but he had been determined that Katie wasn't going to foster care or anywhere else—she was his cousin's child. He had been wonderful; he had done his best to ease the past, to make sure she was doing well in school, to encourage her involvement in activities. He was, at forty-two now, a tall and attractive man with sandy hair and hazel eyes, a well-structured, clean-shaven face, and a lean but solid build.

"You're that FDLE officer," Jeremy said. He didn't seem displeased, but he didn't wait for an answer. He turned back to Katie, and his distress was suddenly evident in his tone. "Katie, I have been calling you and calling you."

"What?" she asked.

"I've been calling you."

"I'm... Wow, I'm sorry. I didn't see that you had called. I've..." She was going to say that she had been incredibly busy, but she knew that was no excuse.

Of course he would have been calling her.

And of course she should have called him.

"I have no excuse. I'm so sorry!" she said.

Their waiter stood a bit away from the table, refills for their iced tea in his hands.

"Please!" Dan said. "We're at a table for four. Will you join us?"

"I..."

Jeremy paused, realizing he might be making a scene. He winced and sat.

"Katie Delaney!" he said firmly.

"I know!" she said sheepishly. "I can't apologize enough, Jeremy."

He turned then to look at Dan curiously. "I thought you were from Florida."

"My mother's family was from Florida. My dad's family were longtime New Orleans people. I'm sorry to say that most are gone now, but I have a home here. I moved here six years ago."

"Ah," Jeremy said, looking as if that explained nothing at all.

"Are you meeting people? How did you find me?" Katie asked.

He pointed at his phone. "Family locator app," he said briefly. "Remember? We share our locations? But you two are together. Here."

"Yeah," Dan said. It seemed like he didn't really want to get into it with Jeremy.

"He isn't after George anymore. He believes me about the other couple on the boat," Katie said.

"Ah." And still, Jeremy looked confused.

"I did sketches of them for the police and the FBI," Katie offered.

"So...are you a NOLA cop now?" Jeremy asked Dan.

Dan shook his head. "Private investigator, but at the moment, I'm a consultant with the FBI."

Jeremy nodded and looked at Katie again. "Maybe you should come home with me until this all blows over. I know that you're right next to the carriage company, but this is serious. You know it's serious."

"Jeremy, I'm safe. I'm good," she promised. "Come on, you've seen the dogs. Those guys would take a man down, even a big man."

Jeremy didn't appear to be pleased. "I just want you... safe."

"We all want Katie safe," Dan said.

"Should I take you home?" Jeremy asked.

Their main courses arrived. Katie gave him a half smile and arched a brow. "Um, we were going to eat this stuff we've ordered."

"And, Jeremy, please join us. What would you like?" Dan asked.

Jeremy let out a sigh. "Thank you, but I have a business meeting down the street. Katie, I have just been so worried!"

"And I can't apologize enough," Katie said. "I was wrong and careless and selfish. And I am truly, truly sorry."

"Please, keep in touch. I want to hear from you at least

once a day," Jeremy said, rising. He stopped, looking down at Dan.

"You're watching over her?" he asked.

"I am," Dan confirmed.

Jeremy dipped down, kissing Katie on the cheek. "Once a day!" he said firmly.

"I swear!" she promised.

He looked at Dan. "You were the enemy," he said quietly. "Now I'm counting on you."

He turned and walked out of the restaurant.

For a moment, Katie and Dan were both silent.

"I'm so…ashamed!" she said. "He was—is—the best. He saw to it that I had counseling. He has always been so caring. I was horrible! How did I not think to let him know right away that I was doing okay?"

"We all get caught up," Dan said, glancing at his watch. "Have some fish, and I'll take some shrimp. And don't worry, I'll ask you every day if you've called him."

Katie grinned. "Thanks."

Antoine's was legendary for its sauces—they were delicious. But as they shared food, Katie grinned, thinking they might have asked for the dishes to be shared in the kitchen. Sauce was falling on the white tablecloth.

She met Dan's gaze. He grinned. "Hey, don't worry. They really do wash these things every night."

The food was excellent. They discussed it, other restaurants, the last Mardi Gras, shops and places they loved… and then Katie found herself pausing.

"Mardi Gras was supposed to be low-key in 1918," she told Dan. "World War I was in swing, and with US troops overseas, too much of a celebration seemed wrong. And in 1919. But while the paper announced that the holiday would be calmer, people just didn't get it. So revelers were everywhere. I wonder if the killer walked around at Mardi Gras. If he followed people, knew who they were."

Dan nodded his head. "I think the killer was local. He knew neighborhoods. He knew places to break in, and back then almost everyone had an axe. I don't believe the Mob-connection theory. No hit man kills a two-year-old child." He stopped to mop up the last bites of his dinner. "And I don't think again that there was any particular hatred for the old couple and their help. But the killer knew them. Knew their home, their habits. Busy streets, I believe, are safe. This guy likes darkness and shadows and an escape route. Dessert? Or should we get going?" he asked.

Katie looked at the time on her phone. They'd been there a while.

"The desserts are amazing," she said.

"Okay, what—"

"But we should get going."

Dan smiled. "I'll ask for the check."

He swiveled in his chair to look for their waiter. Katie gazed out the front door. Their table happened to be positioned at one of the few angles allowing her to do so.

There was a woman in front of the door. She had waist-length, very dark hair. She was slim, maybe five foot six.

She was wearing jeans and a peasant-style blouse and carried a shoulder bag.

She moved impatiently, as if she was waiting for someone.

And she didn't like waiting.

There was something about her...

Katie vaguely heard Dan speaking to the waiter, handing him a credit card.

She stood.

"Katie?"

She barely heard him. She turned and moved toward the front door.

She wasn't sure, but she thought the woman looked through the door and into the restaurant. Looked at Katie.

For a minute, or forever, Katie felt as if their gazes locked.

Then the woman moved.

Katie went flying out the door after her.

People...there were so many people about. Of course. It was a tourist area; it was the French Quarter. They might be scared, but many had probably taken their work breaks and their savings to come here.

They'd told themselves they weren't residents, they didn't have homes here, they didn't need to be afraid on the streets of New Orleans.

Katie was afraid she'd lost the woman in the crowd.

Then she saw her, heading down St. Louis Street toward the river.

Katie went tearing after her.

Seven

Dan wondered what on earth had happened to Katie.

Their waiter, in a dignified manner, was returning with his credit card. He made eye contact with the man and cried out, "I'll be back!"

He couldn't pause to sign the bill, and at least he wasn't running out without paying it.

One thing for certain: he didn't want Katie running loose on the streets alone.

Katie could move. Fast.

She was racing up toward Bourbon Street, doing an amazing job of zigzagging around pedestrians.

He caught up to her just as she reached Bourbon Street. She stood there, dismayed, staring in both directions.

"Katie, what the hell is going on?"

She didn't hear him at first, then she seemed to jolt out of whatever she was in.

"I saw her."

"Katie—"

"Her!" she snapped angrily. "The woman. The woman who was with Dr. Neil Browne on my father's boat. Jennie!"

"Katie, we were in a restaurant—"

"Don't, dammit! Don't start doubting me. I'm telling you the truth. Look, you think you're into all this. That you have to clear your conscience or something. No. That's not enough. I want the killer caught. I want him caught before he does this to anyone else. I'm not blind, and I'm not stupid. I saw her. She's different. She had extremely long, almost black hair when she was out there, but I imagine it's a wig. She can probably change like a chameleon. But I saw her."

"All right," he said. "So, she's on Bourbon Street...somewhere."

Katie nodded. "But I don't know if she went toward Canal Street or Esplanade. I don't know which way she went."

"All right. I really don't want you off alone. I'll get Axel. He was going to hang out in the Marigny, see if he could learn anything there. He can be here in minutes—"

"She can be gone in minutes."

"Then, pick a direction, and we'll give your description of her to the first mounted policeman we find."

She let out a sigh. "Okay. Toward Esplanade."

They started walking, moving at a good clip but slowly enough to try to peek into the different venues along the way.

This was impossible, unless they had a small army. But while he walked, he called Axel.

Axel promised to be right there—with an army.

Katie wasn't listening; she wasn't paying any attention. She was determined to find the mystery woman.

They'd only gone a block and a half—past music venues, shops and two strip clubs—when he saw five police officers on foot approaching them.

"We need a description, ma'am," one of them said, nodding to Dan and looking at Katie.

She gave the description quickly, looking back at him with a little bit of wonder.

"I'm Officer Forte. My guys and I are going to fan out and catch the places between here and Canal. Your FBI buddies are behind me. I'll text them the description you gave me. They'll be fanning in from Esplanade."

"I… Thank you!" Katie said earnestly.

"No, thank you, ma'am," Forte said, and nodding to her and Dan, he was off.

"We still need to keep going," Katie said.

"We'll keep going."

They were down another block when Dan noted a trash can out on the corner by one of the crowded club venues.

He paused and looked in.

Either a dark-haired yeti had been shedding or there was a wig in the can.

"Katie!"

He pulled the hair from the garbage. It was a wig—a very long, very dark wig.

"Damn!" she cried.

He nodded toward the nearest club, heading straight for the door with her behind him. The bouncer at the door was a big man—ready to throw out the unruly or the underage—but disinterested otherwise.

"Katie, you know her better. Describe her to the bartender," Dan said.

The bartender was a very pretty topless woman with little specks of silver on her nipples. It didn't give Katie pause.

"I… Wow, I think I did see your friend!" she told Katie after hearing the description. "Her hair was all messy, and she looked as if she was in a hurry. She headed out the back. It leads to a new place down the back, an all-night diner. If you hurry—"

"Thank you!" Katie called, already heading out.

But the back door just led to the side street off Bourbon. The diner was a door down. Katie hurried toward it, rushing in.

Couples and groups sat about at tables, many looking the worse for wear from their night on Bourbon Street already.

There was no single woman there.

And she wasn't with any group there.

They hurried back out to the street. But away from Bourbon, all was quiet. There were dozens of directions in which she might have gone.

"Hey. We'll find her again," Dan told Katie.

She looked at him, frowning, then lowering her head and nodding. "It was her."

"I believe you," he said.

"Maybe the wig can give us something? DNA?"

"Possibly. I'll make sure Axel gets it into the lab right away."

"But her DNA might not be in the system."

"Right again. Katie, we will find her. The likenesses you gave us of Neil Browne and Jennie were excellent. They haven't put them out to the public yet, but officers everywhere have them. They may well find her tonight. And anyway, now we know she's here. We will find her."

"Okay," she said and breathed deeply. "You believe I saw her, right?"

He smiled. "Yes, I believe...in you. And we have the wig."

"Right," she said. "Of course you believe me now. We found the wig."

Well, maybe it was natural that she didn't trust him.

Their time together had been intense, but it had barely been a day since she had accepted the fact they might be on the same side.

He was surprised himself when he took her face in his hands. "I said I believed in you. We were on the hunt before we found the wig. So, if it's all right with you, we'll leave this to the police and the agents for now. We'll go back and get my credit card and then we'll head out to see George, all right?"

"Ah, right."

He dropped his hands.

She looked at him curiously. "You forgot your credit card?"

He stared at her, gritting his teeth, then shaking his head.

"No. I chose you over the card, but now that I know you're all right, I'd really like to get that card back. Now..."

"Right," she said, and turned back in the direction of the restaurant. "Oh! What about the wig?"

He had his phone out. "It's okay. I'll have Axel meet us at the restaurant."

Axel was already near. He'd come with a group of agents to join with the police in the hunt for the mystery woman.

He made it to Antoine's before them and was waiting at the door with an evidence bag.

"The woman you knew as Jennie, she knows you saw her," Axel said, looking gravely at Katie as they waited for the confused waiter to get Dan's card and the receipt for him to sign.

"I... Yeah, she saw me," Katie admitted.

"And she ran," Axel said. "She knows we're looking for her. If we don't find her tonight, she'll go deep underground."

"We're heading across to Gretna to meet up with George Calabria," Dan told him.

"Right. Well, I'm heading back to help the local agents search for our chameleon," Axel said.

"The wig—" Dan started.

"I'll have an agent get it straight to the lab," Axel promised. They went out to the street. Axel offered Katie an encouraging smile and gave Dan a look he understood too well.

Katie could be in trouble.

She was the only one—besides George Calabria-now-Calhoun—who could identify the woman who had been on the boat twelve years ago.

That could mean an even greater danger for her.

"Let's go to my place and get my car," Dan suggested when Axel had gone on.

"All right," she mumbled.

She was silent as they walked. Finally, she blurted, "None of this makes any sense. A killer who struck twelve years ago, six years, and then now. But here, there was a killer who acted in the same manner, but over a hundred years ago. And the number six. Dead goats years back—six dead goats. I mean, I majored in history, but the world has seen crime shows. Serial killers don't just stop, unless they're caught or killed or…or on the moon or something. What could make someone kill strangers in different places and…do it in such a manner?"

"You know, I had a case in Florida once when a man poisoned five people in order to kill his wife and make it look like the work of a crazed serial killer. Motives are not always easy to find. This may be random, but there have been a lot of coincidences. Don't be so disheartened. Mystery Jennie is here. They might find her tonight."

"She's going to have disappeared into the Bourbon Street crowd."

"Maybe. But we know she's here."

They'd reached his house. It was an old building, constructed after the fires that had ravaged the French Quarter at the end of the 1700s and early 1800s.

Dan had always loved it. The place had a small front porch with columns and a balcony that ran the width of the second floor. His grandfather had always kept it painted a soft mauve, and he did the same, with white trim work. A wall surrounded the courtyard to the side of the main entrance, dividing the open side of the horseshoe from the street.

"This is yours?" she asked.

"Yes. I didn't live here growing up, but I visited often enough. My sister and I are all that's left, though, and as I said, she's in Baton Rouge." He paused. "She's a media consultant. You'd like her."

"The house is really nice," she said.

"Thank you. You'll have to see the whole thing one day. But right now we need to get out to Gretna to see George."

"Yes, of course."

They went through the courtyard to the garage. Soon, he'd maneuvered the one-way streets to exit the French Quarter, and then they were on their way to the bridge.

"George will tell you," she said as they drove.

"George will tell me...what?" he asked.

"She's real. Jennie is real. And if she's here, Dan...then I think the man I knew as Dr. Neil Browne could be the current Axeman."

They reached the little shotgun house where George was living in Gretna. The door opened as they arrived.

The man had been waiting.

He had gotten old, Dan thought. Not that he'd been young when he'd seen them last. Now, however, Dan figured he had to be in his late sixties.

A thought nagged at Dan.

Could he have performed such gruesome murders—could he have swung an axe with the strength needed?

He might have simply retired, but he'd told Katie he was working for the film industry.

As Dan had expected, the man's face turned white when he saw Dan was with Katie. He'd started to greet her with a hug.

Then he'd seen Dan.

"Oh, God!" he exclaimed, as he seemed to freeze.

"It's all right, George, it's all right," Katie assured him.

"No, no, no," the man muttered painfully.

"Sir," Dan calmly addressed him, "Katie has changed my mind. We're here to see how we can help you, and I hope you can help us."

George looked at Katie. His eyes were a light powdery blue. His hair was thinning. Once, he had been all bluster and fury.

Now, he just looked tired.

He stared at Dan distrustfully.

"George, it's true. George, I saw her. Jennie. She's here. In New Orleans."

They were still just standing at the front of his house. "Let's just go in," he said.

It was a simple place, a single story, and there was a dining table just beyond the small parlor. George led them there. He'd made a pot of coffee. It was on the table along with containers of milk and sugar—and two cups.

He left them to sit, muttering that he'd get another cup. He did, and they all sat.

George stared at Dan. His tone was dull and dry when he said, "You didn't want to come and arrest me the minute you heard there were more axe murders and I was in the area?"

"Part of me did, yes," Dan said. "But Katie asked me to have an open mind. And I'll be honest, we all doubted the existence of the other couple on the boat with you. It wasn't just me. My superiors believed Katie was young, you were all that was left, and she'd support anything you had to say in your defense. So I guess right now I'm going to ask you to forgive me. Because I need to know everything you remember."

"You heard it all in court."

"I need to hear it all again."

George nodded and then shook his head. "Anita had just come back from her dive. I knew there was a boat next to ours when she came up, but I didn't realize anyone else had boarded." He took a deep breath. "I don't know how I survived. There was just a shadow, a big shadow behind me. I turned, not expecting anything except maybe Lou, and instead…something smashed my head. I was by the hull, and I fell…and I vaguely remember feeling the water as I hit it again. I didn't see who hit me. I didn't know… I didn't know what had happened to my wife and Katie's folks until I was in the hospital. And I asked about Dr. Neil Browne and Jennie, and they all acted like I was crazy. Oh, they searched. And bodies have just disappeared out at sea like that. But…"

He exhaled. "I couldn't bear my home without Anita. I moved to Orlando. And then…well, after Orlando, with half those who knew me still suspicious, I changed my name. A friend there knew some people up here who were new to the movie business and hiring and…it was something to do. I had to have something to do. I couldn't bear living with just myself hour after hour, thinking about the past."

"Okay," Dan said. "Tell me again what you can remember about what happened on the boat before you were struck."

George was thoughtful.

"Anita had just come up, wondering if Katie had returned to the boat. She was distressed, not sure how she could have lost Katie. So I was on the dive platform, watching for Katie, while Anita ran down to talk to Lou and the group. She was going to get them all out and looking for Katie in the water. She had to be near." He grimaced, looking at Katie. "You were a good diver, but Anita was worried. She just didn't understand how you had lost each other."

Katie shook her head and took his hand. "George, I'm so sorry."

"Katie, you're alive because you were in the water, and you didn't cause any of what happened," Dan said sharply. "If you had come up with Anita, you'd have been dead, too."

"Katie, that's true," George told her. "I was aft. The scariest part of it now is that I was curious, not frightened, when I sensed the darkness of a shadow behind me. And all I remember—I've tried, I've tried so hard—is that darkness. And before that... I'd been in the water, too, for a while. I knew there were other boats around, but it was a popular dive spot." He paused again. "That's why I believed Neil and Jennie had been killed, too. I believed someone came off another boat, and maybe they'd been struck or killed and thrown over."

"But their bodies never turned up," Dan said.

"Right," George agreed. "And there was a massive

search for them." He shook his head again. "They seemed like the nicest people in the world when we met them. And Lou was always so welcoming to new people. Your parents were great, Katie."

"I know," she said.

"I will forever be so sorry and hate myself for believing in strangers."

"We've all believed the best in people who haven't deserved to be trusted," Dan assured him.

"I have an alibi for the night of the murders here, though! We worked until one in the morning," he said. "This football star was ending the filming with a free kick. The star player couldn't make the kick that night to save his life!"

Dan was quiet. Mr. and Mrs. Rodenberry might have been killed around midnight—or up to two hours after. But he had promised to have an open mind. George was staring into space, as if he could see back in time. He shook his head. "I don't really blame you for connecting me when the second murders happened. I lived two blocks from the house where they occurred, and there are many more people than you, Dan Oliver, who figured everything about me was a sham. Please understand. I thought about taking a handful of pills several times. Then... I found out I like working long hours. Don't ever want to be in front of a camera, but I love being a grunt when pictures are being made. I was almost...happy. And now this. But what is so bizarre now is after what happened, with everyone talking, I looked up the old Axeman of New Orleans. Witnesses saw *a dark figure*. It couldn't have been. But whoever was behind me, they weren't in a black dive skin or suit of any kind. They were wearing black, enough to appear to be a giant shadow sweeping down."

"Here's my suggestion, George. I'm going to inform the team you are living here. If I don't, they'll find out, and they'll want to know why you didn't come forward. Now I can say you did," Dan told him.

"There goes my job," George said.

"Why?" Dan asked him.

"People will associate me with—"

"No. Law enforcement needs to know, not the general public. Do you have any money?"

George frowned, and swinging around to look at him, Katie frowned, too.

"I, uh, yeah… I'm comfortable. Not rich, comfortable."

"Here's my suggestion. You check into a hotel that uses key cards. You get yourself into bed as early as possible, and you don't open your door again. That way, if someone wants to bring you to court, you have technical proof that you weren't out killing people in the middle of the night."

"Because this killer will kill again…here?" George asked.

"I think so. I think New Orleans and the similarity to the old Axeman were always in the killer's mind. Where else to go into a final frenzy?" Dan asked softly.

"All right. I'll get some things. I'll head over to one of the big chain hotels on Canal Street. That will work, right? I can leave my car here and grab the trolley when I need to get somewhere," George said.

Dan was afraid Katie was going to suggest that George should stay with her.

"I'd have you with one of us, George, except our hours on this might be ragged, and it's best if you're covered."

He wasn't sure if Katie bought it or not. She was just staring at him.

George nodded again and then rose, heading for his bedroom to pack a few things.

Dan saw Katie was still staring at him.

"Is that real?"

"Yes. When you have key cards, there is a record of when doors open and close."

"Even if you don't lock them?"

"Katie, he needs to be seen by people. There are cameras in the large hotels as well. If he's accused of something, police will have access to key-card records and security footage. It's best for George. Trust me. Safer for him, too."

"You think he's in danger."

He stared at her hard across the table. She seemed to be trusting in him.

"Not as much as you," he said softly.

"Me?"

"You saw the woman you knew as Jennie. She saw you. If she's alive, then she's now a key suspect in your parents' murders. Yes, you're in danger now."

"Thank God for the boys," she murmured.

"Katie, the dogs may not be enough."

"I am not going to a hotel, too. Dan. Believe me, I don't want to be anyone's victim, but—"

"Here comes George. We'll talk about it later."

George was coming out of his room with a small suitcase. "I'm ready. Hey, you can put an ankle monitor on me, if you like."

"George, at the moment, I'm looking after you."

"I see that," George said. He glanced at Katie. "How in God's name did you convince him I'm not a crazed murderer?"

"I'm not sure I did," Katie said. "But I do believe he's

trying to protect you. So, we need to lock up and get you to safety."

They all stood and headed for the door. They waited as George locked up his house. He looked back at it as they walked to Dan's car.

"The old Axeman chiseled out panels to get in houses. He used the axes owned by the people he attacked," he said. He looked at Katie woefully. "Thankfully, I don't own an axe."

Katie gave him a weak smile, and they all piled into the SUV.

As they drove, Katie asked him, "Does the number six mean anything to you?" she asked.

"Six?" George said. He shrugged. "I'm sure it's something in numerology. And I'm willing to bet there are a dozen mediums working their shops or out by the cathedral and Jackson Square who could tell you about the number. I mean, I guess all numbers mean something. Why?"

"Curious. It just seems to be a thing around the city," Katie said.

"Six. Hm. Don't know. Bet your father would have, Katie," he said.

"Maybe."

Dan headed back across the bridge, and as they came to Canal, he asked George which hotel he would like.

George shrugged and grinned. "Harrah's. No, not a good idea now. I might be out in the middle of the night. I like cards. Discovered that a little late, but yeah, I like cards."

"So—"

"Right there. That one is good!"

Dan drove around the corner from Canal onto Chartres Street to bring George through the driveway and valet of a hotel that was part of a big national chain.

A young bellhop came to help him.

"You're going to believe that I'm going to check in?" George asked Dan dryly.

"I'm thinking that yeah, you're going to," Dan said pleasantly. "For your own safety, and because you know I'll have access to all the security cameras."

"He's good," George told Katie, standing by her window and leaning down to talk to them both. "Then again, if he is so damned good, why didn't he catch the real killer in Orlando?"

He patted at the car door and walked away, following the bellhop into the lobby.

"You don't think he's innocent," Katie accused Dan when George had disappeared through the hotel doors.

"I think there's a chance he's innocent, Katie. Yes, I really do," he told her.

He headed back out to the street, navigating the one-way streets to head to Rampart and cross over to Treme and then on to Katie's house.

He parked in front, turning off the ignition.

"You're coming in?" she said.

"You bet."

"To check out the house."

He nodded gravely.

"The dogs—"

"Where are they? They're usually barking away and wagging their tails at the fence when the gate between the two properties is open," he reminded her.

"Hm. The boys aren't out," Katie said. She exited the car and opened her gate.

Dan followed her.

It was dark and quiet next door at the stables.

Katie opened her door. He was glad to see at least she had locks on it, one a solid bolt. But he remembered what George had said—remembered the crimes of the past.

The killer had gained access by cutting out panels in doors. And he also remembered the window in her downstairs bathroom. It was large, looking out over a pretty magnolia bush and covered with a solid plastic drape.

But it was easy access to the house.

He followed her in, and she turned on the hall lights. He stepped ahead of her and started with the left side of the house and then the right.

She followed him.

He headed upstairs next, going room to room.

She had her bedroom, while another bedroom had been transformed into an office. The third, the guest room, offered an inflatable bed and small television. Back out in the upstairs hall, he noted there was an attic. A cord pulled down the stairway to it.

"Dan! If someone was in the attic, how would they get the stairs down?" she asked him as he yanked on the rope.

He ignored her, headed up the dusty stairs, found the chain for the single electric bulb and pulled it. Light flooded the space. It was clean and neat with only a few boxes.

No one was hiding there.

He headed back down. She was waiting for him in the hallway.

"Okay?" she asked him.

He headed back down the stairs, determined to check out the back door, the kitchen door, again.

He remembered there had been a second door.

The house was built up on pilings, so there might well be a basement. There was. Like the attic, it was clean and neat. It contained yard tools, an extra refrigerator, a Ping-Pong table and heating equipment.

Little windows looked to the outside.

They could be broken.

A man—not a giant, but even a man his size—might be able to crawl through them.

He came back up the basement stairs. Katie was waiting in the kitchen, leaning on the counter.

"It's a basement, right?" Her tone was sarcastic. "We're at water level, but the house was built up. And yes, it has flooded, so I move stuff up when a storm is coming. But no one was in it, right?"

"Nope."

"Would you like coffee or something before you leave?" she asked him.

He shook his head.

"No, you don't want coffee? Would you like something else?"

"Coffee is fine," he told her. "Nope, I'm not leaving."

She looked at him, frowning. Then she sighed. "Listen, you've gotten to where you're bearable, but I'm not—"

"Hey. I'm staying because there are no dogs out in the yard and your house is a veritable sieve."

"But—"

"Katie, do you have any damned common sense? You could be a target! Do you have a death wish? Did you want to invite an axe murderer in?"

She seemed to freeze where she stood. "No," she said. "My apologies. The guest room has a blow-up bed, but it's a good one, and the sheets are clean. Please, make yourself at home. Oh, and it has its own little bathroom. You'll barely fit in it, but I get nice hot water, and the water pressure is surprisingly decent, too. Towels on the hooks in there are clean, too. Coffee…well, you know how to fix coffee, I'm sure."

She walked out of the kitchen, and he heard her footsteps as she hurried upstairs.

And then the click as she closed her bedroom door.

Eight

Dan Oliver wasn't a bad guest, and Katie wasn't sure why'd she'd been so sharp with him the night before. She'd heard him walk around, and she was certain he was checking all the windows. She'd heard him in the kitchen.

He had made coffee. She thought about going back down; coffee never kept her awake.

And now she was embarrassed. She'd made assumptions when he'd spoken, and it had really been idiotic. She'd just been so nervous.

She was, in truth, glad he had insisted on staying, she admitted to herself once she'd showered and curled into her bed. The dogs didn't seem to be out.

Her house might well be full of holes.

She'd never learned to shoot and didn't own a gun. Living in Jeremy's house until she'd gone into a dorm at college, she had always felt safe.

Jeremy did have a shotgun, and locks and a high-tech alarm system.

She wondered as she lay awake why—after what she had witnessed—she hadn't headed straight out to a shooting range. She should have learned to defend herself. Maybe she'd resolve now that she would do so.

Jeremy had even suggested it after college. But she had decided to buy the house next to the stables, and Monty was there, and the dogs were there…and it was easier to lose herself in the busyness of working the stables, of talking to new and different people every day.

She'd got caught up in building this life, and she was proud of her tours, that she knew how to make her stories both accurate and fun. Even her weird ability to see the dead had worked out for her because she could add bits and pieces of lore she had learned from the ghosts she sometimes found wandering through the city.

"Why aren't you being more helpful now?" she whispered aloud, to no spirit in particular.

She didn't know. But as she lay there, she realized she would have been awake all night if Dan hadn't stayed.

She heard when he checked the front door, and she knew he checked the rear door, too.

And she heard him when he came up the stairs and softly closed the door to the guest room.

She was tired, so tired. And now she had showered, and the hot water had been delicious, and she felt wonderfully comfortable, and while her thoughts raced, she was relaxed.

And she even wondered at herself.

He'd made her laugh a few times. He'd made her feel competent and important…

She let out an oath of aggravation with herself, slammed her pillow and curled around again to get comfortable.

She wished she had more experience with men. After moving to New Orleans, she'd dated a boy named Len Trotsky in high school, but that had faded away her first year of college; she'd been a dedicated student. And Jeremy had been like a watchdog, and maybe people even thought she was strange, if they knew her history.

She'd had a couple casual relationships with men who had come and gone; both had been musicians, and their schedules had gotten in the way...

Relationships were scary for her because of her ability to see the dead. She'd learned to hide it in everyday life, pretend she was talking on her phone so she could converse with a spirit, but to live a full life with someone... It would be such a lie to omit something like that about herself. And if she revealed it? Surely they'd back away faster than they could say *boo*.

Nothing had ever ended badly. No one had broken her heart. They had just faded away, and she had known she had just been biding time. She had never allowed anything more than friendship to develop between her and Matt or their friend Benny. Friendships were hard to come by, and they were good friends.

And now... She laughed inwardly at herself and smiled in the darkness.

She didn't really know how to handle herself with a mature male. Especially one she never thought she'd tolerate, much less come to like and respect.

She gave her head a shake. Maybe she was doomed to being likable and maybe even a bit charming—and alone.

Whatever...

It had been a long day. A hard day. But she had seen Jennie. And it seemed Dan believed her. George was here, and Dan was respecting his promise regarding George.

And still...

She felt she was living and breathing pure tension.

But over that, exhaustion.

Finally, she felt the comfort coming, the inability to open her eyes, the sweetness of sleep.

It must have been a deep sleep, because when she opened her eyes, she didn't know why.

Then she heard it. Movement downstairs.

She shot out of bed, barely daring to breathe, terrified at first, and then remembering Dan was down the hall. She paused on the landing, her heart thudding so she was sure it could be heard all the way down to Bourbon Street.

"Katie."

She heard his voice as he spoke her name quietly.

"You can come to me. I'm at the foot of the stairs."

She pattered down quickly. He was just inside the front door. He had on his jeans, but his chest and feet were bare.

He had his gun in his hand.

"What is it?" she whispered.

"Someone was here," he said, and he let out a sigh. "Around back. He was going for the back door."

"But—"

"I heard him, but he heard me coming. He was gone before I could reach the door and get out. I've called Ryder and Axel. They'll start a search of the neighborhood."

She nodded. "Thank you," she said. He was telling her a killer had come for her; the killer had been at her back door.

And she couldn't seem to distract herself from his chest. He was very tightly muscled. He was bronze, and in the soft light, his muscles seemed to ripple and gleam.

She inhaled and exhaled. "You're sure...you're sure there was someone there?" she asked. "Monty might have let the dogs back out. They always like to check and see if I have a bit of a treat for them or something."

"It wasn't the dogs."

"Maybe an ordinary intruder?"

He shook his head.

"How do you know?"

"He left a calling card. There's an axe by the back steps." He was quiet for a moment. "This wasn't his only stop. There's blood on the axe."

The forensic teams went everywhere. Through the house, around the house, through and around the yard, and on to Monty's place.

Luckily, it had been close to dawn by the time Katie woke and came down, and now it was getting light. Dan had already called in what had happened, and the teams quickly arrived.

Monty, up and over when he saw the commotion, was worried.

"It's my fault! I let the boys stay in the house when I was out last night. I should have had them in the yard. It's a mistake I won't make again. And let the cops tear my place apart. If there's anything to be found, I will be relieved and grateful to help in any way."

He had an arm around Katie as if he were her father. Katie was trying to be appreciative and extract herself at the same time.

Lorna arrived for her carriage and mule, but once she heard what had happened, she joined Monty in the kitchen, comforting and keeping Katie company.

Dan stood outside with Axel and Ryder.

"We already got the axe into the lab," Ryder told Dan. "We're calling precedent on this with everything. The wig is already being tested, and I believe we will get DNA, but if it's not in the system..."

"I know," Dan told him. "And even if it is…we have to find this woman and prove she's involved."

"The problem with finding her is that she changes with the wind," Axel added. "She could have a fine supply of wigs, different-colored contact lenses, sunglasses, scarves… We did have an army on the street last night, and we didn't find her. But even with that many police going venue to venue, it's easy to slip outside of the French Quarter with a crowd, get to the backstreets, to wherever she's staying. Also we know a man is doing the killing—or a big, tall woman—and that isn't Katie's Jennie. So she has an accomplice here. I imagine they thought they could go around the city without being noticed. They'd think a girl—as Katie was twelve years ago—wouldn't remember them that clearly. She'd only met them that day."

"We've made a number of different images based off of the one Katie created," Ryder said. "The woman with different hair and eyes. If she's here and part of this, we will find her."

"Great," Dan said.

The other men were silent for a minute, watching as the forensic teams went through the yards, seeking the tiniest piece of evidence.

Then Axel asked, "Do you think that she targeted Katie because Katie saw her? Or was she on the agenda already?"

"I don't know," Dan said. He had already told them he'd seen George Calabria/Calhoun. "There are many possibilities. Was it just chance that Jennie was outside the restaurant? Or was she trying to watch Katie? We know there were two of them. The killing, however, does seem to be done by one man. Still, it may be a joint effort. What I don't understand is the geography with what went on here.

Florida, Florida, Louisiana. And the number six that keeps coming up. Speaking of which, anything on the goats?"

"It was three years ago," Ryder replied. "The goats were found with their throats slit. Drained of blood. They were found right off the road. At the time, there was an outcry, of course. But we know people here. We know the key people who really practice voodoo, and they're damned honest. Love spells, good spells…and it wasn't witches or anyone who thinks they're vampires. We have had a lot of groups who are wannabe vampires. Some of them are so-called spiritual vampires. They suck good vibes out of the air. Other groups drink blood, but they don't kill for it, they donate to one another. It's all a bit bizarre. But we investigated and couldn't find out who was responsible. This is a city that has gone through a lot. We still have major crime. The goats…well, it was a single incident, and it wasn't high on the list of what we needed to be investigating," Ryder said.

"Right. Like now. The blood on the axe. Nothing has been reported?" Dan asked.

"Not yet," Ryder said, shaking his head. "We've got the info out to our officers. They are doing their best."

"Agents, too," Axel said. "I'm going to head back in." He hesitated. "It was a good thing you were here last night," he told Dan.

"Yeah."

"Katie should be in a safe house," Axel said.

"This is a safe house if Monty remembers to leave the dogs out, Dan stays and you and I keep our people on it," Ryder said.

"I wish she was somewhere else," Dan said, shaking his head.

"Well, I don't think he'll come back to a place where he can't just slip in and surprise an unarmed woman," Ryder said.

"There's no telling," Axel said. He turned to Dan. "So I guess you're going to stay close with Katie. What's your plan?"

Dan smiled. "She's a tour guide. We'll tour."

Axel nodded. "And look for the woman."

"All right. I'm heading back to talk to the troops," Ryder said. He lifted a hand as he left them and they nodded.

When he was gone, Dan added, "We're going to be looking for two women. One living, and one dead. That was rude of Mabel to appear and say she was going to help and then disappear. Are ghosts always that rude?"

Axel grinned. "See if you can find her, too. She's been prowling around, I'm sure. She has the luxury of not fearing for her life."

Dan looked at the man he had worked with before and called a friend. He'd never known or suspected there was anything out of the ordinary about him. He knew they had often been referred to as the ghostbusters unit, but he'd assumed that was because they dealt with cases having to do with supposedly haunted houses and crimes where the bizarre came into play.

He'd never thought that…that they were ghostbusters. Except it didn't sound as if the ghosts needed busting—their role was to help the living prevent more death.

"How do you just…deal with dead people?" Dan asked.

"Ah, well, I grew up knowing there was more," Axel told him. "Maybe that makes it easier. It may not seem like it, but…well, it makes it easier to help sometimes. Hopefully you'll find Mabel, and maybe she'll have some insight."

"One can only hope. It looks like the forensic team is wrapping up. I'm going to see if it's all right to take the carriages and the mules out," Dan said.

"I'll be in touch, and I'm only ever a phone call away."

Axel headed out. Dan found the head of the forensic team. His name was Randy Moliere, and he appeared to be in his midthirties and was lean, energetic and determined. He was the kind of man who had authority and wielded it well with his own determination in getting a job done.

"Find anything?" Dan inquired. "And the folks are asking if they can go to work? We really don't have a connection to Monty's property, and he's been a good guy, letting everyone traipse around."

"We're pulling out now. The only damned thing we found was the axe and a few drops of blood around it. We don't how he got in. Just opened the gate, I imagine. And we do know whoever did it wore gloves. No fingerprints can be found anywhere near the door. And so far, though we have some techniques that might bring something up at the lab, no prints on the axe. No footprints. It's as if this guy just beamed in or over or whatever. As far as the stables go…what a mess. Dozens of prints. Because normal people working don't worry about their fingerprints. Anyway, we'll be making comparisons, and though I doubt we'll be lucky enough to find a match in the system, we will get DNA off the axe and at least find a victim," Moliere said.

"Hopefully."

Moliere was quiet for a minute and then said, "There's more than blood on the axe. We have hair and brain matter, too. There is a victim out there. And I don't believe there's any chance of finding them alive."

"Not to be pessimistic, but you're probably right. Thank you."

"Tell your folks they're good to go," he said and hesitated. "I wonder if that young woman knows how lucky she is."

He waved and headed off.

Dan went on into the house.

Katie was still at the kitchen table with Monty and Lorna. She looked at him anxiously as he came back in.

"All is moving along," he said.

"Thank God you were here!" Lorna told him.

"Thank God," Monty murmured. "Well, I've got the dogs in while the forensic people are here. But we're just sitting here. God forgive me, I know how serious this is, but…we're just sitting here. Being nervous. Think the girls can take their carriages out soon? I'll have to lock the boys back up at the house instead of in the stables, but…"

"You're good to go," Dan assured him. "By the time the mules are in harness and ready, they'll be out."

"Let's do it!" Monty said. "Not that I'd put money ahead of a dire situation, but food for my sweeties doesn't come free. I mean, the mules eat like crazy. And the boys! Yep, dog food is not cheap."

Monty stood, looking a little worn with his wild hair and beard, and his usually easy smile wavered. Lorna and Katie rose as well, but Katie was looking at Dan.

"Nothing yet," he told her.

Monty and Lorna had started for the front door.

"The blood on the axe… It was real blood, right?" she asked.

"Yes."

She shook her head. "He brought it with him. I don't own an axe. Well, I mean, obviously, he brought it with him if it…if it already had blood on it."

"Don't worry, Katie. I'm not leaving. And with your permission, I'm having security cameras installed at your place."

"You've got my permission. What else, what else…"

"The right people are working on it, Katie. We just need to get out there. You know the streets."

"New Orleans is a big city stretching far beyond the French Quarter," she reminded him.

He nodded. "We'll get up to the Garden District later." He grimaced. "Visit my family."

She smiled; she understood.

"All right, then. I'll go start working with Sarah and the carriage—"

"I'm going to help."

His phone buzzed. He grimaced when he saw it was his secretary-slash-assistant, Marleah.

He'd all but forgotten he had an office.

"Dan!" Her voice warbled through the phone.

He loved Marleah. She was about fifteen years his senior, competent and easy, with no hidden agenda. She liked working but also liked the fact he was flexible about her hours and she could take a few days for a vacation with her husband or friends when she chose.

"Marleah, hey, I'm sorry—"

"I know you're working on that awful thing, but you have to do something about Wendy Lawrence. The woman is driving me insane. She calls on the hour to see if you're back to work on her case."

"I'm sorry, Marleah. I'll call her. I'll take care of things now. Oh, please tell me you didn't deposit her last check."

"You're in luck. I didn't. I was trying to catch you early. She must have called thirty times yesterday, and I kept telling her you hadn't been in, and I didn't expect you in. I wanted to see if you'd please do something, before she started calling again this morning."

"Good! And thank you. I'm off her case."

"Officially and really, truly *officially*?"

"Yes."

"Thank the good Lord! Oh, you have pictures of Nathan Lawrence out and working and everywhere you saw him. Want me to ditch them?"

"Uh, no. Just leave them. I'll file them when I'm back in the office," Dan told her.

"In the trash?" Marleah asked.

He laughed. "No. I keep records and everything. Just in case."

"Uh, Dan, you're not going to work for her again, are you?"

"In case anything comes up about past work," Dan assured her. "Just leave them. And if anyone comes in…"

"I know. You're on a consultation case right now."

"Right. And thank you."

"Bye, boss. Get this guy, huh?"

"We've a good team working, Marleah, so I'm hoping. As far as Wendy Lawrence goes, I'll call her now, and hopefully she won't harass you anymore." He bid her goodbye and ended the call, deciding he didn't need to add that, while he was still at a distance from knowing the killer's identity, the killer had certainly come close enough to him.

He hung up and quickly went through his phone's contacts. Finding Wendy's number, he gritted his teeth, swallowed hard and called it.

No answer. He spoke to her voice mail. "Wendy, I am sorry. We didn't cash your check, and I'm afraid I can't continue searching for dirt on your husband. I don't believe there is any, but you should feel free to hire another private investigator. At this time, I can't continue with your case."

Dan ended the call and headed out of the house. Katie was waiting for him on the porch ready to lock up.

"You have someone installing cameras for me today?" she asked.

He nodded. "They'll cover the entire outside of the house, Katie. And they'll go directly to a guard station at the local office. This guy knows old houses and how to remove panels or find basement windows. We'll have it all covered."

She nodded. "I guess it's good to know you."

"I wish. Special Agent Axel Tiger and Assistant Director Adam Harrison are the ones with the power. Well, Ryder, too, but the FBI was made lead on this, so... Anyway, you're the connection they have. They need to look after you."

She cast a dry smile and an inquiring look in his direction, and he was struck by something about her. She was very attractive, but it was more than that. There was something about the energy and life within, maybe even something that spoke about the passion and care in her personality. He wasn't sure.

And now...

Now she meant so much. They were almost friends.

Well, at least she didn't seem to hate, loathe and despise him anymore.

"Do you really think we can do anything by driving the carriage around?" she asked him.

He smiled. "You never know."

They headed over to Monty's. The boys were out, greeting them eagerly with swishing tails and happy barks.

Monty and Lorna had rigged the carriages.

"Hey, wow, thanks. You all didn't have to do that," Katie told them. "But thank you."

"Hey, get out there and bring home the mule and dog food," Monty said.

"Will do," Katie promised.

"Monty," Lorna called, climbing into her rig, "I'm not going off the beaten track for anyone today or until the monster is caught. My people get French Quarter tours today, and that's it. I'm not even going to take them by St. Louis No. 1 or 2 or 3, for that matter. Canal to Esplanade and the river to Rampart Street. That is it."

"I think that's where you go most of the time," Monty said.

Lorna made a face at him. "We usually strive to please," she said. "Anyway…today I will strive to please—in the French Quarter."

She waved and headed out. Monty watched as Katie climbed into her own rig and Dan followed.

"You're going with her?" Monty asked.

"She had a traumatic morning," Dan said cheerfully. "Company is a good thing. And I kind-of-almost grew up here. I've got some stories in me, too."

"But that's not why you're going with her," Monty said. "I saw you on the news. You're with the cops."

"Officially, a consultant to the FBI. And I'm working for Katie."

"For Katie?"

"Of course. She wants this solved."

"Right. Naturally," Monty said, and he gave them a solemn wave. "I'll make sure the boys stay out at night from here on out."

"Thanks, Monty," Katie said.

Monty shook his head. "Katie…that axe. He was close. So close. But the dogs would die for you. I wasn't thinking, I…"

"Monty, it's okay. And I adore the dogs and don't want

them dying for me. We're going to make it all safe. And get the guy," Katie said.

Dan nudged Katie so they'd get going. She waved to Monty, released the brake and made a clicking sound for Sarah.

When they were headed out of Treme and toward Rampart, Katie turned to him. "So do I really head down in front of Jackson Square and find some tourists?" she asked.

He nodded. "Let's see what we get through your usual haunts. The practical things are being done. Forensic tests will be completed, and every cop in the city will know that we're looking for another victim via our new Axeman. Jennie was running through the French Quarter last night. She might be there again, just in a different guise. But I think we'll know her when we see her now."

But they saw nothing passing through the French Quarter down to Decatur Street and Katie's position in front of Jackson Square.

Lorna had evidently arrived just before them. She was standing on the sidewalk with Benny, now in silver, clean-shaven and evidently doing a personification of Andrew Jackson that day. Beneath his silver coloring, his attire was the same as that worn by Jackson as he sat on his steed in the famous statue in the square.

"Beignets!" Benny said, greeting them both. "I saw all the commotion at Katie's place and all the police and forensic vehicles that pulled up in front of Monty's. I figured something had happened and that..." He paused and shrugged. "That you might need beignets. And café au lait." He frowned. "I got plenty of beignets. I, uh, didn't know you'd be here, too, Mr. Oliver, so I'm short a café au lait. I can run back over—"

"Benny, we can share, thank you," Katie told him. "That was so sweet of you."

Benny grinned. "Beignets, yeah, they're sweet."

"Nice, kind, thoughtful," Katie said.

"Dan can have my café au lait—" Lorna began.

"Katie and I can share just fine," Dan assured her, agreeing with Katie. Did she really want to share with him? Swap DNA through a paper cup?

He kind of liked the idea.

"Please!" Benny said, passing the box of the powdery doughnutlike creations that were the specialty of Café du Monde.

Dan accepted the box just as Lorna enthusiastically grabbed a pastry, throwing a dusting of powdered sugar over the four of them.

"Oh, Lord! I'm so sorry!" Lorna said, appearing horrified.

"It's powdered sugar." Dan assured her. "It will all blow off soon enough."

Katie was looking at him. She reached out and touched his face, wiping away at the substance that must have gotten all over his nose and cheeks.

He liked her touch. The way her eyes touched his, even the amusement she was allowing herself to feel.

"Well," Benny said, "I, um, well… I mean, wow. At least…at least people aren't leaving the city in droves. I mean, I'm making out okay, moneywise. And it seems you guys are still doing okay on the carriage tours."

"So far," Lorna said. "But…well, I at least am leaving it to Matt to do the night shift. Hey, speaking of which, Benny, do you want a ride later? Your house is right by the stables. Let's go back together. Katie has Dan. Want to come with me?"

"Sure. I'll be ready when you are. Well, guess I'm off to be Old Hickory for a while."

They all called out a thank-you to him for the beignets, and Benny headed to the corner and the little stump he used for his podium.

Katie finished off a beignet and sipped the café au lait, then handed the cup to him.

"Thanks. You don't mind?"

She shook her head. He sipped. He tried to tell himself there was nothing all that intimate about sharing a café au lait.

A large group of tourists was headed their way. One woman stepped toward them and said they were part of a convention and obviously they wouldn't fit in one carriage.

Katie and Lorna assured her they could divide up however they chose, and the carriages would follow one another.

She also wondered if they would be so kind as to leave them—for an extra fee, of course—at the World War II Museum.

Katie looked at Lorna, and Lorna grinned. They'd be following one another. It wasn't far out of the French Quarter.

They assured the group they could do as they chose.

Dan sat back, listening to Katie as they drove. She knew her history; she loved the city. She talked about all aspects with ease. The tour group was good: people asked the right questions. None seemed to be into sensationalism, blood, guts, ghosts or the current murders.

While the carriage was moving down Bourbon Street again, almost at Lafitte's, he looked out around casually—and saw her.

At first, he just noted the woman. And then he noted her swinging haircut and her clothing and the way she moved…

Pausing with a sigh of disgust as a staggering man ran through her rather than around her.

"Katie, I've got to hop out!" Dan said.

She wasn't moving fast; it was easy for him just to balance on the carriage and hop off. He caught her eyes and promised, "I'll meet you back at Jackson Square."

He hurried across the street in pursuit, hoping his ghost would have something that just might help in some way.

Nine

At least he had left her with what remained of the café au lait.

Katie watched Dan leap down with an easy agility. He looked back at her, and she knew he *had* seen someone on the streets who had drawn his attention.

Living or dead?

She didn't know, but she decided she was going to have to find one of her friends in the city who had also departed the physical plane long ago. She glanced out the way he had gone, but the only people she saw on the streets were those hurrying about on regular, living-person errands. "Is everything all right?" one of the women asked her.

"Oh, yes. The Great New Orleans Fire of 1788 destroyed eight hundred and fifty-six of eleven hundred buildings, and another fire, in 1794, destroyed another two hundred and twelve. Because it was a religious holiday, Good Friday, in 1788 priests felt they couldn't ring the bells in warning. But as you see, the city rebuilt. And a lot of the rebuilding was done while the Spanish flag waved over the city."

She went on; she answered questions.

Ahead of her, Lorna was moving her carriage around;

they were ready to cross Canal Street and drop their convention guests off at the National World War II Museum.

When they reached the museum, Lorna hopped out of her carriage and hurried over to Katie.

"Where did Dan go?"

"I'm not sure, Lorna. I think he saw a friend when we were on Bourbon Street in front of Lafitte's. But he'll meet us at Jackson Square."

"Good, good," Lorna said. "Katie, I don't like this. The more I think about it… Maybe we should head to Las Vegas for a girls' weekend or something. Aren't you scared? Terrified? Shouldn't you be the hell out of your house?"

"I'm going to be okay."

"He was there. At your house. A killer. And after what you went through as a kid… Oh, my God, Katie! Could it be the same guy? Could it be that he thinks you might know who he is or that he needs to finish what he started and… Oh, my God."

"Let's get back, Lorna, okay? Of course I'm scared. Everyone here is scared. But we need to behave in a sensible manner. And the cops or the FBI are going to rig my place with cameras. They'll have people around it all the time." She hesitated, not wanting to tell her Dan Oliver was staying with her, but then he had been at her house at the crack of dawn, so…

"Dan is staying over?" Lorna asked.

Katie nodded.

Lorna smiled. "Just don't get so carried away that you're not listening for danger."

"Lorna, it's nothing like that—"

"Sure, it is. Look at the two of you."

"Lorna, it's an arrangement."

Lorna laughed at that. "*Arrangement*. I like that."

"He's working for me."

"He works for me, too."

"Lorna!"

"Okay, whatever you say." Lorna gave her a look that said she absolutely did not believe Katie. "Listen, when you two go in for the night, Benny and I will come, too. All right? Do you mind?"

"Not at all."

"I still think a Vegas vacation would be a good idea. With me…or Dan."

"Lorna!"

"Okay!"

With a grin, Lorna returned to her rig, and they headed back to Jackson Square.

Dan hadn't yet returned. But seeing her, Benny came over to the rig as Katie jumped down.

"The fortune-teller was out again," he told her. "She told me the number six was coming around again. And you know what else she told me?" he asked.

Lorna had joined Katie on the sidewalk then. "What?" she asked anxiously.

"She said it was coming again. It… Something supernatural, a demon, a spirit. And it liked jazz. So tomorrow, I should dress up as a famous jazz musician from New Orleans."

"Satchmo. Louis Armstrong," Katie said.

"Yes!" Lorna agreed. Satchmo, Louis Armstrong, born in New Orleans on August 4, 1901, and probably one of the greatest jazz musicians to ever live. He was still revered and honored in his city. The airport was named in his honor.

Satchmo would have been in the city at the time the Axeman had been striking.

He might well have been playing on the jazz night demanded by the killer.

"I'm doing it." Benny said. "Hell, I'm going to be Satchmo. I'm not taking any chances! Of course, the man was amazing with the many instruments he could play, but I can play a sax. I'm not the best, but I'm not the worst. If there's any chance the killer is a crazy guy reenacting the Axeman and he wants jazz, I'm going to give him jazz."

Ten

"Well, hello, handsome."

Mabel stopped and waited, grinning when she saw Dan coming.

"So," she added, "it seems you now want my help."

They were in the middle of a sidewalk, and while Bourbon wasn't as busy as it might be at night, people were walking around.

He smiled as he took his phone out of his pocket and pretended to speak on it.

"Mabel, forgive me. Yes, I have come for your help, and I'm praying you can give me something."

The superior amusement she had shown when she'd seen him approaching her seemed to fade. "I wish I had more," she said quietly.

"I'm grateful for anything," he said.

She studied him for a minute. "I suppose you are a decent sort, and perhaps you were a bit thrown when I approached you at Lafayette Cemetery. I saw you there, and I knew who you were, and I thought that… Well, I suppose I expected you knew you might see me or, rather, that you might have even been hoping for a chat with a relative."

"Could I have a chat with one of my relatives?"

"I'm so sorry; I haven't met any of the Oliver family. Not from before." She smiled again. "Let's wander a bit. You're welcome to still pretend you're on the phone. Better yet, there's a lovely place on Royal that makes the best shrimp and grits ever."

"You can...you can eat shrimp and grits?" he asked.

"No, but I believe I can smell them and enjoy them vicariously through you."

"All right," he said. "Lead the way."

"They play nice soft jazz, too," she murmured, heading down the block to Royal Street and the restaurant she'd referred to.

He was a single person, but he was led to a table for two. Mabel sat across from him.

"If you wouldn't mind, please tell me what you know and what you're seeking. Just set your phone down and speak softly. People will believe you're conducting business on Speaker."

She'd really been pretty in life, he thought.

She set her chin in her hand, leaning forward on the table, attention on him as he told her about the crime scene Ryder had called him to. He told her about the crimes in Florida. He told her about the strange recurrence of the number six, and how Katie had believed she'd seen Jennie and they'd found a long dark wig.

He also told her about the axe left at Katie's house.

"You must take serious care for that young woman!" Mabel said.

He nodded. "Yes. Mabel, please—"

"Back to the number six," she said. "A few years back, they found six goats with their throats slit, drained of blood."

"I know that," he said, a little disappointed.

"Everyone cried out it had to be a voodoo thing, but it wasn't. The city is host to many Latin Americans, so they cried Santeria. Then they blamed it on the city's Wiccans, and then the so-called vampires."

"Yes, I heard."

She shook her head. "Here's where I may be able to help you." She took a deep breath. "I didn't really think this meant anything at the time, but…in my day, there was more of a…well, a bigger difference between the rich and the poor. The city was filled with immigrants, but we had the old guard, too. There were still older people living who remembered the Civil War, and some hated the North for the invasion of the South, and most hated the South for slavery and the death toll of the war. And we were involved in another war, World War I. But there was a man named Allan Pierce who was, to the best of my knowledge, born and raised here. He…he was fascinated by the legends of Marie Laveau, the famous voodoo priestess. You know about her, of course."

"Yes, of course. People still perform little rites at her tomb, even those who do it just for fun. They leave her coins and do three circles and the like," Dan said. He was growing a little impatient—he was so desperate for help, and she was telling him NOLA tales.

He'd ordered the shrimp and grits. When they arrived, she leaned back, smiling and closing her eyes for a minute, as if she could inhale the aroma of the dish he'd ordered.

"Mabel, you know my dad was from here, his family… I've known NOLA since I was a kid," he reminded her.

"Pay attention. Yes, it's a long story, but it may help you. Okay, so… Allan Pierce had delusions of grandeur. His family had lived in the city during the Civil War but owned a plantation down the river, and they had been very rich. Then they'd lost it and been all but penniless. I met him because he used to play checkers with some of the old-sters I knew. He used to talk about Marie Laveau, saying how she had powers of second sight and the ability to tell the future because she was the world's best listener. Also, she was excellent at making a prediction that was more of an instruction—if you're expecting something, it just might happen because you make it. Are you following me?"

"I think so," he said. "Not sure where you're going, but I'm following so far."

"Pierce had a bet with one of the old men he played checkers with. He said he could make something happen by saying so. As it *happened*, I stopped by the old fellows on the stoop one day when he predicted that people could be made to do just about anything. He said, 'Take the num-ber six. If I just tell people the number six matters, that it's *important*, they'll believe it. I can even convince them I'm some kind of an angel or demon, and six is the number of days a man must work, must wait, must do everything, be-cause man was created on the sixth day.'"

"Did you think he was the Axeman?" Dan asked her.

"I didn't think anything of it at the time. And no, I don't think Allan Pierce was the Axeman. But I later found out he had convinced a lot of people—mainly poor immigrants—that he was something preternatural, maybe a demon, and they all did his bidding, down to stealing, striking others and starting fights." She paused, drumming her fingers on the table. "The man did love jazz, too. I don't know if he could have been the Axeman. I know the people arrested for being the Axeman were not. I don't know…it might have been the fellow Mrs. Pepitone supposedly killed in Los Angeles, but how did they both just wind up in LA? I just don't have the answers to all that." She watched him eat for a couple bites, then continued. "But back to the number six. I know Pierce had a young apprentice, you might say. And the kid went on to say he could do all the same things... Convince people about the number, and you'd get them awed or scared enough to believe they were doing the right thing by doing the wrong thing. I've been all around the city, and I do believe someone is running around getting the rumor going that there is something in that number. I heard a lady down by the square recently claiming the Time of Six was coming again and that people needed to repent. There was a book written in the thirties, I believe. They might be able to help at the library. Anyway, it has chapters on the various strange beliefs embraced by people in this city at times. There is a chapter about Allan Pierce in it. You might find it interesting. Because, when I heard about the slain goats, I wondered if someone wasn't taking Pierce's concept to a new level. Then again, remember, Allan was doing it just for fun. He was a bitter man and liked to manipulate others."

"I'll look for the book," he told her.

She smiled. "I'll keep cruising different areas of the city by day. I may hang out at your friend's place at night. Though... Well, you were rather dense when we met. I hope you'd hear me if I were to give you warning."

He smiled, inclining his head. "*Dense.* Thanks."

"But you're handsome, darling. So cute."

"Thank you for that, too, but you needn't worry. Katie can see...um..."

"The dead, honey. Spit it out. I've been accustomed to it for a very long time. But you say she'd see me, too? Of course, like that charming friend of yours, the Native American boy."

Dan didn't think Axel Tiger often thought of himself as a boy.

"Yes, like him, too," he said.

"Charming. Well, I'm delighted about Miss Delaney." She paused. "Worried, as well. You are staying with her, and you're taking care that she's safe? I mean, this is a maniac or psychopath who has an agenda and doesn't care who he hurts."

"I'm staying at the house, and I don't believe he wants to take chances with anyone who might hurt him instead. Like the old Axeman, he found vulnerable people."

"Even you have to sleep, darling."

"I wake easily. And cameras are being installed that send video straight to the police station. There will always be a cruiser within close range."

"Isn't she scared? Doesn't she want to leave?"

He sighed. "If she wanted to leave, I'd encourage her. Except I don't think she wants to live her life in fear. Mabel, her parents were killed twelve years ago. Now, a bloodied axe was left at her back door. She could leave—and if this guy wasn't caught, a year from now, six years from now, twelve years from now—and the whole thing could start again. It has to end here." He paused, frowning. "I wonder if it could have begun here?"

"You said it began in Florida."

"Yes, but the infamous Axeman of New Orleans struck here first."

"You think someone planned to go to Florida and kill people and then kill here twelve years later?" she asked, a frown creasing her forehead.

"I don't know what I think. We must look at every angle. Our only clue so far is a strange woman named Jennie. Katie met her in Florida, and she's finally seen her again on the streets here, in New Orleans." He shook his head. "And while he may be imitating a killer from a hundred years ago, he's learned modern forensic techniques. He wears gloves and leaves no fingerprints. The ground hasn't been wet, but so far, no footprints. Not a hair, not a fiber."

"But eventually he'll leave something," Mabel said. "It's impossible... Someone had a theory on that."

"Locard's exchange principle," Dan said. "At a crime scene, a perpetrator will take something and leave something behind."

"Eventually he will. Anyway, my dense, handsome friend, you need to get on it. And to watch over Miss Delaney like a hawk. You shouldn't be sitting here with me."

"I needed you."

"I hope so! I hope I can help. And as for Miss Delaney, well, I look forward to meeting her."

Dan glanced at the time on his phone. He needed to get back to Jackson Square. He didn't believe anything would happen to anyone by day, but he was still worried Katie was alone.

Well, she wasn't on her own, but she wasn't with him.

"Go!" Mabel told him. "Somehow, the answers lie with her. And thank you. I believe I could almost taste that delicious meal."

She drifted to her feet. He watched as she left the restaurant, passing close by a man in a business suit.

The man shivered. But he didn't see Mabel.

Dan paid the bill and hurried out, anxious then to get back to Katie. As he walked, he called Axel and quickly filled him in on his meeting with Mabel.

"Allan Pierce?" Axel said. "Well, he didn't come down the line in legend like Marie Laveau or Madame Delphine

LaLaurie. But we have people who can dig to the bottom of anything. I'll get on it."

"If possible, I'll head to the library later," Dan told him. "I'm not with Katie right now, and I'm anxious to get back to her."

"This guy strikes in darkness," Axel said. "And away from the public eye."

"I know. That's why I dared chase down my ghost. Anyway, get back to me. Anything yet on the blood on the axe or anything else?"

"Not yet," Axel told him.

"Thanks." He hesitated. "Axel, what are the possibilities this whole thing started in New Orleans? What if the murderer is from here, if something about the legend brought him down to Florida? Maybe to Lou Delaney's boat, and Lou Delaney?"

"That's a stretch."

"Anything on this is a stretch."

"Did Delaney have any ties to New Orleans?" Axel asked.

"Well, his cousin lives here. That's why Katie moved here. I'll have to find out more."

"Back at my headquarters, Jackson Crow's wife, Angela Hawkins, is researching anything she can find on Allan Pierce, his so-called power of six and anyone who followed in his footsteps. I'll also have her search out anything she can find on an association with Louis Delaney."

Dan and Axel ended their call, and Dan strode urgently down the street. He'd been on Royal Street just a few blocks from the square, but it seemed a great distance to him suddenly.

He hurried along the park and came out on Decatur Street, annoyed at the sense of fear he was feeling, that his heart was racing, and he could hear his own breathing almost as if he was scuba diving.

He burst around the corner.

And it was all right.

Katie was there, on the sidewalk, chatting with a passerby.

He smiled, striding over to her.

"Hey!" she said cheerfully, seeing him. "You're just in time."

"For?"

"Well, this lovely young woman and her friends want to head over to the Irish Channel. It's not a big tourist destination, but the ruins of an old mansion and the family cemetery are there. I was explaining that, as far as I know, it's private property and there's a big fence up around it all, but they'd like to just go by." She grimaced, indicating the one cheerful-looking girl with dark curls and rosy cheeks. "Brenda is a medium. She just wants to get to the old place and see if she can feel anything."

"Oh, okay," Dan said.

A medium? The way Katie had said the word, he didn't think she believed this woman had any special abilities at all.

She was far too polite to say so.

"Are you game?" Katie asked.

"Sure."

The Irish Channel was a fine-enough area in which to live.

It wasn't a tourist area, and the streets weren't thronged with people as they tended to be in the French Quarter. It seemed Katie wasn't against taking her carriage there, but Dan figured she hadn't wanted to go alone.

"Let's head on out," he said.

Curly-haired Brenda was with a group of five, all explaining they were mediums, and yes, they had a small conference here where there were so many interesting places to be explored.

Where so many spirits cried out, unheard, seeking help.

He glanced at Katie and just nodded and smiled.

They hadn't been in the carriage long before one of the men in the group—a thin, sandy and shaggy-haired man around twenty-five years old, leaned forward.

"Um, excuse me? You're the cop, right? From the press conference? Do you think you could get us into the morgue? If one of us could touch the victim, we might be able to help. I mean, the spirits of the dead might be able to give us information."

"I'm afraid I'm not a cop," Dan said. "I can't get anyone in anywhere. Sorry."

"But we saw you on the news," Brenda said.

He shook his head, glancing at Katie. "I was voted the spokesperson in the group," he said. "But I'm sorry, I'm a consultant on this and nothing more."

"Damn!" Brenda said. "It's so frustrating. I mean, we could help. Oh, well. I have really wanted to see the ruins of this mansion. It comes with all kinds of rumors, scandals and ghosts."

Dan arched a brow to Katie. She shrugged and rolled her eyes.

Still, she gamely launched into her best tour-guide voice. "What I know about the Medford Mansion is this. Jonathan Medford was in the Confederate military. The Union took the city in 1862. Jonathan had a beautiful young wife. She fell in love with one of the Union soldiers occupying the city. Maybe. Or maybe she felt she had no other choice than to give in to him, the man they called Beast Butler, a

General Benjamin Butler who was running the city under his Union military. And for Southern women, it was bleak. If they mocked Union soldiers in any way, they could face punishments, be labeled as prostitutes and so on. Butler was reviled in the South, but he was an interesting man. He claimed he was for Southern rights and against Southern wrong. He was Union army all the way, but I doubt President Lincoln would have approved of some of his tactics. Anyway, Jonathan Medford's brother, Isiah, heard about it. He was older, and he had made his fortune in real estate and cotton, neither of which was doing well then, but he lived—seething with indignation, I imagine—just a few blocks away from Jonathan's home. One night he went to the house. There was an argument. The wife, the lover and the brother were all killed, and when he heard about it, Jonathan Medford walked straight into the enemy lines and a bullet went through his heart. The family is supposed to still lie in the little cemetery, but the vaults there are falling apart. There was no more family, there was a fire...and, of course, they were interred in a vault. And in time here, bodies are cremated in the intense heat. So the place just went to ruin, but people kept buying the land, I guess everyone planning to either restore and clean up or demolish the place. I'm not sure who owns it now. A holding company, I believe. But it is fenced off because..." She broke off, looking at Dan.

Brenda giggled. "Because a lot of people think mediums are crazy or the vampires in the city will use it for a ritual place or even some voodoo sect. That's okay. I just want to be in the area."

"I have a feeling the owners are also afraid of the liability," Dan said.

"Well, of course. We don't have to go in," Brenda said. "We just have to get near."

"And so we will!" Katie said cheerfully.

"Have you ever met anyone there?" he asked her softly.

She glanced at him and smiled and shook her head. "I don't even believe the story. Jonathan Medford was killed at the Battle of Gettysburg. He wife died the year before. Public records have her death attributed to illness, and there were plenty of fevers that ravaged this city. There is no record of an altercation between a Medford and a Union officer. Jonathan's brother succumbed to heart disease, according to what records we do have from the mid-1800s."

He smiled and whispered, "But no one has come back to tell the truth, the whole truth and nothing but the truth, I take it?"

She looked at him quickly, as if wondering if he was mocking her.

"Did you see your ghost again?" she whispered. "Is that why you took off?"

He nodded.

"Did she tell you anything?" she asked softly.

"Maybe. Have you ever heard of Allan Pierce?"

"Uh, vaguely. He was around during the original Axeman crimes. He claimed that..."

Her voice trailed, and she stared at him. "He was all about the number six. He was never accused of being the Axeman, but he was certain the Axeman was a super being, created on the same day as man but given will and power. I think people claimed that he made them commit a lot of robberies and assaults, but... I forgot. Yes," she said softly. "The number six. Can it mean anything?"

"Anything can mean something when someone makes it mean something."

They were moving closer to the Irish Channel section of the city.

He asked her, "Katie, what is your family's connection to New Orleans? I know your parents were both in the military and you were born in Florida. But Jeremy Delaney is your cousin, or second cousin. Your father's cousin. Did you have relatives—"

"Yes. My grandparents—they died when I was young—were from New Orleans. My parents wanted to live in Florida because they loved the ocean so much. Jeremy has always been here, but he and my dad were the last of the family." She studied him. "I visited a few times growing up because my dad and Jeremy were always close. And I didn't come with him, but my dad came up after Katrina and the flood to help find survivors. Jeremy has always had a boat, and they went out together. I think they did help. But that was the last time my dad was here before he, my mom and Anita were murdered. Why?"

"I was curious," he said. He smiled. Katie was an excellent carriage driver, courteous of cars and pedestrians, and careful regarding her mule and carriage.

Outside the tourist area, he noted that the few homeowners out—retrieving mail, doing yard work, or just playing on their lawns—stopped to note the carriage as it went by. They weren't as common a sight in the Irish Channel as in the French Quarter or Garden District.

The group in the back was chatting, each saying with certainty that they could contact Jonathan Medford or his brother or perhaps his wife.

Her name had been Gazelle.

"Where did he meet her?" one of the young men asked. "I admit I don't know this story that well!"

"Ah, well, because it's not in the mainstream!" Brenda told him.

"They met at a ball at Oak Alley," Katie said. "They both had the same social stature at the time, and they were considered lucky since the marriage wasn't arranged. It was love at first sight, or so the story goes." Katie turned to look at her group. "We're just about there. And please remember, you can't visit the house or even the cemetery since they're in ruins."

Katie drew the carriage up in front of the mansion. As she had told Brenda, a fence surrounded it, but it had been constructed of cheap wire and plastic, and in areas, it looked as if it had been trampled halfway down by small herds of animals.

Local kids, probably, daring one another to sneak onto the property.

As Katie stopped the carriage, Dan could see the walls of the house that remained. Empty windows looked out like dead eyes.

The cemetery, to the rear and side of the remnants of the house, had a few aboveground tombs and a few vaults.

"To the best of my knowledge, the remains of the family were moved out to one of the cemeteries in Metairie. But... I don't know that much about remains after a hundred years, or if the remains were even moved," Katie told Dan quietly as her group moved along the fence, excitedly looking in and talking to one another.

Brenda gained attention, standing by the property, looking in at the graveyard. "Let's close our eyes, join hands... breathe." she said.

Her group gathered around. She began a low chanting sound and then threw her head back and cried out loud, "Gazelle, Gazelle, dearest lost beauty. We're here! We're here to listen to your side of the story! Let us know you're here, with us."

A moment passed, and she spoke again. "Yes! She's here. I feel her. The air around us is charged with her presence. Gazelle, use me, please use me as your mouthpiece. Let us know the truth of what happened! You were left... so alone, so afraid! All was caving in around you, the war was lost, everything you had known... Yes, and the man you loved was fighting, and when it all came about, you had no choice, no choice..."

"That is the biggest crock," Katie murmured to Dan, smiling up at him.

"I, uh... I don't even know what to say," he muttered.

Then he realized his answer didn't matter. Katie was staring into the property.

"What is it?" he asked.

She pointed.

He looked, following the direction of her finger, wondering for a moment if Brenda had managed to arouse the spirit of the long-dead Gazelle.

But there was something by the remains of the old vault there. Something that stuck out in the growing dusk. White...

"Dan?" she whispered.

He didn't reply. Brenda's group was entranced by her performance, so Dan got down from the carriage and stepped over one of the broken chunks of fence. Then he jogged over to the chilling white *thing* they had seen.

He stopped short. It was a leg, or part of a leg, from the knee to the foot.

Beyond it, almost flush against the wall of the old vault, was the rest of the body.

It was a woman, he saw. There was little left of her face:

it appeared an axe had sliced through her skull and between her eyes straight through the nose and mouth.

As he fumbled in his pocket for his phone, he felt Katie come up behind him.

"Don't!" he warned her.

Too late. She was next to him, staring down at the corpse.

"Katie—"

"It's all right. I can handle it."

"But we have a group of tourists over there. Katie!"

She was just staring at the corpse. She hadn't screamed. She was pale as she stared at the blood splatter on the body and the broken bricks and concrete and the twisted remains of the body.

The head bashed in, and nearly severed from the body.

And the left leg, removed jaggedly and just inches from the rest of the corpse.

There was really no telling who the body had once been...

Except Dan had an odd feeling he knew who she was, that he'd been seeking her all through the day.

Axel answered the phone immediately. He would send police, agents and Dr. Vincent right away.

Dan looked at Katie again. "We can't let the group—"

"Right, right!" she mumbled.

She tore her gaze away from the gruesome sight. "I have to get them out of here, but what do I do? How do I get them away? I can't force them all back into the carriage."

"At least don't let them see this or let them get into the yard. Tell them what you told me. History is often told by the victors, and then by those who feel wronged and are bitter and want revenge in legend, at least. Go tell them what might have been the real story, that there was no love triangle, people just tragically died. There are plenty of real horror stories from the Civil War."

She nodded woodenly. But then she did as he asked. He heard her telling the group the different theories that might explain the loss of the beautiful home and family cemetery.

She didn't have to keep them occupied for long.

In minutes, they heard sirens. The group was curious, but before they could start exploring, police arrived.

The mediums in the group might have believed they had their channels to the dead. Certainly, none of them had foretold the future.

Axel arrived with the first group of police who immediately steered the tourists away from the house, down to the end of the other block, setting up perimeters to keep them and any other curiosity seekers at a distance from the scene. The fenced-in ruins were fenced off in another way: crime-scene tape.

Naturally, the tour group began to speculate on what had happened. Katie offered to get them back to the French Quarter in her carriage, but even as she spoke, Ryder arrived. The police would be happy to take them back in patrol cars.

There was nothing to see here, even though they protested they could help if there had been a crime.

They were politely refused.

Dan had little to do at first except set his arm around Katie and stand out on the sidewalk. They would be interviewed and explain how they had found the body.

Media arrived quickly. With or without the internet, sensational news seemed to travel on the air. Still, the public would be held at bay.

Seeing the smashed remains, there was little way to

identify the person. None of them touched the body. That was Dr. Vincent's purview.

The FBI and NOPD had feared from the get-go that there would be more victims. No one was happy that they'd been right.

Dan settled Katie in her carriage, then walked back into the crime scene and hunkered down with Axel by the victim.

Unrecognizable.

But he knew when an analysis was done, it would prove this was the woman who had been attacked by the axe found in Katie's yard.

He'd never seen her before, other than in images.

But he knew who she was.

Katie had seen her. Years before, and then now, here in New Orleans.

Despite the mangled face, Dan was certain they'd found the mysterious Jennie at last, and while she might have been in a partnership with this Axeman, she wasn't anymore.

The partnership had ended.

Lethally.

Eleven

Dr. Vincent or his assistants had cleaned the corpse, making her as presentable as possible.

The blood had been washed away, but that couldn't change the fact there was a massive gash that sliced the face open at an angle, tearing through the forehead, eye, nose, and mouth.

Staring through the glass at the corpse as she was displayed, Katie nodded.

It was the woman she had known as Jennie, the woman she had chased through the streets just the other day.

She couldn't help but wonder if she was dead because of her.

At her side, it seemed Dan read her mind. "Katie, it's very likely the murders are all connected. And if so, the way this woman died is horrific, yes, but there's a good possibility she was instrumental in the brutal murders of at least nine other people. It's horrible, but she chose her path. None of this is your fault in any way."

She nodded. "I know that. It's just…"

"Horrible, yes. But helpful, maybe, for the lives of others. You saw this Jennie in New Orleans. I imagine it means

Dr. Neil Browne is in town somewhere, as well. And because of you, we have a sketch of him."

Again, Katie nodded.

"He could have changed so much in twelve years."

"Right. But we have a dozen or more computer enhancements of the man to work with. He's going to appear somewhere. And you don't know what happened. He may have tired of his accomplice. This might have nothing to do with you."

She nodded again.

She was feeling…tired. And a little numb. But far too anxious to even contemplate sleep.

They'd gotten the carriage and Sarah back to the stables before coming to the morgue. There wouldn't be an autopsy until the morning, but due to the circumstances, the police wanted a solid identification on the woman as quickly as possible.

Monty had been at the stables, and Dan had explained the situation to him. He'd naturally wanted to help, but Katie had needed to tend to Sarah. It was busy work, and she loved the mule. And it was good to have the boys scurrying around her while she brushed Sarah down and saw to her food.

Matt was still out, serving the night crowd with tours. Lorna had brought her carriage in, accompanied by Benny.

The two of them were now at Benny's house, working on his Satchmo apparel for the following day.

It was just past nine o'clock. There wasn't much to do until morning.

"They've done blood work and fingerprints, taken dental impressions. We'll see what we can get," Axel said, joining Dan and Katie at the window. He looked at Katie and maybe realized how restless she was. "It's tough. But sometimes, no way out of it, it's a waiting game."

She gave Axel a weak smile. "Anything from Angela?" Dan asked him.

"She's working through the night. When she has something, she'll get it to us. Have you two eaten?" he asked.

Katie looked from the corpse to him.

"I had a late lunch," Dan said. He looked at Katie. "How are you doing?"

"I, uh…well, I can sit with you, wherever you'd like to go," she said.

"Seems rude, huh? Going from the morgue to dinner?" Axel asked her.

"I mean, I know this is what you deal with all the time—"

"Not quite this," Dan said.

"I don't think I'm hungry," Katie said. "But I probably should try to eat…"

"Beware, if we're not at a music venue, the media will be blasting the fact another corpse, a victim of the Axeman's Protégé, has been found," Axel said. He grimaced. "That's what they've labeled the killer in the media. The Axeman's Protégé."

"Great," Dan muttered.

"Maybe the restaurants will be empty anyway," Katie said.

"Probably not. Very little closes down this city." Dan smiled. "She's tough. NOLA is a tough grand dame. She'll make it through this. And so will we," he added softly.

"Hey, I have an idea," Katie said. "Commander's Palace. It's right next to Lafayette Cemetery. Maybe Mabel will join us."

"I don't think she's just hanging around the cemetery

waiting to meet us," Dan said. "I mean, uh... I don't actually know much about this yet. *Do* ghosts hang around
cemeteries?"

Axel chuckled softly. "I don't think anyone has all the
answers. I've seen people remain because there was something they had to see through, sometimes hoping a killer
will be caught, sometimes just hoping to help a loved one
through a situation. We went to Gettysburg once where I
met a woman—"

"Living or dead?" Dan asked.

"She was long gone and had died of natural causes,
but she stayed because she liked to haunt historians who
twisted history. She told me about other ghosts there, men
who fought the same battle over and over again, all trying
to understand the past. She would try, bit by bit, to convince them that they could move on. She was there during the battle but died several years later of heart failure.
Many like to return to places where they were happy. And
sometimes they do haunt the cemeteries where they were
laid to rest or interred, just as a...home."

"Well, thankfully," Dan murmured, "we made nice
homes for our dead. Anyway, okay, Commander's Palace
it is."

Katie tried a weak grin. "A landmark restaurant that
opened in 1893," she said.

"One of the famous Brennan family has something to
do with the restaurant now, right?" Dan said.

"Yes. I haven't been in a while," Katie said. "But—"

"But?" Axel asked her.

She shrugged. "When I visited with my folks... My
mom was a bit of an amateur artist. She loved to sketch in
Lafayette Cemetery, and we all loved the Garden District

Book Shop. And a meal at Commander's Palace always went with the outing. I do love the place."

Dan looked at Axel. "Hey, she might even eat something."

"Sounds good. Let's do it," Axel said.

They took Axel's car. He apparently knew the city well enough to navigate to Washington Street, but as they started out, Katie commented, "Oh! It's nine fifteen. Will we make it in time?"

"Axel drives fast," Dan assured her. "We'll be there in a few, and the kitchen is open late."

They could see through to the many vaults as they drove around the cemetery to the restaurant; when Axel gave the car to the valet, they could still see through the Washington Street gates. The cemetery was closed by night, and the streets were quiet. There was still something haunting about the bits of the cemetery that could be seen, elegant yet touched with the decay of the passage of time. Katie could remember the first time she had come to New Orleans as a child, falling in love with the zoo and the aquarium, the entertainers on the square, and the music that seemed to come from everywhere. She thought if they could combine the beauty of the Gulf and the Atlantic with the unique history and flair of New Orleans, it would be a perfect place.

"You're actually smiling," Dan told her as they entered the restaurant.

He and Axel were both looking at her, and she shrugged, allowing that smile.

"I was thinking if you could put New Orleans and the Keys into one place, it would be about perfect."

"There's the Mississippi River," Axel noted.

She made a face. "Lousy diving."

"Ah, well, that just means we all have to travel and get to know more places," Dan said.

She looked at curiously. "You dive?"

He nodded. "When I can."

"I read you were an amazing diver," Axel said, looking at her.

"Once. No more. I don't go out anymore. I…uh…" She stammered, wanting to change the subject. "I find it interesting, though. Key West and New Orleans have many things in common. They're both party towns, which means people often miss what's so wonderful about the heart of them. You have Duval Street in Key West, Bourbon Street in New Orleans. The Key West cemetery is in the center of the island on the highest ground…though, it's not very high. But storms have caused bodies to rise and wash through the streets of both cities. And Key West doesn't have NOLA architecture. It has its own style. It also has an amazing array of Victorian houses since once, it was highest on the chart with per-capita income because money was rolling in during the prime days of salvage."

She opened her mouth and closed it, embarrassed as she realized that the hostess was waiting to seat them.

"Wow, that sounds cool!" the young woman said.

Katie flushed. "Uh, thanks."

In a few minutes they were seated. She ordered iced tea while Dan and Axel opted for coffee. They both knew what they wanted right away; obviously, they both knew the restaurant. For Dan, pecan-roasted fish. Axel went for the steak. Katie still wasn't sure she could eat, but they were away from the morgue now, and the aromas coming from the kitchen were enticing, and she knew food was something she probably really needed.

She went with the special, a surf and turf meal.

Their waitress had just left the table when Katie looked to the stairs leading to the second floor. There was a woman at the landing.

She might have been someone dressed for a costumed event in a 1920s outfit.

But Katie knew Dan's ghost had arrived, sweeping in with flair and elegance.

Mabel made her way to the table.

Katie smiled, seeing Dan and Axel were about to stand out of politeness—and then realized they should not. Mabel waved a hand at the two of them, assuring them she appreciated their courtesy but to let it go. With the tiniest scrape of the chair, she took the empty seat next to Axel.

"Miss Delaney! What a pleasure!" Mabel said. "I'm sure these gentlemen have spoken about me. I'm Mabel Greely."

"Yes, I've heard about you," Katie said, unable to resist a smile. Mabel had shaken Dan Oliver in a way no living person could have ever managed. She continued. "It's a pleasure to meet you."

"You're a tour guide in the city," Mabel said.

"Carriage tours."

"Lovely." Mabel grinned. "I imagine we have friends in common?"

"I imagine we do."

"Gray Simmons, the English fellow who sailed with Lafitte?"

"Yes!" Katie said. "I see him on Bourbon Street frequently. He says he loved to hang around the old blacksmith shop. Though, he tells me the building was used in so many different ways."

Mabel explained to Dan and Axel. "Gray died at the Battle of New Orleans, fighting against the British and for

Jackson, though he had been born in Liverpool. So, dear boys—and Miss Delaney—please bring me up to speed."

Dan explained they had found Jennie dead.

Mabel looked at Katie. "You know it was her?"

"You don't forget," Katie said softly.

"No, you don't," Mabel agreed. "I believe, then, that you have been right, that the killings are all associated. And the man you knew as Dr. Neil Browne is the killer. Jennie was his accomplice, except she crossed him or did something wrong."

"I think he knew I saw her," Katie said.

"And you're feeling a little bit guilty, aren't you?" Mabel asked. "You mustn't. I'm sure she participated in the most heinous crimes imaginable."

"Think we'll see her anywhere? Her...uh..." Dan asked cautiously.

"*Ghost*, darling. She's dead. Do just speak plainly. I've assured you I'm not offended," Mabel said. "No, I don't believe she'll be around. I've rarely seen...evil come back," she finished quietly. "Have you looked into Allan Pierce?"

"We have a top researcher doing so. And we'll get into the archives ourselves tomorrow," Dan said.

Mabel nodded. "You got me thinking on the number six."

"And about the fact this may all have started here somehow?" Dan asked.

Mabel stared at Katie. "Your father was from here, isn't that right?"

"Yes, but he and my mom moved to Florida before I was born. He was in the navy. He lived many places through the years," Katie said. "He came back after Katrina, and he and Jeremy went out in Jeremy's boat. I mean, I guess it was my dad's home, and he wanted to help. My mom and

I didn't come with him. The city was hurting, so unless you were going to be able to do something solidly helpful, you weren't needed. I guess my dad didn't want to be worrying about my mother and me. I thought we could have handed out water or done something. But I was barely a teen at the time."

"Interesting. And his family goes way back, right?" Mabel asked.

"I think… I guess they came over with the major Irish immigration after the potato famine in Ireland in 1849," Katie said.

"So someone in your family was probably here back in my time," Mabel said.

"I imagine," Katie said. "But—"

Mabel waved a hand in the air and then went silent.

Their food was arriving. She waited while they thanked their waitress and their plates were arranged on the table. When their waitress left, Mabel said, "I do enjoy the food on the table! I love seeing the delicious meals… Creole, Cajun or just plain whatever American is. Well, to be quite honest, I never did like hot dogs, but thankfully, they're not on the menu here! Ah, that fish…it smells divine. I think it does. I imagine it does. Memory, yes, sensory memory, I believe that's what it is!"

"It's very good," Dan assured her, smiling.

"Yes, I can almost taste it," Mabel said. Then she shook her head. "With what you've told me about people running around the city talking about the number six, it does bring me back to Allan Pierce. I think that this killer had Jennie convinced he was powerful, in a supernatural way. Either that, or she was in love with him…and violence and killing and getting away with it. I doubt she ever thought that he'd turn on her."

"All right," Dan said. "We look to the past. We know about this man, Allan Pierce, who was around at the time of the Axeman. He might or might not have actually been the Axeman. But he wrote about the power of being a special entity created on Day Six, like all men, but with a power above men. So either this killer believes in it all or he likes the legends. And maybe it's even a challenge to him to be using the number six."

"I think the latter, and I don't know why," Katie said. "He murdered six years ago and twelve years ago, and he murdered three people each time. Which makes six. But here in New Orleans, he's murdered three...or four, now, with Jennie."

"But maybe he didn't intend to kill Jennie, so she messed up his number scheme," Axel said. "That may cause him to go into a frenzy."

"Or to commit more murders," Dan said. "Maybe he planned on three deaths first and then another three." He looked at Katie. "Including you. He was at your house."

"Then, I would have been four, but he'd need two more victims. You ruined his plan to kill me."

"But he's killed Jennie. I think we need to find out more about the couple and their niece who were killed in Florida," Axel said to Dan.

Katie inhaled a long breath. "So our theory is this. The killer is from New Orleans, and he planned it all from here. The plan may have included going to Florida specifically to kill my father, then strategically his next kill in Orlando. To the best of my knowledge, my father didn't know the couple in Orlando. But they, too, were retired and older, and if I remember what they said in the papers, the husband—" she looked over at Dan "—Harold Austin?"

"Yes. Harold and Marie Austin, and Harold's niece Hennie, or Henrietta. Harold was seventy-two when he died, his wife, Marie, was sixty-eight, and his niece had just turned fifty."

"Harold was an engineer who had worked in Tulsa, Oklahoma, before retiring to Florida," Katie said.

"Hard to find a connection there," Axel murmured.

"What if the connection is George?" Katie asked.

Dan frowned. "You think George is guilty now?"

She smiled and shook her head. "No. But George was with my parents. George lived just a block or so from Harold, Marie and Henrietta. And George came here because they were making so many movies. He's a perfect man to frame for these murders."

"I say any of it is more than possible," Mabel told them, nodding gravely. "And while I do love the scent of food, I'm not good at all at shuffling papers around. I do suggest you all begin to look at these angles. And find the truth!"

Katie nodded at the woman. She had been beautiful in her day, probably a bit flamboyant, and yet a woman ahead of her time, not about to be put in the background.

And she remained on earth past death. Maybe frustration had kept Mabel there. She had suffered a terrible loss, and maybe her way to deal with the pain was to help now.

Mabel rose. "Ah, my friends! The deliciousness of your meals is fading. I'm going to hitch a ride down to Bourbon Street and find some friends for a rollicking good time. While I see if I see anything!" she added. "You darlings of flesh and blood, get some sleep! You're going to need it. Ciao, my loves!"

She gave them a wave, blew a kiss and departed, half walking and half floating out.

"She's right," Axel said. "We have to find the associations. Because Dr. Neil Browne is someone who has an agenda, or he's the patsy working for someone with an agenda."

Katie shook her head. "I don't get it. My father was a good guy. He served his country. He came as soon as he could when the levees broke after Katrina. Why would anyone want to kill him?"

They were all silent for a minute. Katie looked at her plate. Despite her certainty that she wouldn't be able to eat after they left the morgue, she had cleaned it all up quite well. Axel glanced at Dan. Dan shrugged.

"What? Are you two implying that I didn't know my own father?" she demanded indignantly.

Dan shook his head, turning to her. "No, his very decency might have outraged someone. After something like Katrina and the levees breaking, you get to see the very best in people. And the very worst. There was looting, there were people left behind, there were horrible things that happened. We'll never know the depth of it because of the flooding. People were trapped in areas."

"My father and Jeremy went out in a boat to save people."

"And maybe they missed someone. Or maybe he saw illegal activity and stopped it. Katie, we'll figure it out," Dan said.

"Tomorrow. I'm about to keel over," Axel said. "I'm going to drop you off and go and get some sleep. I suggest you do the same."

"The cameras were installed?" Dan asked him.

"The entire house is covered. An agent will be watching the screens 24-7. No one will be coming near Katie's place, with or without the dogs on the loose," Axel assured them.

Dan nodded. "Sleep," he murmured. "Sounds good."

Axel rose to go pay. "Adam is footing this bill. The case is personal to him, too," he assured them.

"And we're not…taking advantage of Adam?" Katie wondered.

Dan shook his head. "Adam… Adam has the Midas touch. And he's an amazing man. He uses his business acumen for good things and helping people. Of course, he put together Axel's team, the Krewe of Hunters."

"And they all see the dead," she said.

"We do!" Axel said. He was back at the table, answering her but looking at Dan. "And we love to find the right new recruits."

Dan raised his eyebrows. "Let's get through this," he said.

"Right. Let's get through this."

The dogs were out when they reached Katie's place. They were thrilled to greet her and Dan as they returned.

The stables were quiet. Monty's lights were out. He'd probably gone to bed for the night.

Axel waited until they were in the house, then he drove away.

Katie stood in the entry for a minute: she knew Dan was walking around, checking out every room, every window and every nook and cranny.

He returned and met her on the landing.

"All secure?" she asked.

"All secure," he said. He held her gaze.

"And?"

"I don't sleep deeply. I'll be awake at the first little yip the pups let out."

She nodded. "Okay. So…in the morning, I should—"

"Take the day off. We're going to do research."

"I'm not sure that I should."

"Monty will be fine with it, I'm sure."

She nodded and started up the stairs. He followed. When she stopped to ask him how and where they were going to research, he plowed into her.

They were touching for only a second. His hands brushed her waist. She had caused the collision, but he laughed and apologized.

In that second, she thought about him, really thought about him.

She'd despised Dan so much for his persecution of George. But Dan had been such a haunted man himself. And he'd been willing to open his mind and listen, and now...

She liked him. She still didn't really know him, but she'd begun to like a great deal about him.

More than that.

Touching, the way his touch felt. She was embarrassed to realize that she wanted him. In the worst way.

"What is it?" he asked. He must have seen something of her feelings in her face.

"Uh, nothing! I'm so sorry!"

She turned and fled the rest of the way up the stairs, hurrying through the small hallway and to her own room.

She remembered that it had been a long day with a corpse and blood and the morgue... She needed a shower.

A cold one.

She stripped quickly, throwing her clothes in a pile. She might never wear them again. She should burn them. No, that was ridiculous. She could wash everything and then donate it where it was needed. Yes, that's what she would do.

She brushed her teeth almost savagely and headed into the shower, forgetting at first that she wanted it cold and standing in the steam. But the steam made her think of him…

No, no, she told herself, just his body. He had an enticing body, strong, lean, muscled. It had been a long, long time since she'd even accepted a date for coffee or a drink. She was busy. She was…awkward.

She kept too much inside, and she'd always been afraid of getting too close…

Well, she wasn't thinking marriage proposal.

She was just thinking sex.

She shouldn't be. She should be trying to solve the puzzle of her parents, Orlando, New Orleans, Jennie, Dr. Neil Browne, the Axeman…

But thinking like that was making her anxious.

Maybe it was better to think about sex.

She turned off the shower, stepped out and dried off. She knew she was exhausted, but she felt she was too keyed-up to sleep. She thought she would just lie down, turn on something completely diverting to watch…

A ridiculous comedy. But not a romantic one!

Nothing about criminals…

Not the news, which would be about murder…

She was standing by her television, holding the remote before a blank screen and wearing nothing but a towel, when she heard something downstairs. Like a door or a drawer closing.

Pure terror seized her.

While telling herself it was the stupidest thing to do, she raced out into the second-story hallway, ready to bang on Dan's door or go flying down the stairs to meet the danger head-on.

She froze.

Dan was coming up the stairs with a pack of cookies from her cupboard and a bottle of iced tea.

He met her eyes.

He'd showered, too. His hair was dark and slick against his head. He was shirtless, barefoot and in jeans.

He looked at her, frowning.

"Hey, I'm so sorry. I didn't mean to wake you."

"I wasn't sleeping. I just…"

She stopped talking; she just stood there.

He came up the rest of the stairs, setting his tea and cookies on the hardwood floor by his door, then came over to her. He started to put an assuring arm around her shoulders and seemed to realize she was wearing only a towel. He stepped back awkwardly. "Sorry. I, um, just couldn't sleep. I hope you don't mind. I figured I'd watch what they were saying on the news and snack on some sugar."

"No, no, of course not," she said.

Neither one of them moved for a moment.

And then it seemed they moved together, started to speak together, but didn't. They were all but touching. His face hovered close to hers.

She started talking fast, faltering over words that weren't cohesive enough to be understood. "I wanted… I can't sleep… The circumstances… If you wanted… I mean, you could join me…if you want… I'm not even sure… I…"

"Whatever you would like," he told her, smiling slowly.

He was looking down at her with a crooked smile on his face that might have annoyed her at one time but now seemed like the most seductive come-on.

She dropped the towel.

He wrapped his arm under hers and literally swept her off her feet and carried her into the guest bedroom, laying her gently on the bed and leaning above her. He smoothed back a lock of her hair and asked, "You're sure?"

"Yes."

He kissed her. She wondered if he was especially good or if she was just woefully inexperienced. But she wasn't really: she had lived, not promiscuously, but she had dated, been in a few relationships deep enough to care, to become intimate.

It was the tension…

Her fear. And it was Dan.

She forgot thought; she gave way to sensation, the sweet, wet, fire of his lips and tongue, the feel of his hands, masculine and large and a bit rough against her flesh…

Touching him, feeling the pulse and rope of muscles beneath her fingertips.

The air in the room was cool against the growing heat of her flesh. A drape was just slightly open, allowing in a tiny stream of moonlight that seemed to dance over them as he slid out of his jeans. His mouth moved against her throat and her breasts and down her torso, and she gasped and drew her fingers down the length of his body, loving the power in every twist and turn of it. She writhed against him, twisting and turning, took in the sweet, salty taste of his flesh, and she teased and kissed him.

She felt his stroke against her thighs. His movement as he thrust into her, so slowly at first, a tease even there that seemed to elicit an even greater longing until they were locked as one and moving in an electric wave of energy that was sensuous and wild.

He held her, rolled with her, moved with her. Their lips met and their tongues parried and broke away. And it was forever…and it ended too soon, and she lay beside him, still ecstatic at first, heart pounding, breath coming at a million miles an hour...

And then...

What the hell had she done?

She wondered if the trickle of the moonlight showed that she was blushing red from head to toe, so embarrassed she had all but presented herself on a silver platter to him in the hallway.

She couldn't think of a single thing to say.

But it didn't matter. He lay beside her gasping for breath himself. He turned, rising on an elbow at her side, and looked at her with a gentle and tender smile and murmured, "Wow. You're beautiful. And you know what's even better?"

She hoped he didn't expect an answer. She couldn't create sound now and certainly couldn't form words.

"Beautiful inside and out," he murmured.

She should speak, of course. But she still couldn't. He lay down again and pulled her gently to him so that she rested cradled by his side.

He didn't say anything else; they just lay there in that moonlight.

She was almost dozing when she felt him adjusting the way he lay. Then she pressed into him. Bodies slid along each other.

They made love again.

Later, as he held her, she finally slept.

So deeply, and so at ease.

Nothing stirred in the shadows and soft moonlight.

Twelve

Dan wasn't at all sure what it might have been that he ever thought was *un*appealing about Katie Delaney.

Waking early, he pulled the covers tightly around her and left her curled up with a pillow, the fiery streaks of her hair splaying over the soft mauve cover on the second pillow where her head rested.

He forced himself to dress and walk out of the bedroom.

He first called Axel. Agents had watched the cameras through the night. They had seen the dogs chase each other around and nothing more. No one had come near her house or the fence or made any attempt to enter.

"I'm expecting to hear from Angela soon, but while I'm pleased to report that no attempts were made against Katie—"

"God, no, another murder?" Dan asked.

"No. A letter. An exact copy of the letter that was sent to the newspaper years ago was sent again, received at the crack of dawn this morning. There was an addition to it—a single piece of paper claiming the Axeman was immortal, a true demon from the depths of hell, and that anyone who thought he could be caught or killed was sadly mistaken and might well feel the kiss of the axe."

Dan was surprised by the amount of fury the words awakened in him. He knew he had to control it—he simply despised that kind of grotesque arrogance.

"We've got to prove him wrong," he said quietly.

"Yes," Axel agreed. "I'm going to the autopsy for the woman we know as Jennie. So far, we have nothing on her. They pulled prints, but they aren't in the system. We're trying DNA, and because we put it on a desperate rush, we should have results back soon."

"I bet she's not going to be in the system. I'm not a profiler, but I've attended enough lectures. I see Jennie as someone who first came to New Orleans as a lost soul. Maybe she ran away from home, maybe she had an abusive parent or guardian. She wanted to get away from home as soon as possible. Somewhere in the city, she came across Neil Browne, charming and charismatic, and who seemed to be the answer to her prayers. She fell for his doctrine, for his promise of power over others. But she was a pawn, nothing more."

"If that's the case, George Calabria is truly innocent. He wasn't in New Orleans back then," Axel said.

"No. Neil Browne is a separate entity. We know that from Katie." He was quiet for a minute. "What we don't know is whether there is someone else behind Neil Browne. In other words, Browne may be nothing more than a patsy, too. Someone may have been pulling the strings from here all the time, staying safe, even, or waiting for the right time in New Orleans for his end game."

"That's a scary thought. But one way or the other, we need to find Neil Browne. And if Jennie was here in the city, so is he."

"I agree."

"Do you want to come to the autopsy?" Axel asked Dan.

"No, but I'll be waiting to hear what you learn." He hesitated. "I don't think we're even going to go to the archives. I want to get Katie talking. I'd even like to spend time with her and George Calabria and try to find out anything either of them might know about Katie's father."

"Maybe you should bring Jeremy into that conversation. He'd know more about anything that might have happened when Lou Delaney was in New Orleans after the storm."

"True. I'm going to take it step by step. And hope for something."

"All right. We'll keep each other in the loop."

"Axel, that letter. Did the paper print it?"

"No. While it would be the sensation of the year, the paper seems to value human life. They're staying mum on it."

"Wow! Amazing. And great. Except that it's going to infuriate the killer."

"Yes. But we're keeping this as tight as we can be. The city has been warned. I talked to Ryder this morning, too. He was out last night, patrolling until the wee hours. You know what he told me?"

"That all you could hear was jazz?"

Axel laughed. "Right, and jazz is great. But a lot of venues like to blast out rock and pop, old and new. The killer wanted a panic. He wants people to believe the old Axeman was a supernatural being, and that he's returned."

"We need to move fast," Dan said. "We have to stop him before he kills again. We can't let the city fall into this fantasy."

"I agree. That means we need to find the puzzle pieces. When I finish at the morgue, I'm going to continue door-to-door and walk around sketches of Dr. Neil Browne." He hesitated. "Naturally, we have a host of agents and police out day and night. But this guy is striking by darkness." He hesitated again. "I'd have them putting an alarm on Katie's place, too, but I'm not sure it would guarantee safety. The old Axeman chiseled major gaps in door panels and used any conceivable entrance. The dogs and the cameras—and patrols watching through the night—seem to be our best defense. Of course, she could leave her house for a while."

Dan spoke up. "You know I'm not leaving her."

"Right. And don't. But still, we may need to look at somewhere safer for her to stay."

"Yeah," Dan said. "But she loves her place. It's right next to the stables."

"But she's not going to work today."

"No."

"Someone knows something, Dan."

"I'm on it."

They ended the call. Dan started coffee and then put a call through to Corey Crest in tech support at FDLE.

"Corey, I need help again," he said.

"You got it," Corey promised.

"Okay, I need anything at all you can find out about Lou Delaney, George Calabria…and also any info we got on Jennie and Dr. Neil Browne."

"Dan, we didn't get any info on Jennie or Neil Browne. That's why many people didn't believe that they existed."

"Someone else down there had to have seen them," Dan said.

"I'll try to get you what I have on the other two men, but I'd say I'm not going to get anything new. Delaney has been dead for twelve years. Calabria… We had what we had six years ago, and after the trial, he left the state."

"Thanks, Corey. Anything is deeply appreciated."

"You got it. I hear the killer struck again. A woman, and her body was found in an old cemetery that was just about condemned."

"Yes."

"You knew her?"

"No, but we believe that it was Jennie."

"Jennie! Then, she did exist."

"So it seems. Anyway, thank you. Get back to me."

"Will do."

He ended the call and saw that Katie had come downstairs. She looked to have showered and dressed for the day in leggings and a tunic. She looked pale, as if she was suddenly afraid to greet him.

"Hey," he said. "I put coffee on."

"Uh…great," she said. Now her cheeks looked like little rose blossoms.

"They haven't found anything on Jennie yet, her real identity. I believe she stayed under the radar. Axel is heading to the autopsy."

"Are you?"

He shook his head. "Do you have any of your father's records?" he asked. "Did he keep a diary or anything? What about Jeremy? Do you think he'd meet with us? I'd like to talk to him about your father's time here when he came back after the storm."

"My father—" she started.

"Katie, it's important. And there's a clock ticking."

"I know," she said. "All the boxes I have with a few of my parents' personal belongings, paperwork and so on, are at Jeremy's house."

"Could we speak with George?"

"We'll have to ask George."

He smiled. "We will. Do you remember anything about the time when your dad came up here?"

She shrugged. "I know he was happy when he talked to my mom because they'd gotten a few people off rooftops. And pets! He was thrilled when he could help with animals, too. He was a big-time animal person. I think about how my dad would have loved the boys! Let's see, I remember him complaining, too, angry because there was an element out looting. He was sad one day when they pulled a woman out through a window, but she had already died." She shook her head. "I didn't know anything specific."

"But Jeremy would."

"Yes."

"Can you call him?" he asked.

She nodded. "Of course. I, uh, left my phone upstairs."

She turned and hurried on back up the stairs. As she left, his phone rang.

It was Axel. "Someone leaked the news about the letter," he told Dan.

"Figures. Are they worried about a panic?"

"Let's just say the airport is crowded," Axel told him. "And we have the fanatics on Bourbon Street with their signs already, warning that anyone who commits any kind of sin—sneezing wrong is counted with that, I think—is going to hell. I just wanted you forewarned everyone is afraid of the Axeman. There is a segment of the population that really believes he's back."

"Great. Just great."

"Now the paper will print the letter with this Axeman's addendum."

"Of course. Thanks, Axel."

He ended the call. Katie came back down the stairs. "Jeremy is going to meet us, and he'll bring us my boxes. He wants to go to a place he loves. It's called Coffee Science, and it's on Broad Avenue."

"I know it."

"He needs an hour or so."

"Okay. If you don't mind, we'll stop by my office quickly."

"You're working other cases?"

"No, but I want to make sure my assistant isn't being harassed by an old client. Besides, we have an hour to kill."

"I'll just check with Monty, let him know I won't be in the carriage at all today." She smiled. "Thank God for Monty! He's so understanding. I might be in danger of losing my job, otherwise."

"I'm assuming a lot of employers might see their people fleeing the city," Dan said. "I'll be out front if you want to lock up." He started toward the door and then swung around. "Wait a minute! I brewed coffee!"

He went back to pour a cup of coffee. She was staring at him, and for the first time that morning, she gave him a smile. "Hey, I'm standing right here, you know."

"Sorry! How rude!" He poured her a cup, too. She found cream in the refrigerator and added a touch to hers, then offered it to him.

He shook his head and said, "No, thanks."

"Cools it down, you know," she told him.

"Ice cube does the same. And I hate weak coffee."

"That's our city's finest, dark and robust. No weak coffee here," she promised him.

They both sipped the coffee, leaning against the kitchen counter together.

"I don't want to be a cliché—" he said.

"Then, don't be."

"You're good?" he asked her. "With me?"

She looked away, the color growing darker in her cheeks. "Of course," she said, adding, "And look, it was what it was. No commitment."

"No commitment… So, you don't want me saying anything like *About last night...*"

"Lord, no. All right, this coffee was delicious. I'm just running through the gate to Monty's."

"Wait!" he told her.

He drained the last of the coffee from his cup. It was everything she promised. Dark, strong, robust.

"I'll get out the door first. You lock up."

He headed out of the house. The dogs found him as he made his way toward the gate. He heard Katie locking her door as he tried to share some quick attention between the three big dogs until they saw Katie and rushed to her.

He walked out, carefully closing the gate and getting into his car. A minute later, she came running through the gate, telling the dogs to stay, carefully closing the gate as she left.

She wouldn't look at him as she got into the car. He wasn't sure whether to try or talk about what had happened between them or not. She'd said no commitment.

But he wondered if she had meant that because of him or herself.

"Katie…" he began, before turning the key in the ignition.

"Please don't," she whispered. "I'm embarrassed enough as it is."

"Why?"

"Because… I mean, people just don't do things like that."

He didn't mean to laugh; it was just spontaneous. She glared at him.

"Katie, I'm sorry, I'm sorry! But, yes, people do things like that. Rather frequently."

"I don't," she whispered.

"Then, I'm really honored. And it was one of my best nights ever, Katie. Yes, I understand. No, I don't expect anything from you. But in a time and place that seems to be pure hell, you made the world seem right and livable for me again. You are incredible. I won't ask you for any commitments. Just know I think you're wonderful in so many ways. And I'm...grateful for and amazed by last night."

He didn't wait for her reply but twisted the key in the ignition.

He drove down to Rampart and over to the CBD, finagling to find parking on the street. Katie followed him up to his office.

Marleah was behind her desk in the reception area busy at work on her computer. She looked up and smiled a greeting when he entered, standing when she saw that Katie was behind him.

"Well, hello. I didn't expect to see you, Dan. The Axeman case...is it over? Did you catch him?" she asked hopefully.

"No, Marleah, I'm sorry. I just thought I'd stop by and finish up with the Wendy Lawrence paperwork. Did she come by the office?" he asked.

"No. And I left the paperwork and pictures on your desk, and I have it all digitally in the computer." She waited.

Dan turned to Katie. "Katie Delaney, Marleah Darwin, the most amazing office assistant, secretary...receptionist and all to be found on the face of the earth."

Marleah flushed, reaching over to shake Katie's hand. "My main claim to fame and extraordinary powers is that I can sometimes fathom his mind," she said. "Katie, a pleasure to meet you."

Katie smiled, obviously liking the woman immediately.

She turned to him curiously. He wondered if she'd expected him to have a twentysomething secretary with Mardi Gras breasts.

"I'll just clean that all up," Dan said, indicating his office.

"Please, tell me that you won't work for that woman again!" Marleah begged as he and Katie headed into his office. "She called again after you left her a message."

Dan stopped and turned back to her.

"You could have called me. I'd have gotten back to her."

"No need. She just wanted you to know that while you may be the best in the city, she'd make sure that she smeared you everywhere for refusing to find her husband cheating."

Dan shook his head and shrugged. "Not to worry, Marleah."

He went behind his desk. Katie sat in one of the chairs in front of it, a dry smile of amusement on her face.

"So you were chasing cheating husbands?" she asked.

"He actually wasn't cheating. She refused to accept it. Her husband has money. Not from his work. He's a high school teacher. Family money. She only gets a part of it in a divorce if he cheats on her. At first, I thought she was worried about him, that he might have gotten involved with dangerous people or something. Then I found out about the legal agreement they made before their marriage and…that didn't matter so much. I had told her I'd work on it a bit longer, but that I didn't expect to find anything. Except that…"

As he spoke, he found himself staring at one of the pictures he had taken of Nathan Lawrence in what he had assumed to be a business meeting with a well-dressed man and woman.

"What?" Katie asked.

"Am I crazy? Am I seeing that woman now in everything?"

"What woman?" Katie asked.

He passed the picture over. "Jennie," he said.

Katie took the picture from and studied it before looking back at him.

"She has tight black curls there, and I swear she's used stage makeup or something to change her nose. But, yes, Dan! This could be her."

"What about the man?"

Katie studied the picture again.

"It could be Neil Browne. I'm doubting that's his real name now and that he was ever a doctor of anything. He'd be twelve years older than when I saw him. And there's something about the nose on him, too. This guy has short, short hair, and Browne wasn't wearing it that way when I saw him. He had longish hair, with a slash of it over his forehead." She paused to shake her head. "It could have been them. I just can't say for certain."

Dan drummed his fingers on the table.

He needed to call Wendy Lawrence. But she wouldn't help him.

He needed to reach Nathan Lawrence or, rather, get Axel to do so.

He drew out his phone and quickly called Axel, explained what he had found, and asked that he set up a meeting with the man. Thankfully, since he'd been hired to spy on Lawrence, he had all the information Axel needed to reach him.

"I'm at the autopsy on Jennie right now. Haven't learned much yet, other than Dr. Vincent believes the first blow that slammed into her head and through her face would have caused death instantly. The other hacking was done afterward. He estimates she was in her early to midthirties. That would have made her about twenty-one when she was in Florida. I'll get someone on Nathan Lawrence before heading back in. We'll get something set up for this afternoon."

Dan thanked him and ended the call.

"We'll find out," he told Katie, glancing at his watch. "We'd better go."

"Right," she agreed.

Leaving the office, he asked Marleah to leave everything on his desk just as it was. Marleah frowned but didn't question him. She just told Katie again what a pleasure it had been to meet her.

They arrived at Coffee Science with five minutes to spare, but Jeremy was already waiting for them at one of the tables in the restaurant.

"I got coffee for us," he said. "And I put in a few orders of avocado toast. Sound okay?"

"Sounds great," Dan said, waiting for Katie to take a chair and then sliding in next to her.

Jeremy grimaced, looking at him. "I know Katie loves avocado toast… You can order something else."

"I'm fine," he assured Jeremy.

Jeremy nodded and then thanked the server who brought their order over to the table.

Then he said, "I'm glad Katie's being protected under the circumstances plaguing the city right now. She's still my blood, and well, I'm confused. What kind of help do you think that I can give you?"

Dan shook his head. "We're worried there is a connection between the here and now and the past. Can you tell us about the time that Lou came up here to work with you after the flooding?"

"It was awful," Jeremy said. "Worse than you can imagine, even. And Lou was great."

"Jeremy," Katie said, reaching across the table to touch is hand. "We need something a little more specific than that. Did you two offend anyone, possibly make any enemies?"

"We saved lives," Jeremy said flatly.

"I know that. I know! But, please tell us more. It's important, Jeremy."

Jeremy let out a breath and was silent for a minute.

"After the storm," Jeremy said, shaking his head and taking a long sip of coffee, "Lou wasn't here at first. You can't imagine the night, the darkness, the screams...the sound of gunfire. Lou got up here as quick as he could. This place was still his home, you know? Anyway, we went out from the St. Claude Avenue Bridge... I have a bass boat. By then... God, it was awful. Ninth Ward, the water was up to the rooftops. There was a guy on one of the houses, and he was pointing out places where there were people. We weren't the only ones out there, of course, but this one man...he'd tried to help others, and then we saw that he was desperately trying to get kids out of a tiny vent, and the water was still going higher. Lou, man... Lou was the kind of guy who had to do something, and he was a good diver, even when it came to a free dive. Lou jumped off the boat and went to the vent. He got it broken open, and there were three kids in there, and he got them out just before the water kept going up. You can't imagine that night. It was hard to get around because of the treetops, wires, electric poles... Corpses. Bodies floating in the darkness. That was the worst. We kept going. I reckon we brought in about fifty survivors, including those kids." He hesitated.

"Then, there was coming home... I had neighbors who had managed to get out before it hit. Cops were trying,

trying hard. But there was nonstop looting, not that people cared all that much about things when lives were concerned." Jeremy paused. "Some of us had radios. Radios were the best way to communicate as satellites were not working all that great. Anyway, one night, Lou came with me to try to find my friend, Max, down in the French Quarter. Flooding was never that bad there. Guess the Frenchmen who came in to settle the place did find the highest ground. Anyway, Max had a place back then off Esplanade on Royal Street. He got through to me 'cause some weird group had cracked, and they were catching animals that were half-dead and trying to slice them up to eat. I mean, it was bad. You know your father...knew him, that is. I'm so sorry. He got food. He brought it on down there to give to the people, but there was some whacked-out guy there trying to slice up a llama—yeah, a llama. Got loose from one of the farm or stable areas up on the other side of Treme. Your dad had to force him off the llama, gave him one to the jaw to get him to stop and listen and take a sandwich. People went wild after that storm. Crazy. You couldn't blame folks who were starving. Oh, yeah, your dad had me find some cops that night. We got the guy who wanted to slice up the llama and some others with him to get to the arena. Hope they got that fellow medical attention."

Dan looked at Katie.

Katie looked at him.

"Jeremy, do you remember anything about this man?"

"In particular?" he asked. "During that time? Katie, I saw that man on the roof ready to die, if he could only get those kids out of that flooding house. I saw folks screaming and crying that they would rather die than leave their pets. And cops who figured just get the animals in the boats, too, and we'll just keep moving as fast as we can. I saw people who were so heroic it could make you shiver with amazement at the human spirit. And I saw people killing animals, breaking windows, stealing anything that wasn't nailed down. That one guy, though… I guess the storm did something to him. You know the worst of it? I think he was ticked off your dad made the others around him realize they didn't need to go catching pathetic strays in the street to kill for food. He didn't like it that the people around him preferred the arena and handouts to killing in the street."

Katie looked at Dan. "I don't know… We're grasping at straws here, aren't we?" she asked weakly.

"What are you talking about?" Jeremy demanded.

Jeremy was staring hard at Dan, and Dan decided that telling the man the truth was the thing to do.

"We believe that there might be a connection."

"A connection to what?" Jeremy asked.

"We believe Lou might have been targeted by someone who was here after the storm. Someone who found access to enough money to stage the whole thing down in Florida to kill him, who maybe even figured a way to frame George Calabria, at least through circumstantial evidence. Someone who is playing upon the old Axeman who terrorized Louisiana once, and using the concept of the immortal demon and a fixation on power and the number six that was started here about the same time by a man named Allan Pierce."

Jeremy shook his head. He looked at Katie. "I am so lost. Katie, your father was never stupid…or blind. If the Dr. Browne who was on the boat the day they were murdered was the same man, your father would have recognized him."

"He would have," Katie agreed.

"But I don't think that Dr. Browne was the man you were telling us about. I think he was one of the followers, maybe. If you saw this man again, Jeremy, would you recognize him?" Dan asked.

"The man who was going to slice up the llama?" Jeremy asked.

"Yes."

Jeremy inhaled and exhaled slowly, shaking his head. "No. I was dealing with one of the women in the group. She was older and not doing well. Lou told me he'd deal with the most intense of the group while I got her to help. There were EMTs in the area, and she needed attention fast. Most of what I know about the incident was getting the cops to deal with the people and the llama. Turned out the man who owned one of the big carriage companies at the time owned a few exotic pets, and the llama was a beloved pet. The llama was returned and… Well, a llama in the middle of all thàt. But no. I would not recognize the man again because I really didn't see him. Remember, too, there was no light. We had our flashlights. We had the moon on some nights. The world was dark and wet, and you could still stumble upon corpses of cats, dogs, human beings just about anywhere." Jeremy paused, inhaling and exhaling again. "Trust me. If you weren't here, you can only imagine."

"I know it must have been hard," Dan said. "Is there anything else you know about the man or any of the people with him?"

"I just know they were steered toward the arena by cops." He frowned. "But, again, do you think that someone here managed to get followers to kill for them? Wait, I guess it has happened before. But…someone got someone to Florida to murder Katie's mom and dad and Anita Calabria, kill people again in Orlando, and then come here? I mean, it's not like they would have been working up to kill Lou. Lou was murdered twelve years ago."

Dan took a deep breath himself. "Whoever this person is, they might have made sure they were anonymous. From what I've heard, Lou Delaney wouldn't have kept his own identity a secret. I doubt if they exchanged pleasantries, but somehow the man found out who Lou was. Maybe the man could have gone to someone else involved and lied and said something like 'Oh, who was that? I have to thank him for what he did for me!' And there was something that had already begun in his mind or a plan he had in his head. I'm not even sure how to explain this. There had to have been something he had going. If he revered the Axeman and Allan Pierce and had figured that the disaster was a way to manipulate people and situations, it might have seemed to him like a grand design for life, and power was falling into place. Kill Lou and the others, kill again in *six* years, and then come back to New Orleans *six* years later for his end game, his grand finale."

Jeremy nodded gravely. "How could he have known? This killer…how could he have known Katie would move here? Is he targeting Katie? Katie! You need to relocate to Europe or Australia. Somewhere far, far from here."

Katie shook her head. "Jeremy, if we're right, this killer has money. He sent henchmen to do the deeds he wanted done in Florida. He would have done his research. You're my closest relative. He probably knows about you as well as all about me."

"And now Dan?" Jeremey asked.

"Probably," Dan said. "Maybe we're part of the end game, and maybe we're not. But we know this isn't random. And now we're prepared."

"And I can't spend my life running. I just can't," Katie

said and hesitated. "Jeremy, you have to be careful. You could be in danger, too, if this does have anything to do with what you and my dad did here after the storm. You have to be careful."

"I have an alarm system on the house, remember," Jeremy told her. "And I have a gun and a permit," he assured Dan.

"Here is what we have going for us. He wants to make these killings as much like those done by the Axeman as possible. The Axeman always struck late at night or early in the morning. He used the cover of darkness. It would have been easier back then as people didn't have sophisticated alarm systems. They barely had lighting. Most didn't expect any kind of an attack. Now, the city is on edge. People will be prepared."

"Except for those who can't be," Jeremy said quietly. "Those who are older and on fixed incomes. Those who have jobs and little children and must choose between feeding and clothing their families and shoring up their homes. The couple he killed here and their caretaker…they were on a fixed income, right? They wouldn't have expected anyone to come after them. They didn't do anything wrong."

"Jeremy, I can tell you this from many years in law enforcement. It's often the good and the innocent who suffer. But there may be connections. We need to find out if there are, and if so, what they are."

Jeremy shook his head. "It's not that bad things don't happen here," he said. "It's a big city. Things happen. A lot of the bad has to do with the drug trade. But this killer, he isn't after money. You think that he has money. And I doubt he's into drugs. He's just…"

"Probably a narcissist with psychotic traits. I don't think that our missing Dr. Neil Browne is the leader. Though, I do think he could be the one who killed whoever Jennie was. I think he was ordered to kill her, and that it wasn't easy, and that's why his first blow was lethal. He wanted to make her death merciful. Remember, too, we're working on a theory. But having spoken with you, I think it's a very plausible theory."

"George Calabria is here in the city," Katie said.

Jeremy started, staring at Katie with surprise. "What?"

"We found out he is living here now, and we went to see him. He's in a hotel to be safe," Katie told him.

Jeremy's gaze jerked from Katie to Dan. "Then...were you right...back in Orlando? I mean, he's been close to the crimes in three places. I think he has money. I—"

Dan shook his head. "No. I think I was wrong. I think whoever is pulling the strings would love to see George go down for the crimes. We're going to talk to him again."

"I don't know... Why is he here?" Jeremy demanded. "I thought he was going to go off and live on a far, far away island."

"He decided he wanted to do behind-the-scenes work for the movies," Katie said. "Embroil himself in fantasy and get away from reality. I understand that."

"Watch out for him," Jeremy warned.

Dan nodded. "We're watching out at all times."

"But you're going back to Katie's house—"

"With cameras and three large dogs and me," Dan said firmly.

"You have to sleep...dogs can be poisoned," Jeremy said. "Katie should be—"

"Jeremy, please! The FBI is watching us. Police are watching us."

"And you think it's a chance to catch him. At Katie's expense," Jeremy said.

Katie shook her head firmly. "Not at my expense. At my insistence. I told you, I can't spend my life looking over my shoulder. This must be solved. Here and now," she added softly.

Jeremy sighed. "You'd better text me twice a day."

"Yes, and you're to text back!" Katie told him firmly.

He smiled. "Okay. And please keep in close contact. Please, please." He wasn't looking at Katie; he was looking at Dan.

Dan nodded.

"Okay," Jeremy said awkwardly. "So we're...set. Except the news about another letter to the papers and the guy being an immortal demon is out on the streets. We may all need to be worried about people doing nutty things, dangerous things, because they're so worried."

"Maybe," Dan admitted. "But we'll get through it."

Jeremy nodded and almost smiled. "Yes, we will get through it. NOLA strong," he said.

They were silent for a minute.

"Hey, uh, what did I tell you about the avocado toast?" he asked.

"Best I've ever had," Dan assured him.

"What now?" Jeremy asked. "We sit and wait for him to strike again?"

"No. We're going to see George again, and...a man who just might have had a meeting with Jennie and the man we know as Neil Browne," Katie said.

Dan felt his phone vibrating in his jacket pocket and reached for it. He excused himself and rose to take the call from Axel.

"Can you get to the office now?" Axel asked.

"Yeah. What's up?"

"Ryder found your man, Nathan Lawrence. We have

him in one of the interrogation rooms, but we don't have him on anything, so holding him... So far, he's just scared and confused. But get here as quickly as you can. With your pictures."

"On my way," Dan assured him. He turned back to the table and told Katie, "We have to go. Now. Jeremy, thank you. Sincerely, thank you."

"Wait!" Katie said. "Wait. We've all figured out Jeremy might be in danger, and we're just going to go off—"

"Katie, I'm fine," Jeremy said. "Good alarm system. Shotgun. I'm good."

"But you sleep, too," Katie protested.

"Not through the blare of my alarm," Jeremy assured her. "This takes away nothing from anyone. Most people don't spend their lives afraid of being attacked. And they don't use firearms, and they may not have alarms. I've trained at the shooting range. I know what I'm doing. I'll be all right. In fact, bad as this may sound, I'd love to shoot the blood-soaked bastard who killed your mom and dad."

"I'll tell Ryder and Axel, too. They'll keep an eye on the neighborhood," Dan promised.

"See!" Jeremy said to Katie.

"Katie, please, we have to get moving," Dan said.

"I'll be in here a while longer," Jeremy said. "Can't seem to get enough of that avocado toast!"

Dan managed to extract Katie at last; in the car, she was quiet.

"I know you're worried, but Jeremy is right about one thing. He's not vulnerable. The killer goes after those who are vulnerable."

"My father wasn't a vulnerable person."

"But your father wouldn't have expected a guest on his

boat to be an axe murderer," Dan reminded her. "He would have thought he was with a friend."

Katie didn't reply.

"I'm about to see Axel. He'll make sure Jeremy's house is covered. Okay?"

She looked ahead and nodded. And then she managed "Thank you."

"Katie, we'll solve this. I promise. We'll solve this."

She looked over at him, and he wasn't sure if he saw belief in her eyes or not. But he did see something he wasn't sure he'd seen before. Trust. And maybe even…

Affection.

No commitment, she'd said.

He looked ahead again. He was committed to the case. And whether she wanted it or not, he couldn't help it.

He was committed to her.

Thirteen

They went through security at the FBI offices. There was a reception area with a comfortable sofa. Axel met them there, asking Katie if he could get her anything and pointing out that since she was the only one there at the time, there was a television and she could control it any way she liked.

Then he led Dan down a hallway to an interrogation room.

Adam Harrison was in the room; three chairs faced the one side of the table where Nathan Lawrence was sitting.

He looked up hopefully when Dan and Axel returned to the room.

"I swear!" the man said passionately. "I don't know anything about the axe murders! You all think I know something, someone, that I can help... I have a wife! A good life, and I... Oh, my God! That's awful, I would never, never..."

Dan sent down the folder he'd stuffed into his jacket pocket, opening it and displaying the picture he'd taken of him, Jennie and the unknown man, presumably Neil Browne.

Nathan Lawrence sat back in confusion. He was a well-dressed man in casual designer clothes, well-groomed, with a nice face, brown hair with a touch of gray, and a lean, gym-toned body.

A match for his wife, Wendy. They lived to a certain style, Dan thought, and considered themselves entitled to that lifestyle. Except that Wendy might want a divorce... and was therefore determined to catch him cheating.

Dan had never thought that the man was cheating. He had family money, but from all appearances, he liked his job as a teacher.

"I don't understand. That's Missy and Franklin Turner," he said, looking up at Dan. Then he frowned. "I've seen you. On the streets. Um, in the French Quarter."

"Yes, that's where I took this picture. You were having dinner near the river."

"Yes, of course. That's where I met Missy and Franklin," he said.

"Who are Missy and Franklin? Friends?" Dan asked.

"Well, no. I mean, not really. They befriended me on social media and then asked me to meet. They have a group that meets, and it's just about finding the best in ourselves. It sounded interesting to me. Getting together with others, finding out where help is needed in the city and beyond."

"Just a group that meets to help others in the city?" Dan asked.

Adam cleared his throat and said, "Nathan likes the idea of community outreach. You know that he's a teacher. He devotes his free time to their wrestling team."

"You're a wrestler?"

Nathan laughed at that, shaking his head. "No, no, I do the arrangements for the team to travel, and I set up their meets."

"And he helps out at a church soup kitchen," Adam said.

"Great. So, when was your last meet with the wrestling team?" Dan asked.

"Oh, a couple of months back," Nathan said, frowning. "Midwinter."

Before Dan had started watching him. Maybe his travels with the team had spurred his wife's determination to watch him.

"And the soup kitchen?" he asked politely.

"Protestant church in Metairie," he said. "You can ask them. I haven't been there for several weeks now because Wendy—my wife—seems to have plans on Friday nights, and that was when I put in my hours."

"Let's get back to Franklin and Missy," Dan said. "They found you on social media?"

"Sure. All kinds of people meet on social media."

Dan glanced at Axel. Axel pressed a piece of paper across the table.

"Write down how you're connected."

"It's a business site," Nathan said, writing as directed. "The site is letsdoit.com. All kinds of people are on it. Some do a little to help the community, and some do a lot." He hesitated. "I guess some are looking for friends, and some are looking for recruits."

"This couple, Franklin and Missy, they wanted you to come to a meeting?" Dan asked.

"Yes."

"And did you go?"

"No, I couldn't. Wendy had something planned already. I apologized online… I guess they weren't happy. I haven't received another invitation." He sighed. "Look, I love what I do, but it's hard. Dealing with teenagers? Some girls are in high school and already have kids, while others are pregnant. Some of the guys are in gangs already pushing drugs.

This sounded like a nice group. Just a nice group of people finding power and giving with one another."

"*Finding power.* That phrase was used?" Dan asked.

Axel leaned forward. "Did the number six come up in your conversation?"

"What? Uh…yeah, actually." Lawrence looked confused. "They said they were a solid group and didn't ask just anyone in. They liked to keep their number at six. They didn't consider themselves to be elite or anything. It was just the right number of people to be able to get things done."

"Where were you supposed to meet them?" Dan asked.

"Oh, that I don't know," Nathan said.

"How could you be expected to meet them and not know where?" Axel asked him.

"They tell you where to come right before they meet, and of course, I'd sent my apologies, and they never told me."

"That's convenient," Axel said.

"I swear!" Nathan vowed passionately. "Look, you don't think that—"

"The woman is dead," Dan said flatly. "The victim you read about, Jane Doe in the decrepit old family cemetery." He pointed to her in the picture. "She's dead, hacked to death. So, yes, these people do have something to do with what's going on. And you had really best tell us anything you know. You don't want this killer running around the city, especially when he's someone who knows you."

Katie hated sitting in the reception area waiting.

She should have stayed with Jeremy. Now that they had talked, she was equally concerned about Jeremy as she was for herself. And no matter how he blustered that he was fine and could take care of himself, Katie was frightened for him.

She knew she had Dan with her, and she was being watched and had a great deal of protection going for her.

Jeremy was on his own.

George was also on his own.

She'd called George; they would meet up later at his hotel.

A phone rang, and she heard the receptionist answer the call. "Yes, yes, of course. Yes, they're both in interrogation right now, but I'll have them with you as soon as possible... I'm sure, Detective... We've been getting calls here, too, of course. The paper had no choice once the information was leaked... Yes, Detective."

The young woman behind the desk was speaking in low, careful tones.

Katie could still hear her.

Katie stood when the call ended and approached the young woman's desk. It was behind a counter with windows that could be closed. Maybe bulletproof. But maybe not. No one could reach this floor without going through security and receiving a special clearance.

The young woman looked at Katie warily when she approached, and then she sighed, realizing that no matter how careful she had been, Katie had heard her.

"Tips. I'm starting to think now everyone in the city has seen something. At first, we couldn't find a witness for anything in the world, and now suddenly, half of the city has seen the killer, seen someone suspicious. Putting all the law-enforcement agencies in the world together, we haven't the resources to check out every single tip that's now coming in. But we have good people! And so do the cops. They can weed through a lot."

"That was Detective Stapleton?" Katie asked.

The young woman nodded. "He thinks he has a solid lead. He's looking for Axel and Dan. I'll be right back—I have to signal to them that Ryder has called."

She left her post and apparently spoke to someone down the hall who in turn managed to get the message through.

A minute later, Dan and Axel were exiting the inner sanctum of the offices.

They both thanked the receptionist who nodded to them gravely.

"I play jazz every minute of the time I'm home," she assured them.

"Maybe not a bad idea," Dan said, smiling. "Okay, let's go see Ryder." He set an arm absently around Katie's shoulders to lead her out of the offices. Axel followed.

"There's a tip he thinks is real?" Katie asked as they headed downstairs.

Dan nodded.

They left his car and headed straight for Axel's. He had plates on his car that would allow him parking anywhere in the city, Katie knew. Maybe even anywhere in the country.

"Is Ryder meeting us?" Katie asked as they drove.

Dan shook his head and glanced at her, a grim, dry smile slightly curving his lips.

"Ryder is on to another possibly credible tip. Even after weeding out the sensationalists and attention-seekers, there are a lot of people to follow up with now that the letter to the paper is public knowledge."

They drove to the Marigny, to an old home in a residential neighborhood that had charming trees and foliage growing in every yard.

They parked and walked up an old brick path to the porch and the front door.

The door opened as they arrived; the woman inside had been waiting for them.

She was in her early sixties, Katie thought, and she looked as if she enjoyed the outside and physical activity. She was thin but wiry, had sandy-colored, slightly graying hair in a stylish, short cut. Her eyes were sharp and blue, and she assessed them quickly.

"Special Agent Axel Tiger?" she asked.

Axel produced his credentials.

"I feel like an idiot. Why this didn't occur to me before… Uh, sorry, sorry! Come in. My husband is just in the parlor. Please."

"We're a block down from the first murders here," Dan whispered to Katie.

She nodded, feeling a sense of unease trickle down her spine. She hated it; she hated being anywhere near the place where the killer had struck; she'd hated coming upon Jennie's corpse.

But she'd do just about anything to make it all stop.

"I'm Mona, Mona Lusk, and this is my husband, Rene," she said, leading the way into the parlor.

Rene Lusk was about the same age as his wife. He was tall and thin and wiry like her. They might have run marathons together or perhaps enjoyed fishing, boating or power walking.

Rene had been sitting on a big chesterfield sofa. He rose when they came in, shaking hands with them all.

"I'm afraid being late on this is my fault. And even now…" He glanced over at his wife. "Even now I'm afraid you're going to think we're alarmists seeing things that aren't there, making things up."

"When I first saw the man, Rene just laughed and said this was New Orleans. We're both from here, a bit jaded.

I mean, people are often in costume, and sometimes the more bizarre the costume the better, they seem to think," Mona said.

"Even when it's not Mardi Gras or Halloween," Rene said dryly. "I mean…it's just New Orleans. Oh, and we have a historic voodoo temple or house near here, about two blocks over."

"And it's great! Nothing evil there. Matisse Renoir is the high priestess there for her congregation. They don't do anything bad, trust me. They adhere to the tenet that anything hurtful done to others comes back on oneself threefold. But the house there… She has wonderful historic displays, about the religions in Africa and Haiti and how old religions came together with Christianity, and how the saints work in and—"

"Sweetheart," Rene said, interrupting his wife. "I don't think we need to give them all a lesson in voodoo or even the history of the world," he said softly.

"I'm sorry, I'm sorry. It's just nothing bad goes on there, and people have a tendency to think that voodoo is all about curses."

"It's okay. Katie and I both live here. And our families go way back," Dan assured her.

"Please, sit," Rene said.

They all did so, Katie, Dan and Axel taking the sofa, Rene and Mona in the chairs across from it.

"So," Rene began, looking at his wife, "I was in the kitchen, pouring my cup of morning coffee. I heard Mona out here, muttering." He grimaced at his wife. "She talks to herself a lot, getting crotchety in her old age."

"Hey!" Mona protested.

"And?" Dan asked.

"I poured us both a cup of coffee and brought them out here and asked what she was bitching about now," Rene said.

"Rene didn't see him at first," Mona said.

"*Him* who?" Axel persisted gently.

"The Axeman," Mona said. "Well, of course, I didn't know it was the Axeman. I thought it was some weirdo who thought he was in Chicago or something. I mean, we're not into the dead heat of summer or anything like that yet, but it's not cold around here, either."

"Temperature has been darned great," her husband said.

"Yes, yes, and that's why I was muttering about all the crazies we manage to get in New Orleans. And I was wondering why he wasn't running around Bourbon Street or a party area if he was going to be all dressed up."

"Dressed up how?" Katie asked.

"Big slouchy hat! And a trench coat or an old railway frock coat or something of the like," Mona explained. "Everything he wore was black. He looked kind of like a giant in a full-length black coat, with a hat that dipped low over his face. Now, I didn't think *Axeman* when I saw him. I just thought another crazy guy was running around New Orleans."

"And he didn't come anywhere near the house," Rene said.

"What was he doing?" Dan asked.

"When I saw him, he was just leaning against a tree. It looked like he was resting or waiting for someone," Mona said.

"Later, when we heard about what happened to the old couple—" Rene began.

"And so very near us!" Mona said with a shiver.

"Well, I still didn't think of it at first," Rene said.

"But then there was another body found, hacked up, and

the news came out someone seems to think that he's the Axeman returned," Mona said.

"Well, we knew the legend, but I looked up information on the Axeman," Rene told them. "And the few eyewitness descriptions that there are… Well, they coincided on describing him as a dark figure in a dark something and a slouch hat. So, you see, I started thinking the guy who had been leaning on the tree hadn't been resting or waiting for a friend."

"No! What he'd been doing was watching the neighborhood, watching for whoever came and went. Trying to see who did and who didn't have dogs and alarms," Mona said.

"Quite possibly," Dan said gravely. "And thank you. If you see such a man again—"

"He strikes in different places!" Rene said. "The Axeman strikes in different places."

Dan rose. "We don't know for sure," he said. "This isn't a demon or anyone from hell or with a superpower, no immortality. This is simply a very sick human being. And I don't think he always knows what he's doing from day to day, and we don't even know if more than one person is involved."

"He was big, like a super being," Mona said gravely.

"Lots of men are big," Axel said as he stood.

Katie scrambled to her feet to join them; they were leaving.

Again, they thanked the couple with both Dan and Axel leaving their cards behind should the couple think of anything else.

When they reached the car, Dan turned to Katie. "Will you call Jeremy again, please?"

"I… Sure, but—"

"Please."

She got Jeremy on the phone and handed it over to Dan as Axel drove.

Dan asked Jeremy about the day in the French Quarter after the storm when they'd had trouble.

"Among the people there... Was there anyone large?"

He listened to what Jeremy had to say and then ended the call.

"What?" Katie and Axel inquired in unison.

"Well, there are many tall men in New Orleans," Dan said.

"But...what did Jeremy say?"

"The man your father had the altercation with was average-tall, maybe six one, six two. But he thought one of the guys hanging around in the background—he's not even sure if he was with the group or not—seemed to be taller. Notably bigger. It's the only reason he remembers."

"Okay, the Axeman then and now is a big guy, on the taller side of average, and he runs around the city in a long dark coat and slouch hat," Katie said. She shook her head. "We don't know! Mona might have thought the man was taller than he was. And—"

"There's still possibly more than one person involved in this," Dan said. "Six if Nathan Lawrence was telling the truth. They were short one person, and for some reason they thought he might be the right guy to fill their ranks. Maybe because he has family money but is in truth a mild-mannered teacher who is so gullible he's unaware his wife is out to get him. Either that, or he's a damned good liar, and he's laughing his ass off at us right now, or hurrying to tell his god or demon or leader that we fell for everything that he said."

"There's someone calling the shots. The others adhere to him. Nathan Lawrence may be hapless and innocent, which means someone else was contacted after him," Axel said. He glanced over at Katie, in the passenger's seat next to him. "We got a social website from him. We're trolling it, trying to see if we get a bite."

Katie nodded. "So now…" she mused.

"Axel is taking us to George's hotel on Canal. Easy walking distance to my house. We'll see George and then get my car for anything else we're going to try to accomplish today."

Axel dropped them off. "I'm on to see the fortune-teller who works the square and who is certain that the number six is coming and we all need to repent. I'll let you know if it's anything or if we should see her together," he added to Dan.

Dan nodded. They headed into the hotel. It was a nice place. Katie had always liked it; though, if she knew people were coming for something other than a convention, she liked to suggest the independent NOLA hotels. They tended to be historic, charming and unique.

But George's choice of hotel on Canal had been a good one: a large lobby offered plenty of room for people to sit and chat, and the nearby bar and coffee corner allowed for either libation that might be the right thing. She headed to a housephone to let George know they were there. He asked if they wanted to head up or him to come down. Then he suggested the restaurant in the hotel; he didn't want to go out.

He'd come to feel safe there.

They met him in the restaurant. Katie wasn't hungry. She was pretty sure she'd eaten quite enough at Coffee Science, but she decided to pick at an appetizer to share with Dan.

George ordered a hearty late lunch/early dinner, and when their waiter had gone to put in their orders, he leaned low and asked anxiously, "Have we learned anything?"

"Maybe."

"There was an exodus out of the hotel this morning. Lots of people are leaving the city," George said.

"And many will stay…and/or hurry back," Katie said.

"You knew Lou Delaney and his wife—and Katie—for years, right?" Dan asked.

"I met Katie's parents when they moved to Florida, before Katie was born. We all…well, we all loved a lot of the same things. I was in the navy, too, way back. Not career, but I did my time. We loved boats, diving…all kinds of things about the water. And then, of course, sun and sand. Resting under swaying palms while the water lapped on the shore. That kind of thing. Even the study of sharks," George said. He winced. "We actually met in a chat room— old navy guys—before we met in person. Why?"

"Did Lou talk to you about the time he came up here to help Jeremy after the storm?"

"Ah, yes. Of course. He couldn't wait to help. He wanted to see Jeremy, he wanted to be here. First, lives were at stake, and the country was kind of a mess over it. You know, everyone had thought New Orleans had dodged the worst bullet the storm could bring, but then the levees broke all over the place, and it was a true disaster. He was anxious to do something. When he came home, he was both pleased and disheartened. He told me most of the time, people were decent. Damned decent. He saw young, healthy people sharing water and whatever they had with children and the elderly. He saw people risking their lives to save others. And then he saw looting and those who were greedy. But for the most part, he was encouraged. Most people, he truly believed after the experience, were good people. Decent. Willing to help others. Then, of course, there were those who were the opposite. And there was one guy he struck right in the face, some guy with a bunch of thugs in the streets. They weren't just looting, they knocked over an old man to take something that he was eating. You didn't do a thing like that in front of Lou."

"Did he mention a particular event, George? Or a particular person?"

George was thoughtful. "Just what I was telling you about—they were near Esplanade but in the French Quarter. People could walk in the streets, but businesses were down. An invitation to lowlifes, I guess. He was furious to see an old man knocked down. And he socked someone in the jaw."

Katie looked at Dan. "That sounds like my dad. This is like what Jeremy told us…"

"I wasn't in NOLA then," George reminded them. "I only know what he told me, but…"

"What?" Dan asked as George's voice trailed.

"He said something about it being a small group of horrible people. He and Jeremy wound up getting the cops. I don't know if they got them at all because your dad and Jeremy reported them and moved on. But he said the man he punched had taken a few wild slams at him first, and he was disgusted because there was a big guy with him. But they were all a bunch of cowards because the rest of them lurked in the shadows when he got his blow in and warned them all he was going to the cops."

"A small group," Dan said. "Maybe a small group of six."

Dan reached into his jacket pocket. He again produced the pictures he'd taken of the man—Neil Browne, as they knew him—and Jennie meeting with Nathan Lawrence in the restaurant.

"You know movie magic, George. Could this man be wearing prosthetics?" Dan asked him.

George stared at the picture a long time.

"That looks like him, yes, and… Well, the nose. The nose and the ridge on the brow—when done well, it can really change everything." He looked at Dan. "That's him. The last show I was working on…well, not a show, but the movie that just wrapped up. They were using a lot of prosthetics. It was something of a mystery sci-fi thing. Time travel. The writer is convinced, I think, that Neanderthals didn't disappear, they just intermarried, and we all went happily on to become the Homo sapiens we are today. And I—"

He stopped speaking. His color went red, and then he seemed to become pale as ash.

"The movie," he whispered.

"Yes?" Katie pushed.

"He-he…this man. He might have been in the movie. There was a day about a month ago when they hired on dozens of extras. They were showing time and time travel and…he might have been there. Right in the group. Oh, my God. Both. I mean, it was kind of a zoo. They had so many extras in, and there were three makeup trailers, and everyone had to be done… Silicone."

"Silicone?" Katie said.

"They were using tons and tons of silicone."

"So," Dan said, "you think Neil Browne and Jennie worked on the movie? Was there a public invitation for extras? How would they have been hired?"

"It was in the newspaper. I think they advertised for sixty extras. I mean some, of course, needed very little makeup. But they'd advertised for all ages, all ethnicities, male and female." George suddenly started scribbling on a napkin. "Carly Britton. She was the casting director on the picture. She would know. And she would know if there was someone who took the documentation for paychecks and the IRS and all that. If they were there—"

"They would have given fake names. But your Carly Britton may still be able to help us, George."

He nodded glumly.

"What is it?"

"The production company," George said sadly.

"What about them?"

"They're going to start up again. This time, something like a Hitchcock thriller. They asked me if I wanted to be a PA."

"And?" Katie asked him.

George sat back, shaking his head. "Not until this is over. Nope. I am not leaving this hotel until this is over!"

Katie nodded, understanding.

Dan had his phone out.

"Wait!" George said. "I'll call Carly for you, set you up with her." George leaned back in his chair to hear clearly as he put a call through to the casting director.

While George was still speaking with Carly, Dan's phone rang. He answered it and then looked at Katie.

"Ryder."

"And?" she asked hopefully.

"We have an appointment right now."

"With?"

"A fortune-teller."

"A fortune-teller?" Katie said. "You mean…one of the mediums working on Jackson Square in front of the cathedral?"

"I'm not sure. Why?"

"Because Benny was approached by someone talking about the number six and saying a demon was coming or warning people to repent. I don't remember the exact conversation. I didn't think anything of it at the time. I mean, this was going on, but that might well mean that anyone working on the square as a palm reader, tarot reader or anyone with a crystal ball might be zeroing in on the situation we have going." She hesitated. "I think Benny said she was warning about something supernatural... I guess it could be the same person."

"Maybe," Dan said softly. George was still speaking with the casting director.

He waited for George to finish his call.

George looked at the two of them. "Carly says that she's available after four this afternoon. She has an office on Magazine Street. I'll text it to you."

"George, thank you," Dan said.

As they prepared to leave, Dan absently took Katie's hand.

It was...a gesture.

She'd made a point of not letting him think that she'd become...clingy. Expecting anything.

And yet...

Holding his hand felt natural, good. Like being with him... When she'd hated him, she just hadn't seen how striking he was, even charming at times, honest, determined, strong...

Perfect.

She lowered her head, sighing.

This was not a time to think that she was falling into... whatever it was that she was falling into. But she was glad of his hand.

Fourteen

"He just looked at me. And I knew!" the woman whispered.

Her name was Greta Marks; she was forty-six, an attractive woman with long dark hair and eyes as dark as coal.

If someone was looking for a stereotype, she did appear to be the perfect medium. And she knew it; she was dressed in a peasant blouse and colorful skirt and carried a large black bag. She'd opened it for them, displaying her crystal ball, tarot cards, and several books on discerning tarots, reading palms and understanding the messages that could be found in a crystal ball.

She was at Ryder's station, and they weren't in an interrogation room; they were talking to her in his office.

Dan had asked Ryder earlier how he had come to know about the woman. Had she been one of the hundreds to call in a tip, or had something happened with her?

She had been part of a tip. A tourist had called in to tell about a reading on the square at which she'd become afraid. The medium had told her the gates of hell were breaking loose, subtly, and that her lifeline wasn't very long. She was susceptible to a demon, and an immortal demon was in the city.

Greta Marks hadn't protested when Ryder had found her and asked her to come into the station. But Ryder had done it the right way: he'd asked for her help. He wanted to know anything she could tell him about the demon and the number six and what was happening with the gates of hell.

"Did you meet the demon?" Dan asked her, after they had been introduced and were all seated in Ryder's office, including Katie.

"Well, of course I saw him. He came to me," Greta told them earnestly.

Ryder produced one of the sketches drawn from Katie's memory of Neil Browne and showed it to Greta.

"Is that him?" Ryder asked.

"Oh, um. Hm… Maybe. The face is…different. But the eyes… See, that's where you know," Greta explained. "The world is full of charlatans." She laughed. "Take Washington, DC. Look at what goes on up there, eh? Everyone lying, and I'm not picking on any party. They act the good act! We see people here all the time who think they're something special, or unique or…" She paused, shrugging. "But when he came to me, I knew. I just knew. I looked into his eyes, and I knew he was the real thing."

"Did he ask for a reading? Cards, a palm reading?" Katie asked quietly.

"He asked me to read my crystal. To tell him what I could see in my crystal ball. But he was the one who saw events first…and he showed them to me. First, it appeared that storm clouds filled the space, and lightning jagged, and then…the clouds seemed to grow red. He said death and destruction were coming, and we all needed to adhere to the number six, bow down to the number six. A presence had returned from the bowels of hell. He had come, the immortal one. And I just stared into that ball because I could see it all as he told it! Storms, darkness, shadows, thunder, lightning, blood…and death. I was… I was so scared! But he told me I was safe, protected by six, but I must warn others. Tell them the immortal being was back, that hell was out there, a demon wielding a bloody axe."

"But this was after the first murders, and before the woman was found at the old family cemetery?" Dan asked, glancing at Katie.

Greta nodded somberly. "I… Yes, I believe so. I… I don't know if he was the immortal one, or if he was a prophet for the immortal one. But he promised I would be safe but that I should spread the word, warn others that they had best repent, that they…they needed to adhere to the number six."

"Greta, look at the picture again, will you please?" Ryder asked her. "How did he appear different?"

"His chin and nose…his chin almost had a point. And his nose was larger…or longer. He…he almost had the look of a satyr or something like that," Greta said. "But he wasn't threatening to me. He was kind. He promised I would be safe."

"How many times did you see him?"

"Just that once. Oh, and he gave me cards to give out, cards with the number six written on them. You know, just playing cards, but all with the number six."

"And did you give them all out?" Katie asked softly.

"Yes! I did within the next hour!" Greta said. She frowned suddenly. "I—I want to help. That's why I came in. I don't want people to die. I don't want the city to be in a cloud of blood. I saw this man only once, and as I told you, he's very real and… I made sure to do what he asked of me. Getting the warning out, telling people about the number six, getting those cards out. I know I'll be safe, but Detective, now it's up to you. Please, tell people to honor the number six. And to listen and obey when someone comes, telling them to obey the laws of six, the law of the immortal demon. It's up to you!"

"Greta, what was he wearing?" Dan asked.

"A cotton shirt...trousers. Not jeans, trousers. He was nice-looking, um...smooth."

"Did he wear boots, shoes? Did he wear gloves?"

"Shoes, not boots, not sneakers. Leather dress shoes. And no gloves. He would have looked silly wearing gloves, I think." She shook her head. "He wasn't silly. There was nothing silly about him. Everything about him was...real. You must warn people. The demon will only hurt those who don't know that he must be honored. And honor our great music, too. Jazz must be played. I don't think he cares for modern music. There is a lot of screeching and that kind of thing. Jazz is true music. I think... I can't remember everything that was said! Especially when I was staring into the ball. It was watching something amazing!"

Ryder nodded politely. "Greta, I'd like you to see a friend of mine for a bit of a conversation."

"Oh?" Greta asked.

"Come with me," Ryder said gently. He glanced at Dan and Katie, a nod that indicated he'd be right back.

"I think Benny may have gotten one of those cards," Katie told Dan when the two had left Ryder's office.

"This probably is the same woman who approached him. Would he have kept the card?" Dan asked her.

"I can call him, but if he's working, his phone will be off. It will vibrate. That way he knows he needs to check his phone when he takes a break. But he was going to be

Satchmo today… The same woman told him he should be Satchmo. Louis Armstrong."

Dan smiled warmly. "Yeah, I know Louis Armstrong was Satchmo. Home here in the city, remember?"

"Sorry."

"No worries. Can you go ahead and call Benny, leave him a message?"

"Sure. And we can leave here and maybe have time to swing down to Decatur Street. You can always see him on his little stand, and find out if she did give him a card, and if so, if he still has it. Do you think there might be prints on the card? That's why you asked about his appearance, if he was wearing gloves?"

Dan shrugged. "Might be hard. Greta would have held the cards, some people might have handed them back, whoever did hold them would have left something behind, but… yes. Anything right now is a hope."

Katie pulled her phone out and called Benny, who didn't answer. She left him a message.

Ryder returned to the office.

"Where did you take her?" Dan asked.

"I let her go," Ryder said. "But I feel like I should have taken her to the police psychiatrist. I'm no professional, but I'd say she's suffering from delusions."

"Hypnotism," Dan said.

"What?"

"I think our guy is a talented hypnotist. He took a good look around the square, and he had a great deal of fun with Greta. She was susceptible to hypnotism." Dan shrugged. "I know one young woman who works down there a lot. She reads tarot cards. But what she really reads is people, which I believe is the same talent our famed Marie Laveau possessed. Lacey, the young woman I know, was a psychology major. A lot of the locals bring their young adult children to her. She knows how to fathom a problem someone might be having and then she points out possible solutions. But Greta was an easy mark. She likes the feeling of being a medium, and she loves believing the world is full of mysticism."

"Maybe she can be dehypnotized," Ryder said, shaking his head sadly. "I mean, we're free people, right? Free to believe as we like. But it's just not great when someone is running around spouting the mantra of killer!"

"I hope she can…be helped, I guess. Except that…"

"That what?"

"I believe I'm paranoid, but with good reason. If the person who saw her was the man we know as Neil Browne, and Neil Browne is doing the killing, *Greta* might now be in danger."

"Let's face it. Anyone vulnerable in the area right now is in danger. I still say the killer is basically a coward. He watched the house before he went in to kill the Rodenberry couple and Elle Détente. He made sure they weren't tough enough to fight back."

"Right. But this woman, Greta, Ryder will watch out for her," Dan said, looking at Ryder.

"Yeah, yeah, Ryder will take this one on," Ryder said. Then he sighed. "What do you think?"

"I think Neil Browne talked to her and in this instance, I don't think we need to be afraid. She did exactly what he wanted her to do. Ryder, we're going to head down to the square. Katie has a friend who may have one of those six cards. And then George gave us a heads-up. He thinks that Neil Browne might have been an extra recently in a movie. The casting director Carly Britton just might have a way to find him."

"I'll be back on the streets. We've just begun to investigate all the tips we've received between the FBI and the police hotline."

Dan nodded, and they left the station, driving quickly to the square.

"There he is!" Katie said, pointing to a supposed statue in on the walk near the street.

"How do you know that's Benny?"

"Satchmo," she said. "He's perfect!"

She hopped out of the car while he was still pulling the keys from the ignition, hurrying to the statue.

Benny was a damned good Satchmo, down to the way he held his saxophone. The bucket in front of him, brimming with ones, showed just how much his dead-still performance was appreciated.

But he moved when Katie talked to him, hopping down from his little stand. "Got your message, and I found the card!" he told Katie excitedly. "I had stuffed it into my little case."

He reached into the case next to the bucket and produced the card for her. He looked at Dan with happy triumph. "Here!" he exclaimed.

Of course, his hands were all over it.

Dan smiled his gratitude. "This is great, Benny, thank you," he said, taking it with a handkerchief from his jacket pocket and sliding it into an evidence bag from his jeans. "They'll send someone for your prints, and they'll get Greta's prints. She's the lady who gave it to you. And just maybe they'll be able to pull other prints as well. We just need yours for elimination. Is that all right?"

"Should be fine," Benny said, grinning. "I'm the kid who never even stole a piece of gum, so I don't think there are warrants out for me anywhere."

"Benny, you look great, by the way," Katie told him.

He beamed. "Yeah, and Matt and Lorna are both out with their carriages now. We're all going to head in together once they're back. Monty said he might take Sarah and your rig out later. He's cool with us coming in once it starts getting late."

"Monty is the best," Katie said. "Okay, thank you, thank you. We have an appointment. We'll see you later."

He nodded. "Back to it!" he said, and crawling up on his little stand again, he posed as Satchmo, the great Louis Armstrong.

Neither Lorna's nor Matt's carriages were resting at the curb; both were out with tourists, Dan reckoned.

He looked over the area. It wasn't as busy as it might have been.

But it was still filled with humanity.

"On to Magazine. I'll call Axel, and he'll have someone meet us there to take the card back to the offices so forensics can get on it."

She nodded, watching people on the street.

"What are you thinking?"

She let out a sigh. "I think we all have a tendency to think bad things happen to other people. We never think it will happen to us. I'm sure that made most Londoners feel safe back in the Jack the Ripper days. They weren't prostitutes in the Whitechapel area, so they were going to be okay. They'll stay out by day and run back to their hotels when they start to get nervous. I imagine some of the small bed-and-breakfast places might be losing clientele."

"A lot of people use travel sites where people just own a place and rent it out, too," Dan said. "Houses, rooms. Well, I guess they're paid in advance."

"People who feel they aren't vulnerable will stay," Katie said.

"And we do have our own residents, all of whom are nervous right now, I imagine."

"He's attacking the whole city, attacking the economy. Can you have an agenda against a city?"

"Why not?" Dan asked quietly. "Except—"

"Except you think it has to do with my father."

"Not because he did anything wrong, Katie. But because he was a good man."

"I know," she said softly.

They left the Quarter and headed down Magazine Street. Like the French Quarter, it offered shops, clubs and plenty of great restaurants mixed in with office space.

They found parking and Carly Britton's office. She was on the third floor of a building Dan thought must have been built in the late 1920s or perhaps the 1930s. It had nice deco touches in the arches and paint and was kept in good repair.

When they tapped at the door, they were bidden to enter. There was a reception area with about twenty chairs. The woman was a casting director, so she would have a receptionist out here and perhaps interview people in an inner office. A door to the right of the desk suggested as much.

There was a perfectly coifed blonde of about forty behind the desk; she was in a designer suit, carefully tailored, very businesslike. It fit her slim figure like a glove. She'd accented her look with a bold red lipstick.

She stood, offering them her hand. "I'm Carly Britton," she told them. "I let my secretary go home when our last client left. I understand this might have something to do with the horrible axe murderer plaguing the city?"

"Yes, I'm afraid so," Dan said and then introduced himself and Katie.

"I hope I can help. We had so many extras working on that last picture. I couldn't seem to keep enough people coming. Even with extras, we're careful. We ask for identification, and we verify social security numbers."

"That's great," Dan said. He reached into his jacket pocket, this time to produce the pictures that had been drawn of Neil Browne, with his many possible looks.

Carly Britton looked down at the pictures, and then she looked up at Dan, shock in her eyes.

"Yes!" she said.

"Yes, he was in the movie?" Katie asked.

Carly shivered. "Oh, lord, you think—"

"He's a person of interest," Dan said quickly. "But he was known to accompany the young woman who was discovered murdered yesterday."

"Oh. Oh—oh!" Carly said.

"Yes?" Dan encouraged.

"This man… I must get into my files. I can't remember his name, but…he came in with his girlfriend. They both worked one day when we had a crowd scene that switched time… We had different sets of people, all dressed for two different time periods. His girlfriend…"

Her voice trailed. Dan looked at Katie and pulled more pictures out of his jacket pocket.

He showed Carly the sketches done from Katie's recollections.

"I… Yes, there were so many people that day, but…oh! Oh, how horrible! She's…she's dead now?"

Dan glanced at Katie and nodded.

Carly Britton was shaky; she stood, using the desk as a brace to do so.

"I'll get my computer," she muttered.

When she hurried into the inner office, Katie turned to Dan, looking a little pale, anxious and trembling.

She tried to smile. "What don't you have in those pockets?" she asked.

He shrugged. "I don't have any kind of a bag. Bags get lost too easily. A jacket...well, a jacket stays on the body most of the time."

"They were in a movie, probably watching George!" Katie said with dismay.

"And George is fine and smart and staying in a hotel with cameras and security," he reminded her.

"He knew George was in the city. He knew George could be blamed again," Katie said.

Dan nodded. Carly was returning with her computer. She set it on the desk and used a long, well-manicured finger on the touch screen, frowning for several seconds before she stopped.

"Here, here!" she said.

She turned the computer toward Dan. Katie inched her chair right next to his so she could see, too.

She let out a gasp. Carly jumped.

"I'm sorry... Yes, that's Jennie and Neil Browne."

"Oh, no," Carly said. "That's Brian Denholm and Aubrey Freehold from Baton Rouge. I take copies of their driver's licenses."

Both were there on the screen. Dan pulled out his phone, glancing at Carly.

"I need to get these to the FBI office," he told her. "They can check the identities and check out the addresses."

"My lord, well...at least you can identify that poor woman," Carly said.

Dan assumed the licenses were fakes; the social security numbers were surely faked or stolen as well.

But he shot the pictures over the phone to Axel, who would get them to the right place.

"Thank you," Dan told Carly.

"So he might have murdered her!" Carly said dismayed. "Oh, my God."

"Yes?"

"Murderers *and* thieves!" Carly said.

"What did they steal?"

"Stacey—best makeup artist possible on any set—she had a case stolen, a big case. She had makeup in it, all kinds of foundation and pencils and the like, but she had a supply of silicone. You know, silicone... We did some Neanderthal brows and heavier jawlines on some of the actors and extras and... He was probably a murderer and a thief!"

Dan glanced at Katie.

They were both thinking it was worse to be a murderer than a thief...

And yet it explained so much.

"Ms. Britton, you have been an enormous help," Dan assured her.

"Yes, I... Oh, lord! I worked with those people. I hired those people!"

"You couldn't have known they were...anything other than what they presented themselves as," Katie assured her.

"And we don't have answers. We're investigating," Dan said.

"But she's dead, right?" Carly exclaimed.

There was a knock at the door, and the woman nearly jumped out of her chair. "No, no, I'm not expecting anyone!" she said.

"It's all right. It's an agent from the local FBI office," Dan assured her. Still, he found himself instinctively brushing the SIG Sauer in its holder beneath his jacket as he walked to the door and then waited.

"Mr. Oliver? It's Mike Cody. Axel sent me."

He opened the door and dug in his pocket for the card Benny had given him. The young man at the door was obviously new at the job: he was wearing an impeccable blue suit, hair cut short and slicked back. He had the eager and determined look of a puppy determined to do right.

"They'll get started on this immediately," he told Dan.

He frowned when Dan took his picture quickly with his camera phone.

"Uh, sir—"

"Just making sure you're who you say you are," Dan said, smiling.

He kept his smile in place as he quickly sent the photo to Axel.

Axel got back to him right away with a quick text.

Yes, that's Mike.

Dan smiled at the startled agent. "Thank you. Can't be too careful these days," he said cheerfully.

"Ah, right. Well, if that's all."

"Thank you."

The young agent left.

Dan turned back. Carly Britton didn't look quite as professionally all-together as she had when they walked in.

"I'm scared to leave," she whispered.

"We can take you somewhere," Dan offered.

"No, uh, I have my car... I can't just leave my car. I need it. I work. But I am married. I have a husband. Oh! That didn't help. The killer...he killed the man and wife and the nurse or maid or whoever she was..."

"Ms. Britton—" Dan began.

"Mrs.!" she exclaimed. "I just told you I had a husband. Oh, I'm sorry. I mean, calling me Carly is just fine. We tend to be on a first-name basis in the industry. I'm just… I knew them! I hired them. I'm scared."

"Do you have an alarm system?" Dan asked her.

"Yes, but—"

"He's targeting people who don't have alarms, we believe."

"*Believe!* That's no guarantee."

No, he had no way of guaranteeing anything when it came to a psychopathic killer.

"I'll alert the local police station. They'll watch your property. They're on the alert already, and with what you've given us—"

"You'll catch him tonight?" she asked dryly.

"We're happy to follow you home and see that you get there," Katie told her.

The woman sighed. "Thank you," she said and hesitated. "Would you look around the place, too?"

Dan looked at Katie.

"Sure," he said, hoping he didn't sound as weary as he felt.

They locked up the offices and headed down to the garage with her.

Carly had an expensive car, in a red that matched her lipstick.

Katie went along with Carly, sliding into the leather passenger seat. Dan followed them in his vehicle, falling in behind once Carly pulled out of the garage.

Carly lived in the Garden District, so it wasn't far. She had evidently called her husband as she drove, and he was at the gate to their house, a sumptuous Victorian, when they arrived.

"This nice man is on the case," Carly told her husband, a balding man in his fifties. "He's going to look around the house."

"We do have a state-of-the-art alarm system, Officer…"

"Oliver, just Dan Oliver. I'm a consultant on the case."

"They sent a consultant to see me?" Carly asked, apparently thinking she'd been sent someone second-rate.

He wasn't in the mood for a fight.

"Yes. It's been a very long day for us. If you wouldn't mind…"

"Yes, please!" Carly said.

Her husband led the way in.

It was a big house. It took him thirty minutes to go through it, assure them no one was hiding under any of the beds, and he advised they should set their alarm anytime they were in the house.

They managed to leave at last.

"Where now? What now?"

"We hope the tech and forensic people can get something. We go to your place. We pick up dinner and go to your place. I'm bushed."

"Me, too," she said softly.

They did a drive-through restaurant for a bag of po'boys. When they reached the house, the dogs were waiting at the gate.

Katie and Dan greeted them and went into the house. He looked up for the cameras as he passed—they all seemed to be in place.

In the kitchen, Katie set down the bag of food. She hesitated, looking at it, looking at him.

He didn't know what drove him; they were both exhausted. But he found himself walking over to her and pulling her into his arms. She didn't protest; she looked up at him with no surprise.

"No commitments," he said. "You don't even have to call me in the morning. Oh, wait. I'll be here in the morning."

She didn't speak. She kissed him.

They began shedding their clothing downstairs. She hesitated when she felt his weapon, and he set his hand on it as well.

"Always with me," he told her.

They made it up the stairs, laughing as they entangled with clothing on the way.

He headed to the guest room again. Maybe that meant no commitment.

No commitment, and no discussion, no talking…just breathless whispers that made no sense, sounds of pleasure that escaped. He focused on the feel of her skin, the scent of it, the way she moved, her flesh against his, naked and sweet.

The taste of her.

They made love, kissing, touching, caressing everywhere. It was even better than it had been the first time: it was exciting, it was comfortable, it was knowledge of one another, growing.

Climax, wild, exhilarating, almost violent in the force of it. Lying together, letting time go by, breathing, simply holding each other. Then his phone, in his jacket on a chair in the kitchen, began to ring. He leaped out of bed, heedless of his state of undress and tore down the stairs.

It was Axel.

"Yes, Brian and Aubrey… You found out who they really are? Do they really exist?" he demanded. "Did they manage to get social security numbers into the system—"

"Hey, hold up," Axel told him wearily. "They existed."

"What?"

"The two existed. They were from Baton Rouge. They disappeared about a month ago. Their families looked for them everywhere."

"Then...wait. Is our dead woman Aubrey? And Neil-slash-Brian—"

"No. Two bodies that were dug out of the bayou a day ago just proved to be them. It looks like their throats were slashed. They weren't dismembered. But they've been in the bayou, and the medical examiner is having a hell of a time. They're...decomposed."

"Then, how—"

"Dental records. It's them. The two we knew as Neil and Jennie murdered the real Brian and Aubrey for their identities," Axel stated.

Katie was standing at the top of the stairway, wrapped in a sheet, looking down at him.

"They found bodies to go with those identities Carly gave us," he told her.

"So," she said. "We still have no idea who Neil and Jennie really are...just that they murdered more people than we can begin to know."

"What about the address on their driver's licenses?" Dan asked Axel, remembering he was still on the phone.

Axel let out an aggravated sound and told him, "Empty fields. And there's the irony. The address they gave for Aubrey is right by the Medford Mansion—not a stone's throw from where she died."

Fifteen

Katie gave Sarah a good brushing, enjoying the busy work that allowed her mind to wander. The dogs played near her, loyal guardians to the end, until they tired of their rollicking and lay down at the entry to the large barnlike stable structure that housed the mules and harnesses and other equipment.

Dan was just outside on the phone, catching up with Ryder and Axel. She'd heard they were planning another press conference. Dan wasn't happy about being the spokesperson, but he'd done it once, and it seemed only logical that he would be the one to do it again.

He didn't like being recognized in the city as being on the team. It made any kind of surveillance harder; then again, he'd told her that morning, it could draw a suspect out, if they were to approach him.

She knew Dan was frustrated. She had seen Jennie, and then they had discovered her body. They'd discovered clues to their work for the movie-production company, only to discover the names they had used belonged to people they had killed.

But, she'd reminded Dan, they hadn't been killed with axes. They'd had their throats slit.

It seemed the Axeman's Protégé cases were specific and specifically planned, but the man—or woman—driving the onslaught of blood and death didn't care if their adherents killed others, just so long as they didn't use axes.

Maybe.

Jennie was dead.

They believed that Neil—or Brian—had likely killed her. And he—whatever his real name might be—was still out there. Maybe he hadn't wanted to kill her, but he'd been ordered to do so.

And yet there was more to it; it went deeper. Because so-called Neil was tall, but not extraordinarily so. He was built, but not massively. And it had sounded as if the man in the long black coat with the slouch hat hanging out and watching the Rodenberry house had been big.

Six.

Were there six people involved?

The man Dan had been hired to watch had met with Neil and Jennie—and Neil had wanted him to join with them. So, if there were six in the group imitating both the Axeman's murders and Allan Pierce's belief in the number six, they were now missing at least a couple players.

The dogs began to bark, but their tails were wagging, and Katie heard voices just outside the stables. She set her brush down, gave Sarah a pat and promised that she'd be back and hurried out to the entry.

Lorna and Matt had arrived together, with Benny.

Today, Benny was back in historical attire, dressed as a swashbuckling Jean Lafitte. As he often did, he'd used stage makeup to appear silver-gray from head to toe. He was so good at what he did that Katie and Lorna often enjoyed watching people's surprise and amazement as they realized Benny was actually not a statue but a living man capable of entertaining them and making them laugh at themselves and him.

She thought about Benny and the artists and musicians on the square, along with the tarot readers and others. She loved New Orleans. And she realized that while, yes, she was scared, she wanted justice for what had happened to her parents. And now she was furious anyone could do these horrible things and tear at the fabric of a city that offered so much continual wonder.

"Hi!" Lorna called, seeing her.

"Hey, you guys!" Katie said. "That was good timing. The three of you here at once."

"No, not timing," Matt told her.

"We—Lorna and I—stayed at Matt's place last night," Benny explained.

"Oh," Katie said. "Good idea."

"We figured with three of us, we had a better chance of waking up if something was going on," Benny said.

Matt grimaced. "And Benny brought his costumes and makeup…and swore to clean up the mess this evening."

"Before he makes it again tomorrow," Lorna said, laughing.

Dan had been listening, obviously done with his calls.

"We can't *all* have a drop-dead, hunky G-man guarding us," Lorna said, throwing a wink his way.

"I'm just a consultant," Dan said, grinning.

"Still, you're with the Feds now!" Lorna said. "Oh, and it's cool… I didn't mean it in a bad way."

"No offense taken," Dan told her. "And yes, stay together. There is a certain safety in numbers."

"You're going to get him, right?" Lorna asked.

"Or them," Katie muttered.

"More than one person is doing this?" Benny asked, horrified.

Dan shook his head slightly. He didn't want any of their theories shared.

"Oh, who knows?" Katie said.

"What's going on here?"

They all spun around. Monty was coming toward them. "I've got a business to run here!" he said, but he was smiling. He paid his three drivers, but most of their income came in tips. He seldom cared what hours they worked. He wanted to know when they were and weren't going on, the best they could, so that he could cover their little piece of the action himself.

He was a good employer.

They were good employees.

"We're ready...well, we're almost ready," Lorna told him.

"All three of you are going out today?" Monty asked, scratching his head through the wild thickness of his hair.

Katie glanced at Dan.

"I'm going to ride with Katie again," Dan said. He didn't ask permission; it was a statement.

But Monty didn't mind. He just nodded. "Good. I'm going to do some cleaning up around here today, then. Go forth, children. Do your best. And try not to let anxious tourists get to you." He looked at Dan hopefully. "Are we any closer to catching a madman?"

"Maybe. We have good people on it," Dan said. "Anyway, I am pretty capable. I can help get the mules harnessed."

Dan was a big help. Between them and Benny working carefully in order not to disturb his costuming, they were quickly ready. And with Matt leading the way, they headed toward the French Quarter and their curb at the square across from Café du Monde.

As Katie drove her carriage, she tried to articulate her thoughts to Dan.

"This thing with the number six. We know Neil and Jennie—I'm going to stick with those names until we know their real names—were part of it. We believe there's a big man behind it. Literally. But they'd need three more people if they were going to be a group with the power of six."

"They were trying to recruit Nathan Lawrence. Maybe they did," Dan said. "Mild-mannered schoolteacher by day and vicious axeman by night."

"You think so?"

"No, but it's a group that needs money, and I told you Nathan Lawrence may be a teacher, but he inherited money. All this travel, fake IDs, it takes money."

"Then…who could it be? All we know right now is the big man, who is maybe pulling the strings, and Neil. Jennie is dead. So…"

"They may need new people all the time, since it seems even the members of the group wind up dead if they might endanger the game," Dan said. He was quiet then, thoughtful.

"What?"

"The casting director?" he said.

"What? She was terrified!"

"Or was she? And Nathan Lawrence…innocent and duped? Or maybe he was up to something."

"But you had him under surveillance, and you're supposedly good at what you do," Katie said. She frowned, looking at him. "You still don't think George—"

"No, actually, I don't." He hesitated, looking at her. "Okay, listen, we've had people monitoring the security tapes at his hotel. For his protection as much as anything else. George hasn't left the hotel. He's rented a dozen movies, and he has become friends with everyone working in the restaurant there. George is—"

"Is what?" Katie asked.

"Scared. I mean, maybe he was part of it once and knew even before we did that Jennie was going to wind up dead. But don't be upset with me! I don't think so. George has been used. I believe this thing is twofold. The big man, I guess we'll call him, stepped into the whole Axeman/Allan Pierce legend, as far back as Katrina. Your father happened to be a stand-up guy who got in his way. Everything was planned. The big man either watched and studied your father himself or had his followers do it. Probably the latter, since Jennie and Neil evidently killed your parents. They missed with George, but that turned out to work for them, and they found out where he was living and made their next kill, that we know about, in the Orlando area. Where George fit the bill perfectly. They knew he was here, and they probably laughed at the fact he didn't recognize them when they were both working for the movie. Now..."

"Who is the big man?" Katie whispered.

"We'll drive around, and I'll listen to your wonderful stories of history and beyond, and we'll see what we can find out."

They reached the square. Matt hadn't even had time to cue up on the curb before he'd been hailed. As they pulled in behind Lorna, Dan jumped down and headed away from everyone to make a phone call. She wondered if he was calling Axel or Ryder or if anything else had been discovered. When a smiling woman approached her, she smiled in return and indicated Lorna was the next to go. Lorna nodded her thanks.

Benny was already in place near Decatur Street, where he could be viewed from those sitting street-side at Café du Monde.

But though she had sent the first group on to Lorna's carriage, there was a second group that approached her almost immediately after.

Dan saw; he ended his phone call and jumped back on the carriage to be with her.

"The Axeman! The Axeman! Tell us about the old Axeman," a teen boy in the group demanded immediately.

"Gavin!" his mother said with dismay.

"Well, if he is immortal, maybe it is him again!" the boy said.

"Let our guide—guides—tell their stories," the father chastised. "Please. No more on the Axeman."

They started out. Katie told them about the founding of the city, some of her great stories about the Baroness de Pontalba and how buildings she'd had constructed in the 1840s still formed two sides of Jackson Square, allowing for shops, apartments, restaurants and museums. She talked about the War of 1812, the Civil War, the changes of flags over the city...

And when they went by Lafitte's, she talked about the Lafitte brothers, the good and the bad, the triumphant and the sad. But just as she was ending that segment of her talk, she went silent for a minute, so long that the father cleared his throat and said, "Miss?"

"Oh, sorry. I'm so sorry. Lost my train of thought there

for a minute," Katie said. But she looked at Dan and gave a nod, indicating he needed to look to the street.

He turned his head in the direction she'd gestured to, and she knew he saw what she wanted him to see.

Mabel was strolling down the street, arm in arm with a man.

The man was in breeches, a white shirt, vest, socks and short boots; he wore a jaunty tricorn hat.

It was Gray Simmons, one of the ghosts of the city Katie had come to know.

A man who had lost his life at the Battle of New Orleans but remained to see that the city he had loved so much and died for grew and hopefully would prosper. A pirate, and a hero. That all depended on one's viewpoint, he had told her once.

"I'll jump off," Dan murmured to Katie.

She nodded and slowed the carriage, and Dan jumped off, waving to her crew.

"He, uh, had a meeting," Katie explained, and she quickly went on to talk about Lafitte and his pirating ways and his meetings with Jackson.

Maybe not the murder and mayhem of the Axeman, but the teenaged boy was mollified.

Apparently, he liked pirates.

"Darling!" Mabel said, greeting him, leaning toward him to give him a ghostly kiss on the cheek. "How lovely! I was hoping to run into you today."

"Nothing from the city cops or agents, or whatever the rest of them are, eh?" the man at her side asked.

Dan was standing in the street, looking quite the idiot, he thought, reacting to people that no one else could see.

"Er, in here!" he said, indicating the courtyard area of

the bar, empty now. The bar had barely opened, and while a bar might have patrons at any time during opening hours, which were almost all of them, it didn't mean they'd be busy this early.

Shielded by plants, he indicated one of the benches and pulled out his phone. That way he'd appear much less suspicious.

The ghosts took seats across from him.

Gray Simmons had been a dashing man. Dan thought for a minute it was too bad the kid on the carriage hadn't been able to see him. Gray fit the rakish image of a handsome rogue to perfection.

"I'm delighted, Dan. You're getting so very good at this!" Mabel said. "I see that you do see Gray. Let me introduce you. Gray Simmons, Dan Oliver. Dan, my dear friend, and Katie's friend, Mr. Gray Simmons."

Dan nodded politely in acknowledgment.

"Another one. So rare," Gray said to Mabel.

"Not so rare, I'm learning," Dan said.

"Oh, yes, his friend saw me, too. The handsome fellow?"

"Axel is that," Dan said. "And he's with a group who apparently all see..."

"*The dead*, honey," Mabel said. "Poor boy, you try to be so careful! And yet, Gray, I believe he's supposed to be very good at what he does."

"Which is exactly what?" Gray asked.

Dan realized he didn't know the exact answer to that anymore.

"At the moment, I'm on the hunt for a killer. Or killers," he said.

Gray nodded.

"I think he has something that may help you," Mabel said. She patted Gray's arm.

Dan looked at Gray hopefully.

"I mean, I don't know. I just found Mabel today," Gray said.

"I was looking for you, dear," Mabel said.

Gray rolled his eyes with patience and amusement, not looking away from Dan. "The point is, I was distressed when news about all this got out. And especially distressed for Mabel because I know that years ago, the killings hurt her so badly with the loss of friends."

Dan nodded, waiting for him to go on, glancing at Mabel with sympathy.

"But I didn't know she was trying to help. I mean, how could I? It's so rare when one can find someone who can see them, much less someone who can hear them…and might be trying to do something about what's going on."

"Just talk to people, Gray. You really never know until you do." Now it was Mabel's turn to roll her eyes.

"Anyway, can you help?" Dan asked.

"I saw the picture in the paper and on the news," Gray said.

"The picture?"

"Of the woman. The woman who was killed, left butchered in the ruins of the cemetery," Gray said.

"Yes?"

"Well, I think I saw her." He looked at Dan earnestly.

Dan waited a second and then asked, "Living…or dead?"

"Living," Gray said. "Before she was killed. I doubt we'll see her hanging around. Most of the time…" He broke off and looked at Mabel.

"Well, we don't know much more than you do except that…well, we're here. And we're at peace being here, though we've seen friends who have gone on to something else."

"It really does seem to be with a ray of light," Gray said.

"Take Ginger Holloway," Mabel said, nodding thoughtfully.

"What happened with Ginger Holloway?" Dan asked, without asking who that had been.

"Well, she was waiting. A horrible domestic dispute! Her son-in-law killed her daughter in a fight over a TV remote control. Terrible. Though, rumor is such a thing has happened several times. Anyway, once the jury put him away, Ginger was anxious to go. Her son received custody of the kids and all was… I guess as fixed as it could be," Mabel said. "I don't suppose you can ever really fix anything like that, but once he went to prison, well, all Ginger wanted was to see her daughter."

"She was interred at Lafayette Cemetery, too," Gray offered.

"And we saw her leave. It was beautiful," Mabel said. "I could almost believe I saw a hand reaching out…her daughter's hand."

"But," Gray said softly, "we see those who were injured in life, or who died in battle or for justice…"

"Or the American way!" Mabel said.

"But those who were wicked in life, who killed others or caused great harm or suffering…well, we seldom see them."

"And when we do, they don't last long," Mabel said.

"They leave in darkness," Gray said.

"I see," Dan said. He didn't really see anything at all, but then the ghosts didn't have real answers to whatever came next themselves, so there wasn't much that he could see. And he was worried suddenly, anxious he'd left Katie alone.

"So, back to the woman who was killed," Dan said.

"Right. I saw her on Bourbon Street."

Dan hid his disappointment. They'd known she'd been running around the French Quarter.

Maybe the ghost of Gray Simmons felt his disappointment.

"Not alone!" Gray said. "I saw her with a man."

"And it was the man in the sketches, those police renditions or whatever," Mabel said.

"Two of the mounted police working at night on Bourbon Street had the pictures out on their phones, showing them to each other," Gray explained.

"So the woman who was killed was with the guy in the sketches!" Mabel said.

"Yes," Dan agreed. He could tell they understood this wasn't news to him.

"Well, he works on Bourbon Street," Gray Simmons said. "He doesn't look like the sketch, not really. He looks younger. I think he's taken good care of himself."

"Maybe he had a facial," Mabel said.

"Or a nose job," Gray suggested.

"Okay, works on Bourbon Street where?" Dan asked. Now he was interested.

Gray sighed.

"That I don't know. Somewhere between Conti and here. And I'm sorry, I think closer to the Canal side, but I can't be positive. You see, I saw them before I saw the sketches, so I wasn't paying enough attention."

"How do you know he works here?"

"He told her he was going in and she needed to keep a low profile, because all in all, the French Quarter was a small community. And she just said 'What the hell do you think a dumb kid might remember?' Anyway, he told her to go away, and he had to hurry. He didn't want to be late for a shift until he was ready to quit. He was wearing one of those white jackets. You know the kind that waiters wear? That should help...a lot of the places along here are so casual. I think he's working at one of the more high-end restaurants."

Dan leaned back. That would help.

That would definitely, beyond a doubt, help them in a search.

"Thank you," he told them both. "Sincerely, thank you."

"We're here to help. I mean, I think...we're really here to help," Mabel said, shrugging with a grin. She grew serious. "Get these people, Dan. Please get them."

"I promise you I will do everything in my power," he vowed. He stood. "I'd better go. I don't want to leave Katie alone."

"What? She's alone?" Gray demanded.

"Alone, with half the city. But I'm on my way back to her right now."

"You keep her safe, young man! That is one fine young lady," Gray said. He looked at Mabel then. "And she lost people, people dearest to her in the world. Right this the best you can, young man. But you get back to her now."

"I'm on my way!" he said.

Leaving the ghosts, Dan headed back toward Decatur. As he left, he called Axel.

It was going to be easier to explain his information to Axel than to Ryder.

"We need to go about a quiet search," Axel said. "If Neil realizes we're on to him, he'll disappear before we can get to him."

"Maybe we can start at opposite ends of the street and work toward each other. Bring Adam and Ryder in on it," Dan suggested.

"That's a plan," Axel agreed. "And I may bring in one

more agent, new fellow from Krewe headquarters who has been helping out on this here. He's smart as a whip—"

"And speaks to the dead," Dan said.

"Yeah."

"All right. Katie will want to keep the carriage out until early evening—"

"That's fine. Things don't move here until late. If this guy is still around, the fine-dining places will be getting going after six."

"Meet up then," Dan said.

He ended the call. But then he called Axel back.

"What else?" Axel asked.

"Can you get Angela to do a deep dig on someone for me?" he asked.

"Who?"

"A casting agent, the one who let us know that both Jennie and Neil had been extras in the movie. Mrs. Carly Britton. Oh, yes, and check on her husband, too. She acted all terrified when she found out, but…"

"But?"

"Gut feeling."

"Okay. I'll call it in right now. If anyone can find out anything, it's Angela."

"Thank you."

He was almost back to the curb in front of Jackson Square.

Katie's carriage was just pulling out again.

He ran hard. She turned to see him, smiled and waited.

He leaped up on the carriage to join her.

She introduced him to her group, this time six people from a medical convention.

She raised a brow to him in question, even as she started a history lesson for the group.

He leaned close and whispered to her.

"Fine dining tonight, my love."

And he realized that though he had spoken lightly, he meant that last part.

She'd come to mean so very much to him.

Was it something like love?

He wanted to find out. But first, he had to stop the Axeman's Protégé. Had to protect Katie.

That was the only way he would ever really get to know.

Sixteen

"Wow!"

"Well," Katie said lightly, "you said fine dining. I thought maybe I should dress the part?"

"Wow," Dan repeated.

She smiled. She'd put on a simple, knee-length black dress, but the way it draped always made her feel confident. It was nice to feel admired. And surprising, but then everything about her relationship with him was surprising. She'd never have imagined in a thousand years she would have made a move on him…and realize that she admired him, and maybe they were both haunted by the past, along with souls from the past.

She'd known him only a few days. Yet he was suddenly the most important person in her life.

"You dress up well yourself," she told him.

"Do I? Thanks!"

He was wearing a tailored shirt but open at the throat, a vest, and a casual jacket over dark trousers. He looked as if he might have stepped from the pages of *GQ*.

"Anyway, I think they'll let us in wherever we go. And I know where we should start," Dan said.

"And where is that?" Katie asked him.

"A place called Duffy's Den. It opened recently and supposedly has NOLA power money behind it from famous restaurant owners who have been working in finer establishments for years."

"And why Duffy's Den?"

"It's new. They had to do a lot of hiring," he told her. "Also, Angela gave me a list of places where the Rodenberry couple had eaten recently. They went to Duffy's Den two nights before they were killed."

"What do we do if we see him?" Katie asked.

"Both Axel and Ryder will be close by, somewhere on Bourbon Street. One of them will make the arrest. Or if worse comes to worst, I'll hold him until one of them can get there." He hesitated and shrugged. "I can stop someone, but I'm a consultant, and I don't really have the authority to arrest anyone."

"Ah."

"So…shall we?"

He offered his arm to her.

She smiled and accepted. As they exited the house, Jerry, Ben and Mitch made an appearance on the porch, wagging their tails madly.

"I think Monty went out with a carriage tonight," Katie told Dan. "I keep food here for them. Let me feed them just in case. Everyone seems to be distracted lately."

"Monty loves his dogs."

"Yes, I know. But it won't hurt them to eat twice if he did feed them."

She headed back into the kitchen, finding the dog bowls she kept for special treats or those times when Monty did ask her to feed them. She filled her bowls with dry dog food and added a small tin of special wet food to each and started to balance them on her arm to bring out, but Dan was there. He took two of the bowls from her and carried them out.

She didn't think Monty had fed the dogs—they headed right for the food.

"Okay," she said cheerfully. "I'm happy. We can leave now."

Dan drove, finding parking on the street about three blocks from the restaurant.

She hadn't even known it had opened, and she thought that a bit remiss on her part. But apparently it had been open less than a week.

"Lettie and Randolph Rodenberry must have come for opening night," Dan said.

"Maybe. I'm a guide here. I should have known about this place," Katie said. That didn't mean anything in the grand scheme of things and certainly not tonight. She hesitated. "I'm sorry."

"Don't be. Hopefully, we'll lead normal lives again and…" Now he hesitated.

"What?"

"I'm not sure what *normal* is anymore. I spent part of the day conversing with dead people."

"It's a new normal," she told him.

They reached Bourbon and turned toward Esplanade to reach the restaurant. The streets weren't overly busy, but it was Bourbon Street. And the night life was beginning. They passed a neon sign advertising the best strip club in the city. It was next to a casual pizza joint.

Not far down the street, the French Quarter's busiest karaoke bar was rocking.

They reached Duffy's Den. There was a sign in cursive on the arch over the doorway noting the restaurant's

name. Dan opened the door for Katie. She thanked him
and stepped in.

The place was beautiful. The hostess stand—mahogany
and covered with a red velvet runner—fronted a room full
of tables that were set to look like they were in the middle
of conversation pits. The seating was all black velvet booths
that curved around the tables. Some were large; some were
smaller, more intimate.

She quickly discovered Dan had made a reservation as
they were greeted by a pretty young blonde in a form-fitting
white velvet dress.

They were led to one of the intimate booths. A sommelier arrived at their table with the wine list. Dan glanced at
her, and she knew he didn't want wine but thought maybe
they should order some for appearances.

He asked the sommelier for a recommendation. Dan,
smiling, accepted his suggestion for a moderately priced
bottle of red after consulting with Katie.

She didn't want wine, either; she wanted to watch. But
she smiled and agreed that the body and essence sounded
fine.

Their server appeared next. It wasn't Neil Browne; it
was an older man, impeccable in his white jacket, pleasant in his manner.

But even as he described the various specials, Katie
tensed.

She wasn't sure...but there was a waiter back toward
the door, speaking with a group of five who were seated
at one of the larger pits, and he looked familiar. If it was
Neil Browne, he'd changed a lot...but he used prosthetics.
No one knew what was real about him and what was not.
He was a chameleon.

She fumbled to grab Dan's arm as he politely listened to their server.

"Excuse me," she said to the waiter. "Dan!"

She pointed.

But as she did, the man turned to look at her, almost as if he had sensed her watching him.

He dropped his tray on the table, along with the five drinks on it. The group cried out in dismay, jumping up, trying to avoid the spill of beverages, some milky, some clear, all sliding and sluicing across the table and threatening their clothing.

The man bolted out the door. Dan proved his agility, leaping over their table to tear after him with a startling speed. He yelled over his shoulder to her, "Call Axel!"

But near the door, he found himself blocked, colliding with the disgruntled customers in the way of the exit, who were still trying to sop up the liquids staining their clothing, complaining loudly and vociferously. To complicate matters, the elegant young hostess left her stand…and blocked the exit as well as she tried to calm the patrons despite her own confusion.

Dan made his way through. Katie followed, more slowly slipping through the crowd now at the door. She dialed the phone and listened to it ring as she excused herself, pushing through.

A bizarre thought occurred to her.

Luckily, the wine hadn't arrived. They weren't running out on a check.

Axel answered his phone, and Katie tried not to stammer. "He was here, saw me looking at him, and took off. Here at Duffy's Den. Dan is already in pursuit. He bolted out onto Bourbon Street."

"I'm two blocks away. I'll send out the info. We'll send out the troops. What was he wearing?"

"A white waiter's jacket, but I imagine he's shed it by now," Katie said.

"You're probably right. I'll use the sketches," Axel said. "Stay where you are, Katie, in the middle of lots of people."

"Um…"

She was already outside the restaurant. She doubted she'd be welcomed back in. But she was on Bourbon in front of the restaurant, and there were people milling everywhere. Many were laughing, walking arm in arm and swaying arm in arm, in some cases.

"Right!" she told Axel.

She didn't want the agent worrying about her, not when he needed to get everyone finding the man she knew as Neil Browne.

She ended the call. She wondered if she should call Ryder, too, but Dan had told her both Axel and Ryder would be on the street peeking into different establishments. She was sure they had a communication protocol established.

She looked down the street, watching a group of thirty-somethings piling into the popular karaoke establishment.

Others were ambling into and out of bars and clubs.

Maybe she should wander, not far, just a block or two, peek into bars and anywhere Neil Browne might have fled for cover. But he was probably off of Bourbon Street already.

Or was he?

What better place could one find to join in with a crowd and blend into a group?

A large, popular bar with nightly live music was a stone's throw away.

Katie headed in that direction.

* * *

Neil Browne had disappeared into thin air before Dan had reached the street.

That wasn't possible, so he had ducked in somewhere.

He headed down the street where one bar, despite the killer's copycat Axeman letter, was playing rock music. An AC/DC number was blaring out the doors with such energy they seemed to shiver.

People were filing in. Some to dance, some for the advertised cheap drinks.

He entered. The place was crowded. Tables were spilling over, the floor in front of the cover band was filled to the brim with gyrating singles and couples, and it was about three deep at the bar.

He searched through the crowd, glad of his height. He could see over most people. He reminded himself that according to Katie, the man was about five-eleven or six feet. He looked for the white jacket but instantly knew the first thing the man would have done would have been to toss the waiter's garb he'd been wearing.

Process of elimination. He glanced over singles, couples and groups and then moved toward the bar.

The Aerosmith number segued into a tune from Metallica.

Making his way to the bar wasn't easy. He eased through to the far end and there, head ducked low, was Neil Browne. He edged his eyes up carefully and saw Dan, now trying to make his way down the bar.

The man leaped up and headed for the kitchen.

It was then that Dan saw Katie. She had come in. She apparently knew people in the bar; they were calling out to her, and she was waving and smiling but moving.

Toward the kitchen. Katie must have also caught sight of Browne. He couldn't see exactly where the man had gone.

"Excuse me, excuse me...excuse me," he said, trying to press through the crowd.

"Hey, buddy, wait your turn!" one man shouted at him.

He was desperate. "FBI!" he shouted with authority. Well, he was working for the FBI.

And it looked like Katie and a killer were heading for the same place. He had to get to her.

Why hadn't she stayed in the restaurant?

Because, he knew, whoever else might be involved in this whole thing, she was after the man who had killed her parents.

Dan burst through the swinging kitchen doors at last to see that the ostensible Dr. Neil Browne carried a gun for use when he wasn't wielding an axe.

He had the cooks and bussers and several of the servers lined up on one side of a large, stainless-steel workstation, almost on top of some massive ovens and cooktops. Browne was across from them, his gun leveled at the shaking, crying crowd.

One person wasn't shaking: it was Katie. She stood out in the dress she was wearing, and because she simply was a beautiful young woman. She also stood out because she was staring at the man with the gun with so much disdain.

"You, get over here!" Neil Browne called to her.

He'd been wearing prosthetics, and they were peeling off him now. The kitchen was hot; he'd been hot running. He looked a bit like a zombie, decaying in the steam that rose from pots on the cooktops.

Dan took aim at the man, but Browne had known he was there. He cocked his gun, still aimed at Katie.

"I'm going to get that girl, G-man," he told Dan. "You

lower your weapon, or she dies first and then as many as I can take down."

"But you'll be dead," Dan said.

The man's gun didn't waver but remained directly aimed at Katie as he turned to look at Dan. "I don't really care. I am a creature of the six. I will go on. She will die along with all the rest of these people."

"I'm not a G-man. Lower your weapon."

He could fire...and kill the bastard, here and now, easily. But the man's gun was cocked...

One of the waitresses let out a loud sob. Her knees seemed to give, and she collapsed to the floor. Katie moved to comfort her.

"Get back!" Browne ordered, his gun on the crowd as he moved around the island to reach Katie.

"Let her go. It's your only chance to run. I see a back door. Let her go, and you can run and disappear again," Dan yelled, trying to keep his own gun leveled at the man.

Browne hurried to Katie, wrenching her from the sobbing girl.

Again, he turned to Dan.

"Two seconds. This isn't the way he wanted it, but it's the way that it will have to be. Two seconds... Lower your weapon or—"

Dan saw Katie make a sudden, swift move.

Too fast for Browne.

The sobbing waitress had collapsed in front of one of the massive stovetops, and Katie grabbed hold of one of the boiling pots of liquid cooking there.

She slammed it into Browne's face.

His gun went off, but the bullet flew up into the ceiling as the man shrieked in agony. Dan rushed over as Browne tried to absorb the pain and take aim again.

Dan was ready to shoot to kill, but he veered his aim just a hair, catching the man exactly as he had wanted, shooting his gun hand.

Browne's gun fell to the floor. As Dan progressed around the island to wrench the screaming man from Katie, he heard shouts of "FBI!" and "NOPD!"

The kitchen staff was running out.

Officers and agents were filing in. He reached Katie and Browne, slamming Browne hard in the chest and sending him flying, still wailing and blubbering and screaming with pain.

He pulled Katie into his arms. They were both shaking badly.

"Brave, brilliant girl," he said, pulling her against him. He knew Axel and Ryder were both there. They had called for an ambulance, and despite Browne's screeches, Axel was advising him he was under arrest for the murders of Elle Détente and Lettie and Randolph Rodenberry.

The man was half laughing and half crying as he declared, "I didn't murder them!"

It didn't matter. His denials were nothing.

Axel went on to add the murders of Anita Calabria and Lou and Virginia Delaney.

Dan noted the band had ceased to play. He glanced at Axel who nodded and led Katie out of the kitchen. The bar had emptied quickly. Police officers were blocking the front and the area around it.

"You okay?" he asked Katie.

She looked at him and nodded. "Thank God for gumbo."

"What?"

"Gumbo. I got him with gumbo," she said.

Dan smiled as he saw EMTs rush in, heading to take Browne, who would also have a police escort.

Axel came toward them. "There's paperwork, and Ryder and I will be heading to the hospital with Browne, whoever he may really be, so we'll get together in the morning. Another Krewe agent is here… His name is Andre Broussard, and he'll take a report from you for now. You were a consultant on this, Dan, so…just make sure he knows you and Katie were out for a nice dinner when Katie recognized Browne, and he saw her, and law enforcement was immediately notified, and…well, whatever happened after."

Dan nodded. "Right." Apparently, it didn't go on a report anywhere that a dead man gave you a tip.

Axel paused, staring at Dan.

"Amazing. You disarmed him. You didn't kill him."

"I wanted to kill him," Dan admitted softly.

"But you didn't."

"No." Dan took a breath. "Almost. But we need him alive. He's not the mastermind behind all this. There are others involved, and we don't know how many. I'm not so sure I was being moral or ethical at all. We need him alive."

Axel nodded. "Well, I'm going to the hospital. He's pretty badly burned, but… Hey, Katie. Quick thinking. Well done!"

She gave him a weak smile. "Thank you." She was quiet a minute. "Others are involved, but that man killed my mom and dad. Brutally. He hacked them to pieces. I hope I hurt him badly. I hope he's in pain for as long as he may live. They say that healing comes only through forgiveness, but he planned on killing me, too. I guess… I guess I'm glad we didn't kill him. I never want to be as bad, but I hope he hurts. I can't help it!" she whispered.

"That's okay, Katie," Axel said. He saw the EMTs were carrying the man out on a stretcher. Ryder was right next to it, nodding to them, but not about to leave the suspect—

even burned and shot—without him making sure he wasn't going to try to bolt and run.

"Get some rest," he said softly. "Ah, here's Andre."

The man coming toward them looked to be about thirty-five, and Dan had the feeling that he'd probably been part of some branch of law enforcement or another for a while. He was about Dan's height with dark hair and dark eyes in a lean, sharp face, and he had the look of a man who kept fit, as field agents tended to do.

He offered them a nod as Axel quickly introduced them, and then Axel took off after the stretcher carrying Neil Browne out of the restaurant.

"Shall we sit?" Andre asked Dan and Katie. "The kitchen employees and staff are all giving brief statements, but what they know is a man burst into the kitchen waving a gun at them." He shrugged. "So... I just need you to start at the beginning."

He had an official-looking pad out; he wasn't using a smart phone.

"Wow. Pen and paper," Dan said.

Andre Broussard grimaced. "Old-school. Yeah. I'll need your signatures."

Dan looked at Katie. "Well, we've learned through the investigation this man was in town and was with the murdered woman we found in the old cemetery. Katie knew both of them. They were the couple who disappeared off the boat the day her parents and a friend were murdered... axes and knives used on them," he said quietly.

"We were just about to order dinner. New place in town, you know," Katie said.

Andre Broussard grinned and said in a soft whisper, slightly accented with a bayou twang, "Ghost told you, eh?"

Dan and Katie glanced at each other. "Well, anyway,

when he saw Katie and knew that she had seen him, he took off. She pointed him out to me immediately, and I went after him. This place was crowded, and it seemed as though he might try to hide among the patrons. I came in first, but Katie was closer to the kitchen."

Katie continued the thread. "He had a gun. He forced me in and then terrified the entire staff in the kitchen. He forced us all to one side and then used me and a threat to kill everyone in there to try to force Dan to drop his weapon. I'd gone to help a girl who collapsed, and she happened to do so right by a stovetop. When he came to grab me, I noticed the bubbling gumbo on the stovetop and…" She faltered.

"You stopped him," the agent said.

"Yes, Special Agent Broussard," Katie said quietly.

"Andre, guys, please. Everyone just calls me Andre."

Dan nodded.

"Okay… Read what I've written. If it's what happened as you told it to me, just sign it please," he said.

Dan read the rendition Andre had put down. It was exactly what they'd said.

He looked at the agent. "Uh…damn, you're good."

Andre grimaced. "I can write fast. I guess it's a good ability." He hesitated. "I'm from Louisiana. This is… Well, it can't mean as much to Adam and me as it does to you, Katie, but it means a lot to us. So…any time I can help you, in any way, reach out. I do know the area well. I was raised in Lafayette, did a tour in the military after college, and when I found out about the Krewe of Hunters, I applied to the Academy. Then I worked in New York City with the team there."

They were alone in the bar; employees and management were gone. Police photographers were still in the kitchen, but other agents and officers were out on the street finishing up with the large number of witnesses to the evening's events.

"You...you always knew you wanted to be Krewe?" Dan asked him.

"Long story, but yes," Andre said. "I've had so-called imaginary friends since I was a child. So far, it's an amazing group. Never easy. But you don't go into any of this if you're looking for easy, right?"

"Right," Dan murmured.

Andre stood then and gave them both a card. "That's my cell, on me at all times, and obviously I shadow Axel, but if you can't reach him or need anything...call."

They thanked him and stood as well.

"We can go home?" Katie asked him. "Oh! Dan, did you want to go to the hospital, too? See what Axel can get out of... Neil Browne? Once he stops screaming," she added softly.

Dan did want to help interrogate Browne. But he also didn't. He didn't want Katie anywhere alone. Not that night. Not until it was over. Really over.

And while Jennie might be dead and Neil Browne might be in custody, it was far from over. And he knew that already from the words the man had spoken in the kitchen as he'd waved his gun around.

"No. I'm good. Axel is there for the Feds, and Ryder is there for NOPD."

"You two look exceptionally nice," Andre complimented them, taking in their outfits.

"Thank you, but no more fine dining for me tonight," Katie said. She pulled a face, looking at Dan. "Pizza to-go on the way home?" she asked.

He nodded, glad that after the trauma, she wanted pizza.

Dan gave Andre his hand. "Thank you."

"Glad to meet you both. Sorry for the circumstances," Andre said, indicating the front of the bar. It was time for them all to leave.

A crowd had gathered. They made their way through it, trying to blend in, just as Neil Browne had done earlier at the bar. They got a pizza and then did their best to get through to Dan's car.

"You're going to be a hero," Dan told Katie. "*Heroine*, sorry. Fiercely defending herself and others...with gumbo."

"New Orleans is famous for gumbo, you know," she told him as they got into the car. "I'm actually starting to feel really bad about it. Dan, I did scald him. I mean, it was there. The pot was there, and I had to do something."

"Katie, you defended yourself and others."

"But what if... His burns have to be pretty severe. And he knows more, Dan. Yes, I believe he and Jennie killed my parents. And I feel torn. I never thought I was vicious, and I wanted justice...not revenge."

"We always feel torn. He'll live. And yes, we must learn from him everything there is to learn. Somehow. He isn't going to want to talk. Remember, he didn't care if he died. He was part of *six*. He said that made him immortal."

"'This isn't the way *he* wanted it, but the way it has to be,'" Katie said, repeated the words that had been spoken. "A creature of six...and a *he* who is calling the shots. Oh, Dan, I wonder if that meant I'm supposed to die under an axe, like my parents."

"Katie, we have Browne. Jennie is dead. We believe they were low on their number. Maybe the couple killed in Baton Rouge were part of the group. Jennie was seen, and so she had to die. Come to think of it, I wonder if Neil would have been killed, too. You knew he was in the city. You saw him. Once you saw him, he became a liability...

Interesting. I'm sure Axel and Ryder will see that guards are posted on him at the hospital."

They reached her house. The dogs were waiting.

Katie greeted them with a lot of love. "My knights in furry armor!" she said.

"They do love you," Dan agreed.

"And they seem to like you okay, too," she said.

"I like dogs. They're honest," he told her as they went up the porch steps and then into the house.

They ate the pizza in the kitchen.

Katie climbed up the stairs ahead of him.

But she went straight to the guest bedroom, crashing down on the bed.

"I think *he* is the big man," Dan said, sliding his gun and holster onto the bedside table and walking idly to the dresser to strip off his jacket, vest and shirt. "He wants to recreate the Axeman and revive the belief in immortal creation on the Sixth, or whatever. But I believe different people carry out different crimes. I do believe Neil killed Jennie because he was ordered to do so. And he killed your parents and probably the couple in Orlando. But here in New Orleans, he really went for the Axeman legend. The big man himself seems to have committed the murders of the Rodenberry couple and Elle Détente. I don't know whether *he* knew George before the murders or just knew George was a close friend of your father's, or even if George was really supposed to die, but he turned out to be a very convenient scapegoat."

He sat at the foot of the bed, sliding out of his shoes and socks, thoughtful. He turned to Katie, knowing her mind must be in turmoil and wanting to hold her.

"Katie?"

He curled up next to her.

He'd been talking to himself.

Despite the trauma, Katie was sound asleep.

He lay next to her, careful not to wake her, and held her tenderly in his arms.

Seventeen

Neil Browne sat across the table from Dan, Axel and Ryder. Dan thought that, under normal circumstances, they would have been a formidable trio.

Apparently not to Neil Browne, or whoever he really was.

He just stared at them all as they entered with folders and sat.

And he just kept smiling.

He spoke before any of them could begin to question him.

"I have nothing to tell you. And just what are you going to charge me with? I mean, all the garbled stuff you were saying... A murder in Florida? Come on, man, that's... Wow. That's stretching it. But you want me to say I'm guilty, that I'm the Axeman's Protégé? Okay, if that's what you want." He started to laugh. "Prove it. Prove it in a court of law."

Ryder looked at Dan and Axel and shrugged. "Not sure about all the murders, but there was an eyewitness to one. Except that was when you were Neil Browne. Most recently, you were Brian Denholm, but he's dead and you stole his

ID, and there's a whole cast and crew from a movie who will swear to that."

Dan thought Ryder's words gave Browne concern, though he tried not to show it. Maybe he hadn't known law enforcement had found the bodies of the dead man and woman he and Jennie had presumably killed, and from whom Neil and Jennie had taken their latest identities. Dan leaned forward, glancing at Axel and Ryder and then smiling at Neil Browne.

"Well, let's see... I think there's a lot we can prove. You were armed and attempting murder in the bar. That's enough for them to hold you here for arraignment. And no judge is going to allow bail for a man who might be the Axeman's Protégé. That will give us plenty of time to gather what we need to charge you with... Wow! I'm not even sure how many murders."

"You can hold me. You can't prove anything against me," he said with a shrug.

"Well, actually, we can," Axel said.

Neil Browne shook his head. "No, no, you don't understand. The Axeman comes, and the Axeman goes. He's immortal, created the last on the Sixth Day, given ultimate power. Some call him a demon, and some...well, some say that he is God! Let's face it, fellows, people need God to be a good god. The old Hebrews had it right. God created us in his image—on the Sixth Day. But everyone seems to take God all wrong. I mean, he has a temper and a sense of humor. He gets mad, and he gets playful, and he likes jazz... He really likes jazz. So, you see, demons and gods, all the same thing. Superior beings, and most people just want to believe in goodness and kindness and respect for one's fellow man because they're weak! They are not survivors. The Axeman—a demon, or perhaps a god bored out of his mind, and you must figure, he's vengeful and playful and loves blood. He demands sacrifice. And six! The count of six."

"Jennie was one of your six, right?" Dan asked pleasantly.

At last there was a flicker of emotion in the man's eyes.

"Jennie went on. She will be rewarded. Only a shell was cast aside."

"Yeah, well, you see," Ryder said, sitting back and crossing his arms over his chest, "we mere mortals see that as murder."

Browne shrugged.

Axel leaned in. "We need to know about the rest of your six, Mr. Browne."

The man grinned. "Dr. Browne, remember?"

"Doctor of what?" Ryder asked.

"Does it matter?" Browne asked. "I had the ID."

"Did you kill a Dr. Browne to get it?" Ryder asked.

Browne smiled broadly, displaying a crooked smile that might have often been taken as charming.

"No, made that one with a little help from an ex-con in Mississippi," he said.

"What is your real name?" Axel asked.

Browne started to laugh. "Ah, how brilliant! Neither the cops nor the famed FBI knows who I am. Well, of course not. I'm immortal, I come and go as I please. You'll see! My name is Demon, but you wouldn't understand that. So just call me Browne. Dr. Browne."

"So, this six... There's the one you refer to as *he*. Then there was Jennie... Were the couple you killed in Baton Rouge originally part of the six?" Dan asked.

"Hey, those guys are rising up in immortality, sacrific-

ing pretty decent mortal shells to rise up to be superpowers!"
Browne said.

"So they were. But they're dead—"

"Immortal," Browne corrected.

"Gone, and Jennie's gone. So that's minus three. And
that leaves you, the man you call *he*, and one more. Unless
you did get Nathan Lawrence to join with you," Dan said.

"Nathan Lawrence," Browne said thoughtfully. "No,
he was not deserving, I'm afraid. Sad little guy. So much
power. Money is power, you know, especially when mixed
with immortality."

Ryder turned to Dan and muttered, "We're talking to a
complete maniac."

"But he does know what's going on," Axel said quietly.

"But I'm not telling!" Browne said, and his smile deepened.

There was a tap at the door. Dan saw Special Agent
Andre Broussard through the small paned window high
up on the door.

Axel stood. "Excuse me," he said.

"I understand you're not afraid to die, that you're immortal," Dan said to Browne. "But shedding this skin isn't
easy. I think you were ordered to send Jennie on to her immortality, but what you did was hack her head just about
in two. Must have hurt like a son of a bitch. And she must
have been so surprised…shocked, even."

He thought he might have finally gotten through to the
man, despite Browne's efforts to display minimal emotion.

Dan went on. "Lethal injection is supposed to be the
most humane way to execute murderers… Well, I've been
in the viewing room for a lethal injection. It isn't pretty.
The body jerks and spasms as the organs fail and… Well,
like I said, not pretty."

"He will come for me, long before we reach that point. I mean, if you can even get anything on me. Really. Besides…well, whatever it is you can get me on for last night. People are going to doubt I could have killed anyone."

Dan kept his own face impassive, yet he feared he knew exactly what Browne meant.

There must have been another victim during the night. The big man in the black coat and the slouch hat had probably struck again. There was something to the number six. If different killers were at work, anyone caught would have an alibi.

But Neil Browne still wasn't getting off so easily. He'd been seen by dozens of people wielding a gun and threatening death.

Dan smiled and leaned back. "Pretty sure I've been right so far. Your new identities, they were stolen from the Baton Rouge couple, but live by the sword, die by the sword. So, before New Orleans, you were a lovely little group of six. Killing goats for fun when human beings weren't on the agenda. But it was you and Jennie, we'll say, and the Baton Rouge couple. Now there's also the big *he* and one other. That one other would be…well, someone here. Someone in New Orleans planned the murders, and you think they're all part of some cosmic grand plan. I think they're revenge. Your big *he* wanted to kill Lou Delaney, and it just fell in with all this. You all started killing and believed you were immortal and special. And it became a game. But now, it's just you and the big *he* and one other…unless Nathan Lawrence became part of your little group. You're still short."

"I think I may take that offer for an attorney," Browne said and yawned.

Dan leaned closer again. "Why has it taken you so long to ask? Was your immortal leader supposed to send you one? But he'd be afraid of an association with you, wouldn't he? I mean, he had you kill Jennie, and now he's denying you an attorney!"

"I'll take the lawyer," Browne said flatly. He wasn't smiling. He glared at Dan, and Dan was glad—he had hit a nerve.

Dan nodded. "Think about helping us, though. Keeping that mortal shell of yours. I know you all are careful. Gloves, hair caps probably. You leave nothing behind. But you see, you weren't wearing gloves the whole time you were with Jennie, and there's this amazing way of getting fingerprints off a body now. I believe they found yours, and that puts you with her—"

"Yes, so? That doesn't prove I killed her!"

"Well, yes, it does." He was playing, grabbing at straws, but good ones, Dan hoped. "Because you didn't want to kill Jennie, you were just terrified not to do it. And you touched her face, you had your gloves off, and you touched her face. So you see, there's blood on those prints we're going to get. Won't matter if we know who you really are or not. Your fingerprints here, same prints on Jennie's corpse..."

He let his voice trail.

"Lawyer!" Browne said. His voice had changed.

"Suit yourself," Dan said, standing. Ryder followed suit. He pretended to be oblivious to the fact that Browne was listening as he spoke to Ryder. "We need to figure out that sixth person, and I don't think it will be that hard. We have records on the Baton Rouge couple, and we have Browne's phone now... We can trace some calls. When we don't need this asshole anymore, we won't have to worry about trying to get the federal and state prosecutors to make any kind of concessions."

He let the door close on his last words, feeling just a little bit triumphant.

But that feeling was quickly gone.

Axel and Andre were looking at him and Ryder with grim expressions, and Dan knew; Browne was going to be able to make people doubt his guilt when it came to the axe murders.

Because someone else had been attacked.

"Who? Where?" he asked, feeling his heart sink. "When was it called in. How fast can we get there?"

"The Bywater area. The victims are Jillian and Andy Dean, and Andy's sister Ashley," Axel said. They started walking quickly down the hall away from the interrogation room.

"But," Andre said, keeping pace easily, "here's the good part—"

"There's a good part to axe murders?" Dan asked, feeling numb.

"They're not dead," Andre said. "Seriously injured, but it was almost as if—"

"As if the Axeman's Protégé was never out to kill them?" Dan asked. "They were victims because this group needed something to happen. Something that might help make Neil Browne appear to be different, not one of them, a gun-toting wannabe."

"Dammit!" Ryder hammered his fist against the wall. "We didn't stop him. Agents and officers are combing the city and environs, and we didn't stop this attack." He frowned. "Are any of them conscious? Did they identify anything about the Axeman?"

"Yes," Axel said dryly. "Big tall man, slouch hat, boots, dark coat to his feet."

"The description we already received," Axel said. "This guy wants everyone in the city to believe the Axeman is immortal and he's back."

Katie was waiting in the reception area. She stood as she saw them all coming. Her face paled. "Has there been another attack?"

"Katie, stay here," Dan said.

"Was there another attack while Neil Browne was in custody?"

Dan caught her by the shoulders. "Yes. We're going there now. You need to stay here. Right here. It's safe, Katie."

"I'm coming with you," she said.

"Katie, you're a civilian—" Dan said.

"So are you!" she exclaimed.

"You don't want to see..." Dan realized that his excuse was a poor one, considering all that Katie had already seen.

"Ambulances will already be on scene, so there won't be much to see," Axel explained. "But Katie, we'll have to leave you with one of the patrol officers. The crime-scene investigators won't want any of us destroying possible evidence, so we'll need to tread carefully."

Dan started moving toward the exit. "All right, Katie's in. Let's just get there!"

Axel had a big Bureau SUV; he drove with Andre Broussard in the passenger seat. Dan sat in the back with Katie. Ryder followed in his own vehicle.

When they arrived at the scene, Dan hopped out quickly—an ambulance was about to leave the scene.

"I'm heading in with it!" he said.

"Go," Axel agreed.

Dan left the car, called out to one of the officers to stay with Katie and leaped into the ambulance, surprising the EMT on the scene.

"I'm with the FBI," he said. He looked at the stretcher in place in the ambulance. She was a pretty young girl, maybe seventeen. Or she would have been pretty, if not for the blood dripping down her head. "She's alive and may make it?" he asked quietly.

The EMT nodded. "We have oxygen and a drip going. She's lost a lot of blood. He was going for a major artery in her thigh, I think, but he didn't hit the main. We have the bleeding stopped."

"It's incredibly important that I speak with her. May I? Gently, carefully?"

The young EMT nodded solemnly.

"Thank you. And the others?"

"Andy Dean is unconscious, and they just left with him. He'll need surgery. His wife is unconscious, and until they can stabilize her, they'll probably put her in medically in-duced coma. But Ashley rolled under the bed. She received two good whacks, but she's conscious. She's in pain, but we're getting her to the hospital ASAP. Be brief, because we'll be rushing her into Emergency."

As if to verify his words, the ambulance revved into gear.

"How did she get help?" Dan asked the EMT.

"Smart kid—had her cell phone with her. We arrived about fifteen minutes before you. Once the call was re-ceived, it went out to every agency and to Special Agent Axel Tiger. As far as I know, he was in an interrogation with a suspect and another of his team took the call, but you guys got here almost as fast as we did."

"We hurried," Dan said. The ambulance swayed as it took a corner.

"So, I guess you didn't get him," the EMT said, looking at Dan sorrowfully.

"We got one. And it isn't just a *him*, it's a *them*," Dan explained.

The EMT was shaking his head. He was young, about twenty-five, but had a dignified manner.

"I have a wife. And kids. A two-year-old son and an infant daughter. The Axeman killed a baby. You've gotta stop them."

"We will," Dan vowed. "And we need every bit of help. This isn't an immortal being returned to earth. It's a group of sick people. We will get them all."

Still solemn, the EMT nodded. The ambulance hit a bump, bouncing Dan sideways a step. The EMT indicated Dan could take the little seat by Ashley Dean.

An IV dripped fluids into her.

Her eyes were closed. Dan gently took her hand. "Ashley, my name is Dan Oliver. Your courage is amazing. I know you're in pain. And I know you're worried about your brother and sister-in-law. But you were smart. You got help out here quickly and may have saved your own life and theirs. And I'm so sorry to bother you, but if there's anything you can give me, we need to know."

"The Axeman," she said.

"Yes, a man came in with an axe—"

"He was big. My brother had opened the door to get the paper. He's old fashioned and gets a physical copy delivered. He…he forgot to lock the door. But it was daytime. He walked back up to the bedroom with coffee and then… I guess the man came in behind him. I heard Jillian scream, and I rushed in, and my brother… Andy lying in a pool of blood. The man was going after Jillian. He saw me. He attacked me, but I fell, and he hit me again, and I rolled so he couldn't get me… My phone was in my pocket. I dialed 9-1-1."

"Tell me more about the man."

Her eyes opened. They were enormous and green, with

a dazed light in them. She earnestly told him, "It was the Axeman, exactly as the stories about him go. He was big, his hat was big and low, and he was dressed in a long trench coat of some kind. His face…was dark, as if shadowed, but the hat was so low… I thought I saw his eyes. They were red, and they blazed, and when he heard me talking…heard the emergency operator…he took off. He was just gone."

"He ran back down the stairs?"

"I—I don't know. He was gone."

A big man. Tall and sturdy, and delighting in the fact he was taking on the persona of a long-dead killer. He'd had others do his killing before, but here…now…in New Orleans, he was embracing the legend himself.

Dan thanked her and tried to assure her that she and her family would be okay.

He didn't want to be a liar. He had no idea if her brother and sister-in-law would make it.

But there, in the ambulance, encouragement seemed the best. The EMT nodded at him.

When they reached the hospital, Dan leaped out and called Axel immediately to tell him what he had learned. "Did you find anything?" Dan asked.

"Well, maybe," Axel said.

She was a civilian. Katie understood that perfectly. Dan had gone off in the ambulance. Axel and Andre and Ryder were in the house with the crime-scene investigators.

She leaned against one of the patrol cars surveying the CSI, police, and federal vehicles drawn in on the lawn. Crime-scene tape had been set up around the house.

Officers were canvasing the crowd that had gathered and going door-to-door.

It was daytime. Someone had to have seen something.

She was restless. Everyone was busy, doing something.

No one thought she should be alone now; they thought she needed to be protected at all times. That wasn't a bad thing.

In the middle of the crowd, she saw a woman.

No one else seemed to see her, though a few started as she went by, as if they'd felt a bug or something brush their skin.

It was Mabel. She was watching the scene, too.

Then she saw Katie.

With a grim expression, she made her way to the back of the patrol car where Katie was leaning.

"I know you can't respond or talk to me with all these people around," Mabel told her. "But I've been going through this crowd, listening. And there's a little girl out there who saw him. She saw the man running out of the house. She said he looked like a giant Darkwing Duck. All in black, and he dropped something as he exited the house."

Katie lowered her head and spoke softly. "The axe he used. They found it by the front steps."

"Well, she saw him leave. She saw a car pick him up."

"A car? What kind of a car?"

"I don't know. She was with her parents. They were shushing her and telling her she couldn't be sure of what she saw. She's only about five or six. The parents are terrified, thinking they could make themselves targets."

"Can you point her out to me?" Katie asked.

Mabel pointed. It wasn't easy to see, there were so many people milling about. But finally, behind them all, in front of a single-story shotgun house, she saw the family. It looked as if the young parents were watching the scene worriedly from the sanctity of their yard.

They both held a hand of their child, a little girl with red ringlets and a cherubic but serious face.

Katie pushed silently away from the car and made her way through gawking bystanders, saying "Excuse me," over and over again. Glancing back, she saw she had managed to get away without the officer who was watching her even aware that she had left. But he wasn't supposed to have been worried about her taking off, he was just supposed to make sure no one approached her and hurt her. But nothing was going to happen in a crowd that size.

She reached the family standing on their lawn and quickly introduced herself. She didn't say she was a tour guide and carriage driver; she said she was working with the FBI. In a way, though she hadn't been hired officially as a consultant, she figured it was true.

"We're hoping someone saw the attacker as he was arriving or leaving. Any help, any idea, an inkling of anything might be useful," she said. She knelt by the little girl and offered her a gentle smile. "You have beautiful hair," she said.

"Thank you," the little cherub said. "You have it, too," she continued, smiling. "Like mine, it's red!"

"Yes, I have red hair, too. Mine is a little darker, but we have the same hair!" Katie said.

"Miss… Agent… I'm sorry," her father said. "We…we were just getting ready for the day, you know. Getting Margot here ready for school. Me, needing to head off to work, you know, and my wife was at the coffee machine—"

"I was at the window!" little Margot said. "He was a big black thing, like a giant bat, and he was heading down the street and he was picked up by a sleigh!"

"A sleigh?" Katie asked.

"A fancy, red sleigh, but with no reindeer," Margot said.

"She's just a child," Margot's mother said. "Please, this

is all terribly upsetting! Margot needs to go now. Jubal, you need to take Margot and go—"

"Ooh. Like a flashy sports car?" Katie asked.

"Oh, yeah, maybe!"

"Red and sleek… Did you see who was driving it?" Katie asked.

Margot shook her head.

"Margot, we have to go!" her dad said to the child, and to Katie, "Please! We don't mean to be unhelpful, but… please! She's just a child!" he begged.

"Yes, get Margot to school and…um, lock your doors. Be careful!" she warned. "Day and night now," she added.

Katie turned back to the Dean house, pulling out her phone.

In the middle of the crowd, she found that Axel was coming after her.

"Katie! Oh, my God, what—"

"I know who another of their number is, Axel. The Axeman was a picked up by a sleigh, or a fancy sports car. I was just in such a car, Axel. It belongs to Carly Britton, the casting agent on the movie George was just working. Axel, you've got to bring her in! She put on an act you wouldn't believe, but she's with him. She just aided and abetted the attacker, the big man, the head of this murder ring!"

Axel frowned and said, "Katie, how… Why—"

"Mabel. Mabel overheard the child talking and came to me."

"And you ran off, when you're supposed to be under protection?"

"Axel! We need to get Carly Britton!"

"Yes, right. Come on. Andre is getting the car. I'll let Ryder know. We'll grab Dan on the way. He just called after he reached the hospital." He looked at her exasperated and then smiled. "Well, Dan would take an axe to me if something happened to you. But good work!"

She smiled weakly. "Let's get her," she said.

She turned her head away; she didn't want him to see her shiver.

She had just driven in that car with Carly Britton...to keep Carly safe!

Andre pulled Axel's Bureau car carefully through the crowd, and they slipped in while Axel put a call through to Ryder to let him know where they were going and to have him put out an APB on the woman.

A few minutes later, they picked Dan up on the street and then headed for Carly Britton's office. Ryder was going to get backup and head to her home.

As Dan climbed into the car, he looked at Katie as if quickly assuring himself she was alive and well. Then he turned to Axel. "Was there anything on the computer?"

"The computer?" Katie asked.

"Andy Dean had his computer open. He was about to log in to a remote meeting, and his camera was on. We have people analyzing the data," Axel said.

"I bet all we'll see is a big man in black," Dan said wearily. "We have nothing on the face yet, we just know that it's a big man in black. Ashley Dean was able to talk. She saw him, but that's what she says, too. A big man in black. Slouch hat, floor-length trench coat... But who found out about Carly Britton? Are we sure?"

"A little girl saw the Axeman get picked up on the street," Axel explained, glancing at Katie. "He had a getaway driver."

"She said a sleigh at first, a flashy red sleigh," Katie said.

"You talked to her?" Dan asked Katie.

"Mabel clued me in," Katie told him.

"But you—"

She smiled. "Axel was right behind me," she assured him.

Thankfully, Axel didn't correct her. He glanced back at them. "There's one more thing."

"And that is?" Dan asked.

"The scene investigators found a strange hair. It's being analyzed. May be nothing. Maybe someone was petting a dog or a cat or…who knows? But it was out of place at the Dean residence. Lab techs have it. We'll know soon."

They reached the CBD. Andre parked on the street, and they all jumped out.

Dan looked at Katie, and she knew he was wondering if she would be in danger if he brought her in, or if it would be worse to leave her outside.

"Let's go!" she told him.

They went into the office building. Katie and Dan took the elevator, while Axel and Andre dashed up the stairs. They arrived within seconds of each other at the suite where Carly Britton had her casting-agency office.

The door was ajar.

Dan stretched an arm back to keep Katie behind him, drawing his weapon as Axel and Andre did the same.

He pushed open the door.

Katie didn't scream, but she did let out a gasp.

There was no missing the violence that had gone on. Blood spattered the walls and the desk and covered the woman who lay on the floor, limbs at oddly broken, slashed angles, her head nearly severed from her body.

Eighteen

The city was in a state of sheer panic.

Dan gave another press conference, and in it, he referred to the situation that had occurred in the French Quarter, and he reported he was happy to say some recent victims of an attack were alive. The cunning bravery of a young girl had caused the killer to flee. They believed two of the victims found had been part of the killer's crew, and the mastermind behind numerous killings was now moving with desperation because they were close on his heels. Again, he asked for help from the community and thanked those who had come forward with bits of knowledge or suspicion.

One reporter asked if a forensic team had come up with anything.

Dan could only answer they were working diligently and wouldn't stop.

He gave the citizens of the city and surrounding areas advice again: to make sure homes were locked, to not travel alone, and to avoid dark alleys, parking garages and other isolated spaces. Most importantly, to be careful in their own homes and report anything suspicious immediately.

"And like a brave teenager, keep your cell phones on

you. Law enforcement is ready to move quickly in any direction. Know how to speed dial 9-1-1."

"Aren't you asking for a lot of unnecessary panic by implying people aren't safe in their own homes?" a reporter asked.

"We'd rather be a step ahead than a step behind," Dan said.

At last, he was able to excuse himself.

He joined Katie, Axel, Ryder and Andre in Axel's makeshift office at the NOLA bureau.

"Have they found Carly Britton's husband yet?" he asked Axel as he fell into a chair. It had been a long day.

"No. Not at home. There's an APB out for him," Axel said.

"The man works at home, something with stocks, so there's no office to try," Andre said. "We've asked neighbors and others if they know any of his habits, places he goes, but apparently he and his wife were not friendly neighbors. They stayed in, and most people thought it was because they were snobs."

Dan nodded.

Katie cleared her throat and spoke up.

"I keep thinking about the six. If we're right on this... The real Brian and Aubrey might have been two of the six, with Neil and Jennie being another two. We know there is a head man, the big man who is copying the Axeman in his clothing and attacks. And now Carly aided and abetted the big man, and he killed her for her efforts. We don't know if her husband is involved or not. The others are dead. They tried to recruit Dan's client, Nathan Lawrence, but we don't believe they succeeded. That means—unless they did fill their ranks—that only two remain alive. The big man and

Neil Browne. And Neil Browne is in custody. The big man, the mastermind, whatever, is possibly out there alone."

"Should we take another crack at him?" Axel asked Dan.

Dan looked at Ryder. "Do you want to talk to him? He's being arraigned in the morning on the charges ensuing from the other night. Now might be a good time for him to bargain. With nothing but circumstantial evidence, attorneys from the state and the federal government are still working on how they want to press charges when it comes to the murders."

"I would think they could get him on Brian and Aubrey and Jennie. Since there is written proof they were using their identities," Katie said. "And I am happy to swear in any court of law they were on the boat the day my parents and Anita were murdered."

Axel's phone buzzed, and he excused himself to answer it.

He stood and stepped a few feet away to listen, then returned and sat down again.

"We have something to work with," he said. "Angela has been combing the country and beyond, and the problem has been that Neil Browne has switched identities a dozen times. She managed to trace everything back. Dr. Neil Browne is really Sonny Hartfield, born in New Orleans and, according to records, died in New Orleans during the storm."

"So that's when he ditched his real identity!" Katie said.

"After the storm," Dan said, "there must have been chaos I can only imagine. Say Sonny Hartfield was with the group your father went after, when he was protecting others during the storm, Katie. And Hartfield was already with the *big* man, and they were already working on becoming the super six, immortal beings in the vein of the Axeman and Allan

Pierce. They would have been the core, and they would have added others in. Now that we know his real name…"

"You want me to go in?" Andre asked. "He doesn't know me yet. He's very defensive toward Ryder, Axel and you, Dan."

Dan glanced over at Katie. "He might realize he's in real trouble and could possibly save his supposed mortal shell if he was to turn in evidence now." He took a breath. He really didn't want to say this next bit. "What if we send Katie in? Katie looking right at him will either give him tremendous pleasure…or it could shake him. But, Katie, I don't know if it's something you want to do or can do. I don't want to put you in a bad situation."

Katie stared back at him, firm resolution in her green eyes.

"Yes. I can, and I will."

With Special Agent Andre Broussard at her side, Katie faced the man she had known as Neil Browne and now knew to be Sonny Hartfield.

He wasn't alone; he now had a public defender at his side, a Mr. Rutger.

"Your questions will come through me," Rutger said. "And anything you have to say at all will come through me."

"Fine," Katie said before Andre could speak. "Sonny Hartfield, you piece of scum! In the middle of disaster and tragedy, you went after people who were already down and beaten!"

Hartfield's eyes darted to his attorney.

The public defender was young. He had a blank expression, a miserable expression. He probably wasn't happy about his job, being brought in to represent such a man.

He would still do it to the best of his ability.

"Was that a question?" Rutger asked Katie.

She looked at him. "That man murdered my parents, and I know that he did."

"That's not a question. It's an allegation."

Andre spoke up, smiling. "A public defender, huh? No offense, sir, but…well, we all thought Hartfield here had real power. That he was part of a superpowered group of six people who looked out for each other. One would think someone out there had money. Fake identities, travel… enough money to buy the best attorneys out there. Again, no offense meant, Mr. Rutger."

"Again, is there a question anywhere in there, or are we wasting time?" Rutger asked.

"How do I word this in a question?" Andre mused. "All right. Brian Denholm and Aubrey Freehold were murdered. You and Jennie became them. They were part of your six. You were ordered to kill Jennie, and that hurt you, I believe. You loved her, in your sick way. And you believe in some twisted way that you're immortal. But you're not. You and Jennie easily got jobs on the movie because Carly Britton was one of you. She told law enforcement the truth because she knew we would find out soon enough. And so…it was established that you had worked under assumed identities. Like you, she was totally loyal to the big man, the guy out there who really wants to be the Axeman. But here's something you might not know yet. The Axeman, or the Axeman's Protégé, as they're calling this killer, went out and attacked people today who didn't die. They're not well, but they're not dead. Carly Britton was his getaway girl, and you know what he did for her in return? He killed her. Hacked her to pieces in her office. Now, you're about to go to jail, and we all know jails and prisons can be dangerous places. I'm going to suggest that, if you want to keep this mortal shell you have and not gamble on getting a new one, you tell us who the big man is, the man who ordered you to kill Lou and Virginia Delaney and Anita Calabria, who ordered you to kill again in Orlando, and then started doing the killing here himself with you all obeying his every command, right down to killing one another." He took a breath, then continued. "So here's my question... What can you tell us?"

Katie thought Sonny Hartfield turned a bit white. He wasn't smiling.

He turned to his attorney. She also thought his voice had changed, was wavering.

"I don't want to see these people. They can gather their evidence. They can ask me anything they want, in a court of law."

Rutger looked at the two of them unhappily. He probably didn't want a deranged killer out there, either. He probably had family himself or even worried for his own life. But he did his duty.

"You heard him. Interview is over," he said.

Katie and Andre stood to leave. In the outer offices, they met up with Dan, Axel and Ryder.

"What do we do now?" Katie asked.

"We wait. I believe our Axeman is cleaning house," Dan said, looking at Axel.

"And we're ready," Axel said.

Katie frowned.

Dan explained. "The Axeman's Protégé is trying to tie up loose ends. It's harder to reach Sonny Hartfield when he's being held, but we think he'll make a try at it. And when he does, Sonny might realize that he lived by the axe…and will die by it if he doesn't speak up and get assistance."

Axel, Ryder and Andre nodded at her.

"Time," Dan said. "It's just a matter of time."

"And with that, I'm hitting the hay," Axel said. "I suggest you all do the same. My phone will ring the second anyone has anything. And you're all on speed dial."

"Katie?" Dan asked.

She smiled at him. "Yep. I could go to bed," she agreed, and then she lowered her head. That could mean two things.

And it did.

The team parted ways. Dan drove back to Katie's house.

In the yard, the dogs greeted them happily.

Dan pet the dogs, but he did so absently, looking at the house.

He knew Katie was watching him. "Well, here's the good. No one has come near your place. The cameras are still recording, and their input is seen back at headquarters."

"That must be very boring for someone," Katie said. She also bent to greet the dogs.

"I imagine."

He smiled, looking at her. "Sex first—or food first?" he asked.

"Uh…"

"I'd usually opt for sex. But I'm tired. We're both tired. And we haven't eaten much today, but…last night you were so sound asleep…"

"I didn't mean to be."

"Katie, I'm teasing. You needed the sleep, and I'm glad you were able to. But the days aren't going to get any better. So, how about we go with food, sex and sleep. In that order." He cast his head at an angle, grinning. "I have no real commitment to food. Any old food will do."

She flushed. "I just meant—"

"I know what you meant," he said softly.

"I still mean it. You don't owe me anything, not even a morning-after phone call."

"You know, I don't think either of us has fared well in the relationship department. Busy lives, memories of the past...being haunted. You know. In many ways."

She grinned. "It's good that you met Mabel. She's been great."

"She is great, though she rather turned my world upside down."

"But in a good way, I hope."

"Yeah, I guess. Axel has suggested I join the Krewe. I have the background..."

"You'd be perfect," she said. "You should. I know you weren't happy chasing after errant husbands."

"That would mean I'd have to go to Quantico."

"Yes, I guess so."

"Katie, relationships aren't about anyone owing anyone anything. I want to call you because I want to hear your voice. I want to be with you because... I love being with you. I think I care about you more than I've cared about another woman ever." He gave her a wry smile. "Well, there was Wanda Sterns in high school, and I did have a crush on her, but it fell flat pretty quickly."

"High-school crushes can be crushing," she murmured.

"Katie, I want to see where this goes. I think I'm falling in love with you."

She suddenly felt like she was just made of hot liquid, and she'd melt away...

But in an amazed and grateful way.

"Really?" she whispered.

"I won't ask you for any commitment at this moment,"

he said. "But…would you think about leaving NOLA for a while, coming with me, living in the DC area?"

"I—I—I'd love to, but… I need to figure out the house, leaving… Oh, I'd have to tell Monty, and he's been the best boss ever. He'll need to replace me. I think he's out with a carriage now, but he doesn't like being a full-time guide."

"If you'll just think about it, that's all I need," he said softly. "I just want to be with you."

She smiled. She would have kissed him right there, fallen into his arms…

But Mitch nudged into her side, tail wagging in his urgency to let her know something.

"Let's get inside," Dan suggested.

The dogs followed them to the porch, whining.

"They're acting hungry. I'm pretty sure Monty was out today with Sarah and the carriage that I use. I'm going to feed them."

"Sounds good. Do you have food?"

Katie laughed. "Dog food? Yes."

"I meant people food—for us."

"Yes, I keep food. Look around and see what you'd like. I'm not exactly a gourmet, but I can whip together a few things. Thing is, meat is in the freezer, but we can defrost it quickly."

As Dan prowled in the refrigerator, Katie poured out three bowls of dog food.

"I'll just put these on the porch for the boys," she said.

He nodded absently, then turned to look at her.

"He did kill your parents, Katie. Sonny Hartfield killed your parents along with Jennie, whoever she really was. Jennie has met the same fate. We will get the proof we need. We will get justice for them," he said softly.

She smiled and nodded.

Then she headed out to the porch, balancing the three bowls of dog food.

She'd thought Jerry, Ben and Mitch would be waiting there, hopefully wagging their tails. They knew she was a sucker for them, and even if they'd eaten, they'd wind up being fed again.

"Guys? Come!" she called. "Mitch? Ben, come on. Jerry!"

They didn't respond to her. She thought she heard a whine from around the corner. Setting the bowls down, she worried that one of them had gotten hurt and that the other two were busy trying to help in their doggy way.

"Guys!" she called, and she walked toward the gate between the properties.

She saw the dogs; they were lying on the ground, all three whimpering.

"My guys, what happened?" she demanded.

Mitch was closest to her. She walked to him and knelt at his side. "Poor baby, I don't know—"

The whack on her head was hard. For barely an instant, she felt searing pain.

Then she felt nothing at all.

"Katie?"

Dan had a pack of chicken breasts in his hand.

He dropped them and rushed to the door. She was just putting dog bowls out, for God's sake. She should have been back by now.

He stepped out to the porch. The dog bowls were there, but there was no sign of Katie.

Or the dogs.

He thought he heard something. Drawing his weapon,

he walked around the house, noting that he was stepping out of range of the cameras.

He wanted to kick himself or worse.

He should have never let her step out alone, even on her front porch, even with cameras, even with dogs...

The dogs! What the hell had happened to the dogs?

He moved toward the gate, thinking Katie might have gone that way to find them.

He saw one of the big animals on the ground. The dog saw Dan and tried to lift its head and wag its tail.

It was Mitch, he thought.

Mitch, who couldn't quite move. But there wasn't a mark on him, and there was only one answer that Dan could fathom.

The dogs had been poisoned.

There was something in the animal's fur.

A dart! A damned dart. Dan quickly pulled it from Mitch, hoping that maybe the sedative hadn't had time to work all the way.

He pulled his phone out quickly as he looked around, searching for any approaching danger, ready to call Axel. But as he held the phone in his hand, it began to vibrate.

It was Axel, calling him.

"Dan, get back here. Get Katie, and get back here."

"Wait—"

"The lab identified the mystery hair from the crime scene. Get in here now!"

"Axel! I need backup here, now!" Dan said. As he spoke, he looked across the stables to the building that was Monty's house.

The shadows were waving anxiously.

Mabel Greely stood with Gray Simmons, mere shadows in the dimming sunlight, and the dead were beckoning to him.

"Axel, he has her. I've got to get to her before… Come quietly. He may keep her alive to…to torture her. Axel, don't be seen!"

"Dan, all right, Dan—"

But Dan was moving already, pocketing his phone. The ghosts were beckoning him to make all speed. He drew his weapon.

He'd find Katie, and he would shoot anyone in his way.

The pain in Katie's head was ungodly.

It felt like an axe was sticking into her skull!

But as she slowly regained consciousness, she knew nothing was protruding from her body.

Not yet.

She was tied up, though. Wrists bound together. Her feet, she saw, were free. If she could just manage to get up, she could run…

Where was she? Think! Her head was spinning. She closed her eyes, willing for the spinning and dizziness to stop.

Time might mean everything.

Think! Maybe she was in the stables.

She wasn't. No, she would know the smell of the animals and the hay. No…

She was in a bedroom. Someone's bedroom, and not her own. There was a closet on one wall, a sturdy oak dresser against another, and a window that looked out opposite where she sat. There was a bed, a big one. And…

A chair in front of a small desk. There was a jacket laid over the back of the chair. A big jacket.

A big jacket for a big man.

"Ah, love, you're with me now!"

She swung around.

*A big man. A tall man, and a big man. Oh, dear God,
why hadn't she seen...*

Even now, she couldn't believe.

*Monty? Monty Trudeau, a stone-cold, vicious killer
without an ounce of empathy?*

"Monty," she said. "You?"

He smiled, so pleased with himself.

"Katie, love, I can't tell you what pleasure I derive from
seeing your face right now! You're so stunned! Yes, Katie,
me. This is my place. *My* town. And I learned quickly I
could seize all the power I wanted. I studied the city, you
see. Studied it as you, my guides, never quite did. I learned
so much, and I learned how to earn my way to immortality."

"Monty, you are not going to live forever."

He shook his head, hunching down in front of her.
"Katie, you don't understand the immortality situation.
You see, I am not the Axeman's Protégé. The media just
had to go with that. No, I am the Axeman! I *am* the Axeman. The real thing. He died and was reborn time and time
again, and now he lives in me."

"So, you're the Axeman of New Orleans."

"In this shell."

"Monty... My father... Why? I mean, you were form-
ing this club of yours—"

"Club?" he demanded.

"Sorry, group?"

"The Six," he said. "Just *The Six*. There is nothing else
like us. Immortals."

She started to laugh and then realized she shouldn't. Her
laughter angered him, and she had to figure out some way
to get out. She had to escape, she had to survive...

Dan!

Monty wasn't playing well at all, maybe because he was

growing desperate. Dan was at her house; he would be coming for her, and he would know...

Wouldn't he?

"I'm sorry! I didn't study the past as much as I should have," Katie said. "And honestly, I never seriously connected Allan Pierce with the Axeman. I always felt it was a mystery we'd never get to the bottom of. But I should have read everything out there. It's hard, though, you know. There's so much history."

It was his turn to laugh.

Katie frowned.

"Um—"

"Katie, Katie, Katie. Do you think I really believe all that hogwash?" He leaned closed to her, and she saw he was holding an axe behind his back.

His friendly, bearded, *big* face was just inches from her own.

"Yes, hogwash, Katie, but it's amazing. I had a pack of fools doing whatever I asked, because I convinced them that being with me would turn them into super beings and they would become immortal. Then I convinced Bella—oh, not sure if you know that yet or not, but Jennie's real name was Bella, Bella LaPointe—and that idiot Sonny we'd made a mistake, that Brian and Aubrey were turncoats and traitors and had to be eliminated. Oh, by the way, the real Brian was the one your father knocked around. He was very happy to listen to me about people needing to die and how as one of the six he would be special, and others would die because of him. I had a few problems with him. He wanted to kill your father so badly, and there was no way your dad wouldn't have recognized him from that confrontation. So, well, I had to send Sonny and Bella instead. Oh, watching you all running around trying to catch your own tails! Priceless!"

Katie shook her head. "You knew who I was when you hired me six years ago. You could have killed me so many times over. Let's see, you probably arranged for me to have such a bargain on my house, too, right?"

"Ah, guilty as charged!"

She shook her head. "Why?"

"I always wanted to do the Axeman bit!" he said. "The thing about the power is real. And I can't explain to you what euphoria it is to kill, to watch blood splatter—"

"Why didn't you kill me years ago?"

"Power of six. I had to do it right. Murders, murders, murders... This! The great finale of this part of the game, anyway. The Axeman back in New Orleans!"

"Did you even know George Calabria?" she asked him.

He smiled and shook his head. "The bastard wasn't supposed to survive. Neither were you, actually. But then, when we found George in Orlando...and then that idiot, Dan Oliver! Wow, he made my day going after George the way that he did. I mean, I made sure he was led toward George Calabria all the way, and I'm good at what I do."

"I guess so. You had Carly Britton as your sixth?"

"Carly couldn't get going in business. I managed to set her up. And afterwards, she was happy to be one of The Six, though the most worthless, I'm afraid."

"She saved your ass this morning," Katie noted sweetly. "And then you killed her," she added softly.

He shrugged. "I was afraid the car might have been seen."

"Did you kill her husband, too?"

"No, I couldn't find the lucky bastard. But...hey. He's out there somewhere. Though, Katie, to be honest, I wanted you for the grand finale. You escaped the boat! You got twelve bonus years. I was so anxious, waiting for reports from Sonny. Because you see, you should have been first. Your dad and his precious wife, your mother, should have had the agony of watching you hacked to pieces first. Can you imagine that pain? And your dad would know it was all because he just had to be a hero, couldn't leave us to do what needed to be done…to frankly worthless people. They didn't deserve anything they had. They could have just run crying to FEMA. Your dad! He thought he was powerful that day. I showed him."

"You killed a man. Thousands of thugs have done the same," Katie said. "You're nothing special."

"But I am… I'm the Axeman of New Orleans. And now…"

"You poisoned your own dogs!"

"Well, if you shut up, I can get out of here. I'm just going to shoot Dan Oliver when he comes looking for you. I'm not sure he's even worthy of the axe. Then I can save my dogs. Oh, Katie, I just can't tell you how I've loved this! Watching you admire me, fall in love with the mules and the dogs. And bring in so much money! Thinking you were safe. And all the while, I knew. I knew this day would come… Oh, don't worry. I will get away with it. My dogs were poisoned. The killer was after you. I tried to stop him! I was injured horribly…well, not that horribly, but I do know how to make it look like I was attacked."

She listened to him, scrambling in her mind for more to say.

Dan had to be out there by now. But if he just kicked in the door, Monty would shoot him, then chop her to ribbons, harm himself…

She suddenly saw movement around Monty. She blinked. There was no way Dan had gotten into the bedroom, but…

It was Mabel! And she wasn't alone; she was with the

ghost of Gray Simmons. Her friend, who had just stayed to hang around and watch as his beloved city unfolded…

It was difficult to see them as they motioned to her.

They'd all been such idiots. Looking for a big man. Monty was a big man, blocking her view now.

"My head," she muttered, swinging backward and forward.

"You have a headache, pretty girl? It's going to get worse!" he told her.

She finally heard what Mabel was trying to say to her.

"Kick him, kick him as hard as you can! Knock him over!" Mabel said, kicking out a ghostly foot.

"But…" Katie said aloud.

"But what?" Monty demanded. "Hmm, to shoot him in front of you, or hack you to death in front of him?"

"Kick him over!" Gray cried.

They had a plan, but—

"Monty! Monty!" She suddenly heard Dan; he was calling out. "Monty, was George here? We're going to get him this time!" Dan called. "Where are you guys? Katie? The bastard went after your dogs! Monty, come on, I need to get you and Katie to safety."

Monty looked at her, grinning.

She'd never known the man could look so purely evil. He was always so nice, so polite, so caring and courteous to others…

As he planned their demise.

"Kick him over!" Gray said. "Lass, you can do it!"

And then she knew Dan knew damned well Monty had taken her, and Monty had poisoned his own dogs…

Dan knew that Monty was the big man, the mastermind, the Axeman.

"Monty. I'm still confused," she said, as if she hadn't

heard Dan. "Did this start with the Axeman, or with Allan Pierce's theory of six and being superhuman and immortal. Or were you just sick as can be from the get-go? Because you messed up a lot. I mean, for one, Sonny Hartfield is going to talk eventually. I'm not sure if he can make a fortune with the tabloids from prison, but he'll tell your story soon enough."

"He won't be able to. I can't tell you how easy it is to buy an assassin, Katie. So easy. Of course, it's not the same. I mean, I had to wait to hear about your parents. It's not the same as feeling the axe in your hands, feeling it make impact with human flesh and blood! Oh, to be bathed in the warmth of blood splatter. But shut up now—"

He raised his voice. "Dan, help, help! Help us, for God's sake! He has us, Katie and me. The Axeman has us…"

He was hunched down in front of her but looking toward the door. He had his axe in the one hand behind his back, and he started to draw out the other, in which he held a handgun.

Katie kicked him.

She kicked him hard, with all her strength, and perhaps…

Had just a little superpower of her own.

Revenge? Hatred?

Or the search for real justice, for so many years now.

He didn't just fall. He went flying backward, sliding across the room on his rump, almost hitting the opposite wall.

The door burst open. Dan was there, and even as Monty struggled to right himself and take aim, Dan shot him.

Monty screamed as his hand exploded and his gun went flying.

"No warning! You can't shoot me with no warning, you asshole. You'll face charges. My rights have been—"

"Shut up or I'll shoot to kill," Dan said, keeping his gun trained on Monty as he hunkered down to slice the ropes from Katie's wrists with his free hand. "And I'm just a private investigator. I'm not a cop or any kind of an agent. I'm a citizen standing my ground. I'd shoot you, you bastard, without blinking an eye, and the world—and all immortal beings—would thank me for it!"

Katie hadn't heard the first sound of a siren.

She hadn't heard any kind of commotion.

But suddenly, officers and agents were flooding into the room. Axel was there, asking her if she was all right. Ryder was with him, and Andre Broussard and others, all there to take Monty Trudeau away, to put to rest any concept of an immortal Axeman.

Dan pulled her up and to her feet.

She felt the ghosts behind her, heard Gray complimenting her on her kicking style.

She laughed and replied to them. Dan, Axel and Andre were grinning.

Ryder looked concerned. Katie grinned and went to him, giving him a hug and a kiss on the cheek. "Sorry, yeah, I'm a little wild right now!"

"Of course, of course!" Ryder said.

Katie shook her head, looking at Dan. "How could you know? I mean the dogs were down, and I was gone, but Monty was going to make it look like George got in here and poisoned the dogs and seized us both and killed me—"

"Well, actually," Dan said, "I think I knew—he's definitely a *big man*! But there was something else."

"They'd finally found a piece of trace evidence," Axel said.

"The hair—" Katie began.

Dan was nodding. "A strand of mule hair. We put it together."

"The mules!" Katie said.

"The mules are all fine. The dogs are on their way to the emergency vet," Ryder assured her.

She looked at Dan and said, "It's over. Really over!"

He nodded and, disregarding anyone around them, he walked to her and took her into his arms. His words, too, were only for her.

"This nightmare is really behind us... Well, then, you know the rest. Katie?"

She smiled, looking at him.

"I guess we're going to have to start looking for an apartment in the DC area. It's not going to be easy to find a place that will accept three large dogs."

Dan smiled.

"Let's get tonight over with. And then we can start on the rest of our lives."

Epilogue

The case of the New Orleans Axeman had been studied for years; the case of Monty Trudeau would now be joined with it.

Axel told them that members of the behavioral-analysis unit would be spending time with Monty, trying to figure out just what made such a mind tick.

In a plea deal, Sonny Hartfield admitted to the murders of Lou and Virginia Delaney, Anita Calabria, and Harold, Marie, and Henrietta Austin of Orlando. George Calabria had never had anything to do with the killings, other than conveniently living nearby.

Sonny had helped with the first Axeman Protégé's killing in New Orleans, but Trudeau had done most of the killing; Sonny had been a lookout.

But he had murdered Jennie.

For his confessions, attorneys would not seek the death penalty.

In his boasting confession, Monty Trudeau had let it be known that no legal system would be needed to ensure Sonny Hartfield would die a slow and painful death.

Attorneys were seeking the death penalty for Monty

Trudeau. It turned out not to be necessary. Monty, the self-styled super being, had Stage Four pancreatic cancer. He'd had no idea.

Monty was also being sued in civil court. Matt, Lorna and Katie decided they were going to buy the carriage company when it went up for auction.

Katie, absorbed with the case and Dan, hadn't noted what was going on with her coworkers. Lorna and Matt, friends for years, were now *very* good friends. Lorna excitedly showed Katie her ring. Katie was delighted.

She didn't mind being a silent partner. It would be great if Matt and Lorna managed the company, as long as they took special care of Sarah and didn't mind she had decided she was taking the dogs. And she was keeping her house. She didn't know of any hotels that would take the dogs when she popped back home, which, of course, she would do. Jeremy was there, they were there, and so many friends!

Benny was thrilled about it all and proposed he look after her house in exchange for residency in one of the guest rooms.

That was okay…if Katie chose the room.

There would always be something special about the guest room where she'd first really gotten to know Dan.

When they met up with George once more, he was a happy man.

"Go figure! I know several actors who said Carly Britton was a bit of a haughty bitch, but…wow! Sold her soul to the devil, huh? And lost it to him, too."

George, of course, felt a great deal like Katie. You never, ever got over a loss like the ones they'd experienced. You learned to love the memories.

And you were grateful when justice was served.

He was also glad because he was going back to work for a new movie.

A comedy.

No time travel, no suspense, no murder—no blood. He felt as if he'd been associated with enough of the real stuff.

Carly Britton's husband remained among the missing. When asked about him, Monty Trudeau just smiled.

None of them knew for sure, but it seemed somewhere along the line, a decomposing body might well be found in the bayou and prove to have been Carly Britton's husband.

It took a while for matters to be settled, and then Dan was flying back and forth, filling out everything necessary for the Academy, getting himself into order. He was most worried about Marleah, but she had discovered—thanks to an evening spent with George—that there was a lot of movie-extras work to be had in New Orleans. She could pick what projects she wanted to apply to be involved with and make a little fun money for gambling at Harrah's.

It was late on a Friday afternoon and the sun was beginning its descent when Dan and Katie walked into the cemetery together where his family was interred, and where he had first met Mabel.

She was seated on the steps to her own family's tomb.

She wasn't alone.

Gray Simmons was with her, leaned against a gargoyle, a dashing flirt of ghostly soul.

"Why hello there, " Mabel greeted them. "Thank goodness. We've been trying to find the right time and place to say goodbye!"

"And we've been looking for you," Katie told her. "The two of you. Thank you!"

"Thank you," Mabel said. She hesitated. "I… I will never understand. I couldn't stop the man who killed my friend, and I could never see justice done for her, her family or the others. But in this, well, I feel...fulfilled."

"Mabel wants to go on," Gray said.

"Is that something you can just do?" Dan asked. He lifted a hand. "Remember, I'm new at this. Katie is the old pro!"

"Did you call me *old*?" Katie teased.

Dan groaned, and the ghosts laughed.

"I think so," Mabel said. "Anyway, I'm going to try. I've seen others..."

"I'm... I'm going with her," Gray said, looking at Katie.

"That's lovely," Katie said.

"You'll be all right...yes, you'll be all right. You, lady, you can kick!" Gray told her.

"And she's hell on wheels with a gumbo pot, too," Dan assured him.

"So, then..."

Mabel walked up to Dan, pressing ghostly lips to both his cheeks. "Bye, handsome."

"Thank you, gorgeous," he whispered in return.

Likewise, Gray said goodbye to Katie, hugging her, glancing at Dan mischievously, and kissing her on the lips.

"Thank you!" she told him. "For everything."

"Well, I don't want to be a cliché, but... Love, it's eternal. It never dies. We'll bring yours with us!" he promised.

"And we'll feel like fools, sweetie, if we don't go anywhere!" Mabel said.

But they did go. They stood hand in hand in front of the family tomb.

"It is light, sweet, dazzling, kind, gentle... I can feel it!" Mabel said.

Katie wasn't sure if she really saw the light, but there was a streak, perhaps the setting sun. They were about to throw anyone remaining out of the cemetery. It was late and closing time.

So it was there. That sweeping shaft of light.

And they were gone, and Katie was there alone with Dan, smiling, holding his hand.

He looked down at her and smiled. "Love. I love you."

She smiled in return. "And I love you. Go figure! How the hell did that happen?"

"Because I was always dashing and wonderful," he said. "You were just too busy hating me to notice."

She groaned. Hand in hand, they exited the cemetery and headed across the street. Jeremy had managed to organize a dinner party with George, Benny, Matt and Lorna. A goodbye dinner.

Because in the morning, they'd be leaving NOLA.

Dan looked at her.

"We'll always be back," he said.

She nodded. "Want to know what else?"

"What?"

"I think I'm going to teach you to dive."

"I know how to dive!"

"Good. I won't need to teach you too much, then!" she told him.

Laughing, they headed across to the restaurant.

Whatever their tomorrows might bring, they'd be facing them together. They'd both faced the past, and it was time for the future.

Katie smiled.

Go figure.

It had been in putting her past to rest that she'd found the most amazing future.

She looked up to the sky. It was still blue here and there

as the sun fell. The stars were coming out. She liked to think her parents were there, riding the night sky.

And that, somehow, they saw.

And they were happy.

* * * * *

This winter, look for the latest blood-curdling thriller from *New York Times* bestselling author

HEATHER GRAHAM

On the edge of the Everglades, an eerie crime scene sets off an investigation that sends two agents deep into a world of corrupted faith, greed and deadly secrets.

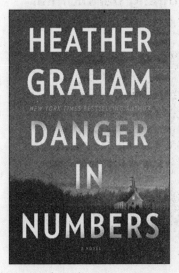

A ritualistic murder on the side of a remote road brings in the Florida state police. Special Agent Amy Larson has never seen worse, and there are indications that this killing could be just the beginning. The crime draws the attention of the FBI in the form of Special Agent Hunter Forrest, a man with insider knowledge of how violent cults operate, and a man who might never be able to escape his own past.

The rural community is devastated by the death in their midst, but people know more than they are saying. As Amy and Hunter join forces, every lead takes them further into the twisted beliefs of a dangerous group that will stop at nothing to see their will done.

Doomsday preppers and small-town secrets collide in this sultry, twisty page-turning thriller.

Available March 23, 2021 from MIRA.